wilderness

wilderness

A TALE OF THE CIVIL WAR

robert penn warren

Introduction by James H. Justus

THE UNIVERSITY OF TENNESSEE PRESS

Knoxville

Te TENNESSEANA EDITIONS

General Editor: James B. Lloyd

Tennesseana Editions is devoted to reprinting publications
about Tennessee or by Tennesseans, including works
concerning current affairs, local histories, or fiction, and
any other volumes that make a significant contribution to
understanding the state's culture or history.

Library of Congress Cataloging-in-Publication Data
Warren, Robert Penn, 1905–
    Wilderness: a tale of the Civil War/Robert Penn Warren;
introduction by James H. Justus.—1st paper ed.
    p.cm.—(Tennesseana editions)
ISBN 1-57233-134-8 (pbk. alk. paper)
1. United States—History—Civil War, 1861–1865—Fiction.
2. Germany—Emigration and immigration—Fiction.
3. Jews—United States—Fiction.
4. Jewish soldiers—Fiction.
5. Immigrants—Fiction. I. Title. II. Series

PS3545.A748 W5 2001
813'.52—dc21   2001018832

J. CAMERON WEST
President, Huntingdon College

1500 E. FAIRVIEW AVENUE, MONTGOMERY, AL 36106
TEL: (334) 833-4409   FAX: (334) 833-4485
CELL: (334) 328-0736   E-MAIL: camwest@huntingdon.edu

Introduction

1

When readers picked up Robert Penn Warren's *Wilderness* in 1961, those who were familiar with the author's earlier fiction saw, some perhaps with relief, that it was much shorter than the six previous novels. Warren went on to write two more novels before his death in 1989, but *Wilderness* would remain his briefest. It manages to sound all the motifs that had become this novelist's signatures, beginning with *Night Rider* in 1939: the hero divided against himself, the fortunes of the Idea in a world of Fact, robust naturalistic detail, and a style compounded of lyric grace and vernacular coarseness. In its Civil War setting, *Wilderness* also explores the high costs of principles and expedience in human behavior and the tangled ambivalences of father-son relationships that we find in Warren's other writing—in his poetry, criticism, and social analysis as well as fiction.

But *Wilderness* also stands out as a unique entry in Warren's body of work. For all his engagement with the Civil War, this is his only "war novel." And Adam Rosenzweig is his only Jewish protagonist, one who views the American Civil War from the perspective of the European revolutions of 1848; and, unlike Warren's other historical reconstructions, this plot moves in linear simplicity. *Wilderness* has no inset stories to break up and comment on its narrative progression, and its modest flashbacks are brief, relived moments of its hero, struggling to reconcile his German strand of humanism with the inchoate messiness of America's great war for the rights of all men. For Adam, to come to America in 1863 to support the Union cause is to continue the stand for enlightenment taken by his father, who, surviving the German barricades, "had lived for human liberty, but had not the luck to die for it." Ailing and disillusioned, Leopold Rosenzweig had returned to his village to be cared for by his brother, an Orthodox teacher, who charged him with blasphemy: "You did not trust God. You trusted man." To trust God is to "await the time" when He alone will bring justice, but Leopold, impatient for men to be "fully man," had stood at the barricades to help speed the process. On his deathbed fifteen years after the failed revolution, Leopold had recanted his mistake, allowing him to die within the Law.

The symbolic clash between inflexible Law and all-too-flexible Freedom would seem to be ready-made for dramatic treatment. Recurring with some frequency in Western thought because it plagues the ethics of both Christian and Jewish societies, the opposition is self-evident without being easy. But a dialectic stemming from such readily discernible principles is almost too simplistic for Warren, a writer who had always been drawn to the ineradicable ironies and smudged overlaps of all Big Issues.

In sentiment Adam may stand with his humanistic father, but the spirit with which he repudiates his father's deathbed recantation comes from the Orthodox uncle, and its rigidity propels the young Bavarian's quest to America. In redeeming Leopold Rosenzweig's commitment to freedom for all, the son does not merely continue that humanistic faith but refines it into something purer. The spiritual signs of Adam's inflexible (and destructive) idealism are ominous. Warren uses such phrases as "cold elation" and "sudden cold thrill of an unexpected joy" to describe the son's vow to carry on his father's cause. Even the Orthodox uncle suggests the extremity of Adam's idealism. When he warns his nephew, "You would enter a world where virtue is not possible," Adam responds with a dispassionate: "So be it."

As readers of Warren's fiction frequently note, his heroes tend to come armed with an "idea" and spend much of their energies in ransacking the world for its confirmation. They meet others armed with opposing convictions, some of them malignant, some merely alternative perspectives, still others that reflect only the tangible business of living. Adam Rosenzweig's arduous journey, from Bremerhaven to New York City to Pennsylvania to Virginia, will test his cold rebirth. In the ruck of a real world indifferent to the virtuous abstractions he clutches so zealously, he will experience the consequences of what most of his fictional brothers in Warren suffer: a "conflict of convictions." The phrase is Melville's, in a poem of that title in *Battle-Pieces* that Warren admired because he conceived many of his protagonists precisely in those terms.

Readers will have to decide for themselves how to evaluate the mix of idealism and naïveté in this hero. In some ways Adam's belief that the American Civil War was an unambiguous assertion of the Good reflects a common conviction among nineteenth-century Americans—and many in the twentieth as well—who argued that warfare conducted from noble motives was worth the tragic carnage suffered on both sides of the conflict. How far does the flawed nature of an actual world taint the virtues that Adam cherishes? Does the expedience of ordinary humans discredit Justice, Truth, Freedom? In bouts of despair Adam will ask, "Was no man, in his simple humanity, more to any other man than a stir or voice, a sloshing in the dark?"

There often seems to be a highly disciplined monkishness about this hero. One of the curious anomalies in *Wilderness* is the conspicuous lack of emphasis on its protagonist's sexuality. Among his southern contemporaries (and to the distress of some of his friends), Warren was the least reticent in his treatment of sexual matters. His early attraction to naturalism meant that the physical body, in both its bewitching attraction and its gross repulsiveness, was an indisputable aspect of his characters' lives. But in this novel even sexual appetite—mostly that of the common soldiers, depicted as a healthy release of young men staving off boredom during a winter encampment—gets less attention than in his other fictions. Is it a reflection of his idealism or his naïveté that makes Adam intolerant of the soldiers' consorting with the washerwoman-whore?

It is in the tattered complexity of the real world that Adam Rosenzweig must earn his self-definition, to acknowledge human frailties, to accept men "in their error," and to affirm their virtues even if they are tinged by compromise and biological need. The

ix

hard course of that process is the substance of the novel—hence the narrative structure that Warren devises, for the first and only time, in *Wilderness*.

2

The publication of Warren's seventh novel may have been the single occasion in which contemporary reviewers, who had been insensitive about all of the novels except *All the King's Men*, inadvertently homed in on the generative core of the one fiction that struck friends and foes alike as the novelist's oddest performance. Appearing in November 1961, the "strangely abstract" *Wilderness* was dismissed as a "philosophical parable" (or a "symbolist parable"), a "prose poem," a "picaresque," an "elaborate literary contrivance," or, finally, *pace* Polonius, a "political historical idealistic allegory." Warren, charged with being "inexorably didactic," was faulted for making meditation do the work of plot in a fiction that was "cramped, stylized, lyric in mode." Although the distaste evidenced by these judgments was of a piece with the general reception of Warren's fiction in the popular press, the consensus about *Wilderness* was cannily pertinent. The reviewers had unwittingly isolated the very characteristics of the book that made it a significant departure from the author's earlier novels.

Beginning his fictional career when the most flourishing American writing concerned itself with social, economic, and political issues, Warren saw his novels judged consistently by the canons of ordinary realism. Meticulous in rendering the feel of his imaginative worlds, he often resorted to the bluntest of detail; yet even his penchant for naturalistic notation fed his tendency to construct his fictions like moral dramas. But in no previous novel did Warren so flagrantly reveal that urgency: even our feeling that Adam is perhaps a colorless hero stems from his creator's conception of *Wilderness* as a parable-like work. He is unabashedly typal. Behind Adam, this aboriginally imperfect man (signified by his lame left foot) suffering his trials in a contingent world, are cultural heroes from Hebrew, Christian, and Greek literature, whose dilemmas come down to us not as psychological case studies but as archetypal representatives. Everyman, Oedipus, Job, even the original Adam lurk in this figurative hero. If Adam Rosenzweig is more passive than some of these models, the passivity is largely a condition of his obsessive drive to meditate on what he sees, to make philosophical sense of experience that seems so inimical to those ideal patterns he thinks experience *should* reveal. That obsessional tic extends to the way his creator appropriates features of his world for metaphorical significance. The local texture of *Wilderness* is thick with symbolic, emblematic, even allegorical objects: the special boot "cunningly" crafted to hide the flawed foot, the snow-capped mountain, the Bavarian neighbor's hogpen, the Virginia wilderness itself (which natives call "the pizen woods").

True to his conception of *Wilderness* as an archetypal moral drama, Warren sends his hero on a journey; but his Adam is not the hero of an updated "education novel," that familiar genre in which the naïf is sent into the world for correction, to fit himself for his eventual place in society. He resembles less the progeny of Goethe's Wilhelm Meister than the stolid pre-formed Christian of John Bunyan. Deep in his intellectual and spiritual conviction, Adam is seen not so much tested by the seductions of the world as he is seen testing them, assessing the extent to which they may fit his ideal vision. Unsurprisingly, he sees that real world, passing by him in detached and self-sufficient segments, as inadequate or contradictory confirmation of his own reality. Adam's symbolic density is so pronounced that his very presence seems stationary; what strikes us as having an ongoing mobility is the life around and behind him. Out of fifteen chapters, in only two— the fourth and the fifteenth—is Adam engaged dramatically in the life that swirls about him. The sea voyage is not only a narrative prologue to the central plot (the trek from New York City to the Virginia battlefield), but it also contains that plot in miniature. On board the *Elmyra* Adam is initiated into a world that is to be his trial: the hostility and condescension of the officers, the amused scorn of the other German recruits, and the disinterested aid of the English seaman who impatiently rejects any idealistic motives for showing Adam how to jump ship.

In later interviews Warren himself addressed the difficulties in the characterization of his hero. *Wilderness* was conceived as a novelette of about thirty thousand words, he explained, but it began "to exfoliate and develop, and the incidental characters began to be more important to me than they had been in the beginning." As the subsidiary figures took up more space, "they became more interesting than the protagonist," and the ratio "shifted along the way." That shift, Warren acknowledged, occurred because he had become "enraptured, as it were, with the world outside" the hero. What resulted was the "strange effect of a central *hollowness* with a rich context, with the central character as an observer who is a *mere* observer."

That rich context, of course, "the world outside," is the Civil War, which Warren declared to be "the great single event of our history" in *The Legacy of the Civil War,* a little book that began as an essay for *Life* magazine the same year that *Wilderness* appeared, 1961. His interest, he remarked, was "the distinction between the historical importance and what might be called the appeal to the national imagination, the symbolic value of the war." It is not surprising that Warren should write that Americans, prior to this great bloodletting, "had no history in the deepest and most inward sense," or that the words *validate, test,* and *cost* all appear on the first page. As we might expect from his subtitle, *Meditations on the Centennial,* that long essay is an assessment of what was left a century after the event, mulled over and articulated by a man of letters whose major concern was always the divisions, contradictions, anxieties, the conflict of convictions, within the self. In this meditation the high cost of enforced awareness, a motif shaping the moral growth of many of his fictional characters, is raised to a national level.

Composed between drafts of *Wilderness, The Legacy of the Civil War* is a distillation of some thirty years of reflection on the subject, but it also demonstrates its author's mastery of the prodigious literature about the war, ranging from soldiers' letters to official histories. Yet the nagging central question that Warren sought to answer in his meditation—"To what extent is man always—or sometimes—trapped in the great texture of causality, of nature and history?"—is the national enlargement of the same issue that his lame protagonist must struggle with on a personal and no less anguished level. Warren's lesson (for it is that): to use the pure ideal of human liberty for measuring what was a human situation, and therefore an impure social and moral situation, is to fall victim to aggressive righteousness. Adam becomes Warren's fictional example of the religious zeal that actually endangered the practical business of carrying on the war. Standing almost alone among the shakers and movers as a compassionate pragmatist, the great man of the time was of course Lincoln, who epitomized the tragedy of commitment as well as its resolution, risks, and moral entrapments. Adam Rosenzweig is, unhappily, no little man with a Lincolnesque vision, but it is clear that his creator saw him as a cousin to all those idealists who badgered the president because he was less the Holy Warrior than they.

In *Wilderness* the shaping medium is space. Even the structure of the journey, that most primitive of spatial processes, de-emphasizes the growth in time of the hero, that most elementary requirement of quest narratives, by converting the protagonist into a virtual abstraction. The effect is similar to that old device of the theater: to create the illusion of movement on the stage, roll the scenic backdrop. The most vital elements in *Wilderness* are those scenic panels, and the most conventionally memorable action involves the self-contained dramas enacted by supporting players in front of them. *Everyman* is the model drama and Dante's *Commedia* the model poem behind all modern versions of the spiritual journey, including the greatest, *The Waste Land*. The very nature of the form requires that subordinate characters and situations, examples and temptations, be dramatically more interesting than the quester himself. So it is with *Wilderness*. Warren's great gift for the creation of eccentrics merges with formal demands to make the part-time characters, those who enact mini-dramas before their respective panels, considerably more interesting than the protagonist whose central story it is.

If in the writing of *Wilderness* Warren became "enraptured" by the world observed by his hero, that world is not the panoramic spectacles of opposing armies, but the brims, margins, and outposts of war, where the costs of the great conflict are domesticated to scale. These vignette-like sequences begin in chapter 5, with Adam's temptation by riches; succeeding episodes serve to deepen the shock and chagrin of the idealist hero. In chapter 7 Adam helps a young woman with farm chores as her husband, a veteran of Chancellorsville, lies dying of his wounds. Chapter 8 is an episode at Gettysburg soon after the battle, dominated by a bloated doctor-preacher who is angling for an appointment in the "business of perambulatory embalming." Chapters 9, 10, and 11 are devoted to the winter encampment, the boredom of which is relieved by a "shindig" in which a drunken war hero taunts and abuses Negroes and an Irish washerwoman receives a public lashing. Throughout the winter Adam observes, with increasing stress, the mutual spying of Jed Hawksworth, the deracinated southern sutler, and his black assistant, Moses Talbutt, that ends with the sutler's murder.

These chapters are the most conventionally novelistic of the book. The period of waiting allows Warren to dramatize the most sustained interaction of the hero with the two most important characters on his difficult journey. The triadic relationship of Adam, Hawksworth, and Talbutt explores the dangers of deracination. All three have repudiated that part of a personal past that has failed to define who they are, and struggling to expunge that failure, they are caught in the toils of a mundane present in which community is only provisional and transient. As the reluctant Jew, Adam must deal with a faith that carries with it a strong reliance upon communal coherence. As the nonconformist southerner, Hawksworth has challenged the racial and class status quo of the society that made him and, when opposed, unmade him. As the free black, Talbutt enjoys a dangerously tangential role; compelled to disguise his previous existence as a slave, he is a man without any community. Both sutler and assistant come together in commercial self-interest and mutual need, but they are linked in more human ways. For personal expedience they take the same stance. Rejecting benevolence as a human impulse, they both deny any motive higher than base self-interest for earlier acts of courage. Refusing to accept *what is said* for *what is*, Adam makes an unlikely third party, a temperamental alien of abstract virtues mediating the alienation of two men who have been damaged by the tangible claims of race and class. The mix turns out to be not merely ambivalent, but volatile.

With the breakup of the winter encampment, the procession-like segments of the novel resume with Adam's encounter with a bushwhacker and his wife, frontier-like figures who recall characters out of *World Enough and Time* and "The Ballad of Billie Potts." Even as backdrop to Adam's inner drama, the Civil War is significant only at the edges of his quest. *Wilderness* conspicuously skirts the obvious events of the war. Just as the sutler's wagons arrive at Gettysburg *after* the battle, so the novel ends just *before* the Battle of the Wilderness. Prior to the final episode, the most dramatic actual involvement we see is that of Adam caught in the civilian anticonscription riots in New York City, an event itself treated by most historians as a kind of footnote to the Civil War. Behind and beneath the heroic scrims of the great battles, the grand disposition of men and their arms and commitments, Warren suggests the mingled underdrama that played concurrently, act for act, scene for scene, with the major event. Indeed, there is about *Wilderness* the purposive air of a counterdrama—a kind of moralist's alternate service in which the central action is assumed to be not in error but incomplete. If the Civil War, the central action in our history, resembles an almost classic engagement between opposing sides of high-minded idealists, Warren's tale resembles a procession of ragtag pragmatists for whom flesh takes precedence over word.

3

Warren has often been seen for his dialectical engagements with some of the more prominent *isms* of his time—idealism, pragmatism, liberalism, mysticism, hedonism, naturalism, political authoritarianism—and just as often charged with smuggling them into fictional situations not entirely suited for them. In the case of *Wilderness*, the most obvious of its triggering issues was the continued fascination among Americans of all stripes with the Civil War, and especially in the moral ambiguity with which its centennial was being observed in 1961. Since it was what Warren called "our only 'felt' history—history lived in the national imagination," its hesitant celebration a hundred years later was itself an index to the very "complexity, depth, and fundamental significance of the event."

One component in that reassessment was the glaring survival of racism, the most recalcitrant issue that had not been disposed of in that conflict. The interplay of racial attitudes in the relationship of Adam, Talbutt, and Hawksworth was not Warren's first exploration of this surviving issue. In *Band of Angels*, the half-black heroine's very identity is conditioned by both official policy and emotional bias; and a year later, in 1956, in the midst of the civil rights movement, the author undertook his own personal analysis of a subject that was dominating the national life, *Segregation: The Inner Conflict of the South*. By 1961 Congress had passed two civil rights bills, with more comprehensive ones to come. Although the Birmingham clashes, the urban riots, the formation of the Black Panthers, and the assassinations of Martin Luther King and Medgar Evers lay in the years ahead, for Warren the matter of race was—and had been for more than a century—"an immediate and contemporary issue." *Wilderness* would be his most profound and disturbing reappraisal, mostly because its author so ruthlessly bared the racism in a "good" man.

By the time of his documentary *Who Speaks for the Negro?* (1965), Warren had already investigated the disastrous assumptions of American whites about African Americans—assumptions that simultaneously sentimentalize and degrade—in the arduous moral journey of Adam Rosenzweig. The false "rebirth" in Bavaria is not redeemed by the real thing until the last page of the novel. There Adam, over the Confederate soldier he has killed, also acknowledges his responsibility for the deaths of his benefactor in New York and Hawksworth in the Rapidan mud. But more deeply impinging on these destructive outcomes is his more personal relationship with Mose Talbutt, whom he has turned into a thief and a murderer. Adam muses on the thought that every man may well be "a sacrifice for every other man," a dour confirmation of words he heard at the outset of his journey: "Everything is part of everything else."

Yet the substantive resolution of Warren's brief novel, an inevitable product of its time, is more tentative, more conditional, than the classic forms that it resembles—the sketch, the parable, the exemplum. In the final segment, when the "eight maniacal scarecrows" burst upon Adam in the clearing, his responses rapidly escalate. At first, even as they assault him, he feels only a "sweet sadness" because, he reasons, they are only hungry, foraging troops. But when one of the scarecrows aims his weapon at a Union soldier, Adam is suddenly filled with "moral repugnance," and he himself picks up a rifle and kills the Confederate. Now to the burden of the previous deaths is added the death of a nameless soldier by his direct hand. His idealism, though not totally shattered, is finally tempered by recognition of what is merely human. The tangled humanity he has resisted so long, in himself and others, coalesces in his own crucial act.

If he begins his journey by clutching his father's political idealism (*we should all be worthy*), this hero ends it by submitting himself to a more comprehensive, and human, requirement (*I must learn to know what a man must know to be a man*). For the first time since he left Germany he picks up his phylactery, the *talith*, and the prayer book from the scattered ruins of his wagon. This late shift in effect makes *Wilderness* a tale of counter-conversion. Adam undertakes his quest, despite the content of his belief, with all the postures of the religious hero. The provisional nature of experience is something this religious hero cannot comprehend, much less accept; when he at long last does understand it, he embraces it, and thereby sheds the absolutism with which he holds his truth. To put oneself in a context of community is not wholly a therapeutic prescription, but a spiritual imperative. Wearing another man's boots means that Adam must sacrifice his own intricately designed boot, which has betrayed him into self-indulgence and which has been a visual reminder of his separation from other men. By putting on an ordinary pair of boots worn by both Union and Confederate soldiers, Adam signifies that the chain of complicity is also a chain of hope.

James H. Justus
Indiana University

wilderness

1

If the mountain had not gleamed so white.

If yonder, under the peaks, the snaggled line of the fir forest had not been so blue-black, against the white.

If the sky above that glitter of snow on the Zelzsteinberg had not been heart-breaking with the innocence of new blue. If one puff of cloud, white as whipped cream, had not lounged high in that washed glitter of blue. If the world had not been absolute in beauty.

If none of these things had been as they were, he, Adam Rosenzweig, might have fled inward into the self, into the ironies of history and knowledge, into that wisdom which is resignation. He might have been able to go back into that house behind him, where the mirrors were now covered, where basins had been emptied of the water in which the Destroying Angel had dipped his blade to cleanse it of blood, where he, Adam Rosenzweig, had stared at the tallow-white face of his father before the black cloth was laid over it, and where, even yet, lingered the smell of the candle that had been lighted for the father's death and set at the head of the body, on the floor.

No, now he could not go back into that room. They would try to make him go in, as was proper and prescribed, but he could not. His father was now in the ground, so why should he go in?

He thought of night coming on. He thought of the loneliness of tonight, this first night in the ground. This, he thought, was the moment when the dead must first feel truly alone. This was the moment when the dead, in loneliness, feel the first stirrings of the long penance of decay. This was the moment when the dead realize the truth: *This is it, it will never be different.*

To be dead, he thought, that was to know that nothing would ever be different.

He thought: *I am alive.*

He thought of the body of his father being lowered, that very afternoon, into the grave, of the first earth being dropped in, of the words uttered: "What doest Thou? O Thou who speakest and doest, of Thy

———

4

grace deal kindly with us, and for the sake of him who was bound like a lamb."

He said the words aloud, and wondered what they meant to him, to Adam Rosenzweig.

He thought of the rest of the prayer, word by word. Again aloud, he said the words that came at the end: "Have mercy upon the remnant of the flock of Thy hand, and say unto the Destroying Angel, Stay thy hand."

He thought: *I am now of the remnant of the flock. I stand where my father once stood.*

He shut his eyes and tried to imagine his father as a young man standing on this same spot, in late winter, and staring at the glittering whiteness of the Zelz-steinberg, that mountain which he, the son, could not now see through his shut lids. With his eyes shut he murmured the opening lines of a poem by his father:

"If I could only be worthy of that mountain I love,
  If I could only be worthy of sun-glitter on snow,
  If man could only be worthy of what he loves."

He opened his eyes. He saw the crooked street and the frozen mud of winter thawing gummily where the sun reached it but freezing again where the shadows of houses lengthened over. He saw the arch of the stone bridge over the Zelz, where the thaw-raddled fragments of ice slid by, like sputum on the black water. He saw, beyond the Zelz, the Schloss, gray, ugly, hulking and improvised, the squat twin towers, each surmounted by a dome the shape of an inverted turnip, the lower wall, where moisture from snow, snagged in crenelation, bled blackly down over the gray stone.

He stared at the castle, and thought that somewhere in that hulking structure an old man, fat and diseased, but a Count, snored in his afternoon sleep, and gathered force to debauch the daughter of a merchant. Standing there, staring at the Schloss, Adam heard a hog grunting from a pen by the hovel which Herr Zellert called his house. Herr Zellert kept swine, and people said he kept them only because he, with his house at the end of the Judenstrasse, and his red-rimmed angry eyes, had to do something to prove that he was not a Jew.

I am a Jew, thought Adam Rosenzweig, and tried to imagine how his father, years ago, had stood on this spot and lifted his gaze above that scene—above the thawing mud, for mud had always thawed in the sun and frozen again in the encroaching shade, above the hovel of Herr Zellert, for there had always been a Herr Zellert keeping swine there, and above the Schloss, for there had always been a Count there, young and arrogant or fat and diseased. His father had lifted his eyes above those things to the glittering whiteness of the mountain, and had yearned in his heart to be worthy of that mountain he loved.

So Adam stood there and stared at the mountain and thought of his father—his father, Leopold Rosenzweig, who years before had left Bavaria, and this street. He had gone to Berlin, and had endured poverty, hunger, nights of study. He had written his poems. He had married. He had had a son. He had named the son Adam. He had taught the son Greek and English, for those, he was accustomed to say, are the tongues of liberty. He had told his son that there was no nobler fate for a man than to live and die for human liberty.

So, long ago, fifteen years ago, March 18, 1848, in Berlin, Leopold Rosenzweig had walked out of his house, leaving his wife, with the beautiful and unforgiving eyes, and his fourteen-year-old son, and had stood with the crowd in the Schlossplatz, when, at 2 P.M., General von Prittwitz had slowly advanced with his squadron of gleaming dragoons, supported on both flanks by Prussian infantry. Later, staring incredulously at the musket in his hand, Leopold Rosenzweig had stood behind the barricades, and then had fired. A year later, somewhat less incredulously, he had handled his musket at Rastatt, in the last grim hours. When Rastatt fell, he, by a whim of chance, had not been among those executed.

Leopold Rosenzweig had lived for human liberty, but had not had the luck to die for it. For years he lived on, in a damp cell, not even knowing that his wife, still unforgiving, had died, and that his son had been sent back to Bavaria. Then, after thirteen years, they had let him out of the cell, to take his prison cough back to Bavaria. His older brother, the brother who had taken in the boy Adam, took him in.

Then as Leopold lay on a cot coughing the last of

his life away, the brother, the *lehrer,* the keeper of the *schule,* said to him: "You have lived without the Law."

Leopold Rosenzweig, lying on the cot, waiting to cough again, answered: "I thought I had something to live for."

And the brother said: "Some say that the old holiness has fled from the world. I pray. I have sat on the floor at midnight with ashes on my head. I have prayed that you may die within the Law."

Adam, crouching in the shadow, held his breath, waiting for the father's answer.

There was no answer.

His father's brother said: "The vase of God's tears is not yet full. You had not the faith to await the time for it to overflow, and the world to be made holy. You did not trust God. You trusted man."

Adam, sitting there in that room where death was encroaching like the dusk, heard the slow râle of his father's breath, and waited.

Then, in almost a whisper, his father said: "Yes, I trusted man."

"And that was blasphemy," the old man said, and leaned at him implacably in the dusk. "Was it not blasphemy? Answer me, was it not?"

Adam felt his heart contract in his bosom. For a long time it seemed that his own breath would not come.

Then, in a voice small and blank, his father said: "Yes."

So his father, in that moment, with that word, had withdrawn the gift given long ago to the son, the gift which had been so preciously confirmed by the years of martyrdom in the cell in Berlin. The father's body had needed six more months to die, but Adam knew that the father's self was already dead. And Adam knew that, in the very moment, in that shadowy room, when his father's self had died, his own self had been born.

Now, six months later, with the father's body finally dead and in the ground, he realized that he, the son, had, in all the years of his youth, lived only in the dream of his father's life, the father's manhood, the father's heroism. So, lifting his face above the mud of the street, the hog pen of Herr Zellert, and the hulking Schloss, he knew more fully what he had known six months before. The knowledge and the obligation had come to him in that darkening room in the moment when his father repudiated all that he had suffered for and had been.

Yes, how could he, the son, now live the life he had previously lived? How could he hunch in a dusty cubicle, surrounded by the rustling sound which was compounded of all the tickings of all the watches and clocks hung on the walls around him, and lean patiently over his table, all the hours of daylight, repairing the timepieces of this miserable huddle of a town lost in Bavaria? How could he now get up from that work table, evening after evening as light failed, and go into his uncle's house and eat boiled cabbage

9

and hear the same words uttered and lie down on the same bed and stare upward into the same darkness and dream of a time to come when he would not be lonely in the dark?

No, he could no longer live that life. He now knew what he would do. He had made his arrangements. All right, he thought with cold elation, his father had repudiated the obligation. But he would not.

Standing there, staring at the mountain, he heard the sound of his uncle coming from the house. Without turning, he knew that it was his uncle who came to stand beside him, small and hunched, under the skull cap. He knew what he would say.

"Come into the house," the old man said.

"No," Adam said.

"It is proper and fitting," the old man said. "It is the time of mourning."

"Listen," Adam said, quietly, "I would not offend you. I have done what is proper and prescribed. I have rent my garments. Look!"

He leaned and plucked at his coat on the upper left side, offering it for inspection.

"Have I not rent it?" Adam demanded. "Did I not bend over the body of my father, even before the feather was laid on the lips, and did I not cut my garment with a penknife and rend it more than a span?"

"Yes," the old man said, "but—"

"But now," Adam retorted, "you wish me to come in and take off my shoes and sit on the floor in a room that smells of tallow and despair."

"Come in," the old man said.

"No. I am going to stand here."

"You would not honor your father?"

"I stand here to honor the man he once was," Adam said, ashamed yet exulting in the anger that made his voice shake. "I look at the mountain to honor him."

"Pah!" his uncle said.

"Do you remember his poem?" Adam asked, feeling again calm. "The one about the mountain?"

"Yes, and he wrote it in German," the old man said. "The language of holiness was not good enough for him."

"It must have been this mountain," Adam said, not really hearing the old man's words. He began to say the poem, in German:

"If I could only be worthy of that mountain I love,
  If I could only be—"

His uncle plucked his sleeve. "Listen," he said. "Your father gave up the holiness of the Law. He trusted to man for the liberty of men. He went to Berlin and studied learning which has nothing to do with holiness. He broke bread with them and they pretended to respect him. But do you know what they did?"

Adam nodded.

"Well, remember it," his uncle said, leaning closer. "They pretended to respect him, those who said they were for the new learning and the new liberty. But when he made his book and praised the mountains and the rivers, it was as when the Jew has to step in the mud and the gentile barks at him: 'Jude, mach Mores,' and the Jew must doff his hat. Yes, I have seen what that paper in Berlin wrote of your father's book, the very men who had broken bread with him. They wrote: 'Jude, mach Mores.' That was the way they began when they wrote: 'Jew, you have no right to praise our mountains and our rivers, for they are ours. It is impertinent for you, Jew, to say you love them.' Do you remember that?"

"Yes," Adam said, "and I remember that then my father said it may take centuries yet for men to be fully man, but one must live for that day, and he took a musket and stood at the barricades beside them and would have died for them to help bring on that day."

"But," his uncle said, "he came back and died within the Law."

"He was old and sick," Adam said.

"He was old and wise. And I have prayed that you in your youth may profit from his wisdom."

Adam said nothing.

"You mean that you are confirmed in your foolishness?"

"If that is what you call it," Adam said, calmly.

"What else can I call it? You being fool enough to go to America." He paused and peered into Adam's face. "Or has my prayer been answered?" he whispered. "And you will not go?"

Adam said: "I will do what I have to do."

———

"Fool," the uncle said, "you go to kill or be killed. In America men now choose to kill one another. But this quarrel is not yours. Do you know what the Talmud says? It says, when two great forces collide, stand aside and wait for the Messiah."

Adam tried to make his tone reasonable and patient. "I am a man," he said. "Would you have a man stand aside and wait? In America now—this minute —men are fighting for freedom."

"Freedom," the old man echoed. "Yes, your father fought for freedom, and you know what that freedom became? In Prague they threw out the Emperor and then turned to killing Jews. Here in Bavaria the heroes marched singing for freedom and stopped singing to save energy to kill Jews. Do you know what the freedom of the world is?" He paused. "Well, I'll tell you. It is freedom to kill Jews."

The old man began to laugh.

Adam thought: *If he doesn't stop laughing I may kill him.*

But the laughter had stopped.

"There is only one thing," the old man said. "We must wait."

"For what?"

"You know for what. For the day when by our example—when by the Jew—all the world will know the Law. And rejoice in its holiness."

Adam looked over the forest and toward the mountain, where the light of evening now reddened on the snow. "I do not want to wait," he said.

———

"What do you want?"

"I want to work for the day."

"When the world will know the Law?"

"No," Adam said, feeling the anger come on him, feeling again betrayed and deprived as when, in the darkening room six months earlier, he had heard his father speak the words which undid the meaning of his own life and martyrdom.

"No," Adam repeated, "I would work for the day when the world will know Justice."

"The Law is just," his uncle said. Then as Adam wheeled on him to say something—something which Adam himself had not yet formulated but knew only as a blackness in his brain and a pain in his heart—the uncle cut in, to continue, lifting his hand: "No—do not say what you are about to say. It would be blasphemy."

"Is it blasphemy to hope for Justice?" Adam asked. He felt close to tears.

"There is justice only in God."

"There may be justice in God," Adam burst out, "but there is none in Bavaria. Yes, you would sit here in this sty and—"

The uncle spat. "Bavaria is the mother of harlots," he said wearily, as though without conviction.

"All right. And you sit here and grunt. Like one of Herr Zellert's hogs. Well, I will not sit here. Where I haven't the rights of a man. Where, today, when I go to bury my father the tax gatherer stands by the grave to take the grave-tax before a Jew can be laid in the earth of Bavaria. Where I cannot even marry unless I get a family-founding permit. Oh, no, there can be only so many Jew-brats born and I have to wait the turn for mine and—"

The uncle was looking down at Adam's left foot. Adam felt the impulse to withdraw it, to hide it. Then that old shame was flooded over by the new, angry shame at having again experienced the old shame.

"All right, look at my foot. Is that because you think no woman would want me? Do you think me not a man because of that foot? Well, look!" He straightened himself, threw back his shoulders, lifted his head. "I can stand on it," he said.

The uncle looked at him sadly, shaking his head.

"America will want me," Adam said.

"You are a fool," the old man said, his sadness now turning into pity.

"Fool or not," Adam declared, "I can march now." He took a step and stamped the heel of his left foot against the frozen mud. "And I can learn to shoot. I can learn to—"

He did not say the next word. He could not, for a terrible elation shook him. He was caught in the sudden cold thrill of an unexpected joy. He could not say the next word. He did not even know what it had been about to be.

His uncle was looking at him, again shaking his head. He was speaking very softly, without any trace of the tone of argument. "Be thou of those," he said, "who hear themselves disgraced, and make no reply. For God is with the persecuted. Know that when even the righteous man righteously persecutes even the wicked, God yet weeps for the persecuted."

"I do not believe that God weeps for that occasion," said Adam, with a last flicker of that cold joy. "I do not believe He weeps when the wicked are persecuted to bring Justice. Nor do I weep for them."

"You would enter a world where virtue is not possible," the old man said.

"So be it," Adam said.

When the uncle had turned, wordlessly, and gone back into the house, where the body lay, Adam continued to stand there. Shadow was gathering now in the fir forest, miles away, and in the street. He looked down at his foot, encased in the bright, strange, clever boot. He regarded the boot with enormous intellectual detachment. He stretched forth his foot, aware, even as he did so, that the motion was comically like that of a fine lady who admires a new slipper, or her own ankle. He admired the cunning design of the boot, the concealed height of the heel, the heel slightly higher on the inner side, the sole slightly thicker on the inner side, the lacings and straps that pulled the ankle straighter. He had a right to admire it. He had invented it. He had borne the pain of wearing it.

He took two strides across the frozen mud. There was no pain now.

He looked down at the boot again and remembered how the idea had come to him that very in-

16

stant when, in the darkening room, six months before, his father had repudiated his own life. So in those months, while the father was bearing the pain of his death, the son had borne the pain of his birth.

For that was the way Adam Rosenzweig had thought of it. When the agony in the foot and ankle was almost too great he would say to himself that that pain was the price of being born into manhood. In the morning when he drew the lacings and the straps just a little tighter than ever before, he would say it. In the evening when he took off the boot and the reaction of the muscles, rather than a relief, was a more exquisite pain, he would say it.

Well, he had paid the price. He could now walk like a man. The examiners would probably not even notice the boot. Or if they did notice, would probably not even care. For people said that the examiners would take anybody who could crawl and had three teeth. The recruiters got a commission per head. Well, he, Adam Rosenzweig, had all his teeth and he had learned to walk. He could march. When he got his new boot tomorrow, the one without so many of the straps and lacings that had been necessary in the beginning, he would look almost like anybody else.

If nobody looked too close.

It was the second morning out of Bremerhaven, on the *Elmyra,* side-wheeler, 1,940 tons gross, English registry, when, after the breakfast of bully beef, hardtack, and tepid coffee, the agent in charge rousted them out on deck, all 125 of them. It was the first time they had been allowed up from the dimness of their quarters, and now in the shock of sunlight and seaglitter they blinked and huddled unsteadily together. A lanky man, with long red mustaches hanging off a ferociously skeletal face, with disheveled mufti but wearing a forage cap that was unfaded blue where insignia had been removed, glared at the gang. The lanky man's eyes were pale blue, and very bloodshot.

"Call 'em off, Pig-eye," the lanky man, in a curious grating English, ordered his assistant, a tub-fat Hollander with one walleye and breeches that hung chronically under the bulge of his belly.

In German, the assistant explained that as each man's name was called he was to move across to face Meinherr Doon-kahn. There, he explained, the men would form a double line. In doing so, he explained, they were to try to achieve dignity.

Meinherr Duncan, meanwhile, removed his forage cap, and it was astonishing, after the thick mat of red hair that had stuck out under the edge of the forage cap, to discover that Meinherr Duncan was bald. He was not bald as an egg. He was, rather, bald as a great knuckle of beef-bone, bony-white streaked with fresh-looking red, as though, lately scalped, he had small hope of recovery.

Meinherr Duncan gingerly fingered his sunburned scalp, and as the men, one by one, moved across the deck to form their ragged line, regarded them with singular unlovingness. Once, as the sway of the deck made him change his own position, it could be seen that he limped, in the left leg. The knee was stiff, like a scantling. Then his attention wandered from the men, and he looked at the forefinger of his right hand, which had been scratching his abused scalp. The forefinger had a streak of blood on it. Meinherr Duncan wiped the blood on the seat of his trousers, and put the forage cap back on his head.

———

At this moment, when the itch and burn of Meinherr Duncan's scalp was beyond help by scratching, Adam Rosenzweig, whose name had just been called, took his first step from the huddle to cross the deck to join the line being formed to face Meinherr Duncan. He took the step decisively, confidently. It was the moment toward which, for months—years, really— his life had been slanting. At this moment his dream would become reality.

The ship had been riding the characteristic easy motion of a long sea, but at this moment the sea broke its rhythm. It gave a little mysterious twitch, the way a horse twitches its hide when a fly lights on it. It was just enough of a twitch to break the easy, predictable lift of the deck, and that was enough to throw Adam Rosenzweig, too confident in his dream, off balance.

He did not fall. Simply, he put out his left foot to brace himself. And the foot came out in that twisting motion which, during all these months, he had so painfully conquered. There he was, frozen before all eyes, with his left toe down sharply, like a dancer's, the heel in the air, his body twisting from the hips, and his right shoulder down for balance, elbows a little out. There was the ingenious boot, with straps and laces, offered for the admiration of all. And all eyes were on it.

Adam felt the old shame flooding his being, and flushing his face. Spasmodically, he shut his eyes as though his private darkness could blot out the external reality. In that instant he thought he might pray. He thought of the little satchel which his uncle had pressed upon him at parting, and which he had not had the heart to refuse—the satchel containing phylacteries, shawl, and prayer book. He thought of himself crouched in the dark, praying.

"You!"

He heard the menace in the voice of Meinherr Duncan, and opened his eyes.

At that moment the ocean twitched again. Somehow Adam Rosenzweig held his dancer's pose, but Meinherr Duncan did not have his stiff leg braced. He promptly sat down, ass-flat on the deck.

Somewhere, in the huddle of recruits, somebody laughed. Or perhaps it was one of the English sailors.

Adam Rosenzweig found the red, ferociously skeletal face of Meinherr Duncan glaring up at him from its blue eyes. He felt the victim of a gigantic conspiracy, in which the whole world participated.

And, in a sense, he was right. If the long sea had not broken its rhythm, and given that mysterious twitch like the twitch of a horse's hide, then Adam Rosenzweig would not have struck that finicking pose and held out his boot for all to admire. If Meinherr Duncan's scalp had not been itching intolerably from the sunburn, his temper, though generally uncertain, especially after too much grog the night before, might have been better this morning. If Meinherr Duncan, at the First Manassas, had not been clipped in the knee by a Rebel rifle slug, then he

might not have been so sensitive about Adam Rosenzweig's special deformity. If, indeed, Meinherr Sergeant Duncan had not, at the First Manassas, discovered himself to be a coward, having been, in fact, the
first man in his company to break and run and then
been clipped reprovingly in the back of the knee even
as he found his stride, he might have been less sensitive. If, on the instant of his discovery of Adam Rosenzweig's deformity, the ocean had not twitched the
second time and set him upon his rear. If somebody
had not laughed. If all these things had not happened in their unique pattern, then things might have
been all right, after all.

There was, in fact, no logical reason why Meinherr
Duncan should have been so outraged by Adam Rosenzweig's physical defect. He knew that the examiners
did not really examine. He knew that he himself had
winked at, and passed farther along, some rather poor
specimens. He knew that food for powder is food for
powder, and that a fellow with a slight limp carried as
many quarts of blood to spill and fetched as high a
commission as the next one. But sitting on the deck,
with his banged coccyx, his sunburned and rum-
bruised head, his bum leg, his cowardice, and the un-
located laugh ringing in his ears, Meinherr Duncan
was in no mood to be logical.

He scrambled to his feet and thrust his red face at
Adam's.

"You!" he screamed. "You God-durn cheat! Steal-
ing a free ride to the U.S.A.! Yeah, with that foot

---

you knew you couldn't fight! Yeah, gonna get rich in America while other folks get shot! Yeah, that was yore notion, wasn't it?"

Adam stared into the red-rimmed eyes that hated him, and could not speak a word. There was nothing to say, for nothing, nothing that was happening to him, was real.

"Speak up, you booger!" Meinherr Duncan was screaming at him. "Wasn't that why you come to America?"

"No," Adam said.

"Well, what was it?" And the red face was thrust more ferociously close.

Nothing was real, and Adam knew that his voice saying what he then said was not real. It was merely his self speaking in the darkness of himself, trying to explain something to himself. "I came," the voice, at a great distance, said, "because I wanted to fight for freedom."

He knew he could not really have said that, not out loud, and when he turned his head slowly toward the other men, those who had answered their names and now stood raggedly in line, and then toward the mass who yet huddled anonymously together, he was expecting no response from them. He was merely trying to read in their faces their own deep, preciously unacknowledged secret: that they, too, wanted to fight for freedom.

Certainly he was not prepared to see Pig-eye, the Hollander, slap his big belly with both hands, as

23

though it were a drum quite detached from his body, and give two hoots of laughter, with a sound richly resembling the interfusion of a belch and a Gargantuan catarrh, and then, pointing at him, at Adam Rosenzweig, turn to the mass of recruits and shout in German: "He wants to fight for freedom. He says he wants to fight for freedom!"

The humor overcame Pig-eye, who had to pause, hoot, and slap his belly, before he got strength enough to yell again: "He wants to fight for freedom!"

Now, however, his words were lost in the general whoops and gales of laughter. The men were laughing. They were looking at him, at Adam Rosenzweig, and laughing. And back in the mob somebody kept yelling: "Für die Freiheit! Für die Freiheit!"

As the *Elmyra* moved up the coast, the green shore to the north slid slowly by, tufted here and there with trees, dotted with white villas and farmsteads, washed in the pure light of a summer morning. Adam Rosenzweig lifted his eyes from his task of chopping rust from a chain and stared at the shore. It was America.

A child, a little boy, stood on a spit of sand near a villa, very small in the distance, wearing blue pantaloons and a white jacket, and a brown dog barked and barked. At least, the distant dog held the stance and made the motion of barking—for the sound could not come to Adam against the brisk onshore breeze. It was a big brown dog, propped on forelegs stiffly forward, with the jaws opening and closing, as accurately timed as a metronome. It must have been a big dog, for it stood nearly as tall as the boy, but at the distance it was like a toy, like a cunning little Bavarian toy, and the jaws opened and shut as though some counterpoise in the hollow interior were moving with a regularity as perfect as that of a pendulum. In the bright light of a summer sea-morning with no haze, he thought he could even make out the tiny red glint of the tongue when the jaws opened.

But Adam Rosenzweig could not hear the sound. No matter how hard he strained, he could not hear the bark. He felt that if, only once, he could hear the sound of the dog's barking something would be real. For nothing seemed real now.

Nothing since that second morning out of Bremerhaven had seemed real. It was as though what he had dreamed, back in Bavaria in the long months while his father was dying and he himself was being born into manhood, had been the reality, and what had actually happened since was only a dream. Or was it even a dream? *For a man's deepest dream is all he is,* Adam had said to himself in the night, *and if that is withdrawn can anything else ever be real?*

After the laughter, that terrible morning, had subsided, Meinherr Duncan had yelled to the English boatswain standing by, "Take him—he's yours! We

26

don't want him, he's yours." At a gesture of the boatswain two seamen had seized Adam.

But Meinherr Duncan had cried: "Wait!" He had come at Adam. "Listen," he said, "if you think they'll just let you overside in New York you're a durn fool. No free ride fer you, you bastard. I do business with this line—and the captain, he'll see you're hauled right back where you come from. But you'll work yore ass off getting back. You get me, you—?"

Meinherr Duncan's strength was spent.

So the two seamen had led Adam away, and put him to work. Yes, he would work over, they told him, and then work back to Bremerhaven, if that was what the captain said, and be thrown off, on his arse, without a bleeding tanner to his name.

Whatever a bleeding tanner was.

By day, Adam scrubbed the deck or chipped saltrust from metal, laxly dragging his boot behind him, accepting again, as it were, a sense of his crippledness, not even aware that his hands were raw and swollen, so painful was the speculation as to what would become of him when he got back to Bremerhaven. What kind of life could he ever have? At night, however, that practical worry was nothing against the waking, or sleeping, nightmare of laughter and the wild cry "Für die Freiheit!" followed by wilder laughter.

He would see the faces and hear the laughter and wake, then lie there sweating while shame flooded

27

over him. But shame for what, he would ask himself. For having said that he wanted to fight for freedom? For being the kind of man who would want to fight for freedom? For having held out, as though for admiration, that ingenious boot? Or simply a mystic shame for being himself?

But one night, in the midst of his shame, a thought came to him. That wild cry "Für die Freiheit!" which had begun in derision—had it turned, in the end, into something else? Perhaps in repeating that cry over and over, the men who had begun it in derision found it springing from their own deepest need. Perhaps that was why they could not stop shouting it, as a soldier must utter his cry as he plunges forward. Perhaps that was why the laughter always got wilder and wilder. The wildness of the laughter must have been an utterance of joy, the joy men feel when they are startled by an inner strength.

If that was true, Adam thought, then he was not so different from other men. They had the same yearning that he had. With that thought, his shame was gone. Then he thought that their yearning, because more secret, was perhaps even stronger than his. And with that thought he felt the sweetness of humility. He wanted to rise and go seek in the dark some man— any man—and tell him that he understood all, and ask forgiveness. He felt like praying to God that God would never remove from his heart this vision of what men were like, for if he could keep this vision, then he,

Adam Rosenzweig, might find a way to live, after all.

With that, however, he seemed to see his uncle staring sadly at him saying: "You would pray to God to give you the delusion of the glory of man, and that is the last foolishness."

Even so, he slept.

Adam lifted his eyes from chipping the salt-rust and looked at the green shore and saw, far off, the little boy on the sand spit and the dog uttering the barks you could not hear.

That green shore, in the glittering light of morning, was America, he thought. In America was a little boy wearing blue pantaloons and a white jacket, standing in front of a white villa and watching a ship sail beautifully by. In America, far off southward, there were men who yelled and charged and died in the smoke of battle. Yes, that was America, he thought, the land where he would never come. For neither peace nor war now, would he ever set foot there.

He looked back at his left foot, stuck out behind him, and remembered Old Jacob. Old Jacob, the cobbler, had made the boot. Adam had sat with him describing the kind of boot he wanted, and the old man, crouched over his bench in the dark cubbyhole of a shop, had nodded, had said, yes, he could make it. He made it, the first boot that would, bit by bit, press the foot nearer to a normal shape. Then, after the pain of that first boot was over, he made the other to replace it, the one with fewer straps, buckles, and laces, the one that would look more like an ordinary boot.

The day after his father's burial Adam had gone to the shop for the new boot. It was ready. He took the two gold coins and laid them on the cobbler's bench, beside the new boot. Sitting there, Old Jacob looked down at the money, but did not touch it. "I will tell you something," he said.

"What?" Adam asked.

"I am an old man," Old Jacob said. "I was born in the time when Napoleon came, and men talked of a new time. We Jews talked of a new time, too. There was a new time. But it did not last. Then things were worse, even, than before. People cried, 'Jude, verreck'!" and Jews died.

"I was a big boy in the bad time. I was ordered to be apprenticed to a cobbler. I wanted to be a teacher, but one did what one was told. I could not stand the smell of the new leather. You know how they tan leather? It is not an agreeable idea. Well, I would smell the new leather when I tried to work with it, and I would vomit. When it got so bad I could not eat or sleep, I ran away.

"I was a fool to run away. The police caught me. They beat me and put me in jail and beat me again. After a while they sent me back to the cobbler. It was not his fault, the cobbler's. Perhaps he himself had never asked to be a cobbler. Perhaps he never asked to be born. That thought came to me, and it helped me to live. A man can learn to live. Look!"

And Old Jacob picked up a piece of new leather and stuck it into his mouth and began to chew it. Adam watched him. The old man took the leather from his mouth. He did not even spit out the saliva that had accumulated in his mouth. His lower lip glinted with moisture.

"See, I have learned to live," the old man said, and in the shadow of that cubbyhole of a shop, a shadow designed to hasten, even at midday, the blindness of age, he burst out laughing. In the laughter there was an awfulness of joy that made Adam's heart freeze.

The old man conquered the laughter, peered at Adam, and said, "Yes, one can learn to live. Even so" —and he pointed at the two gold coins beside the boot on the bench glinting in the gloom—"I cannot take that."

"It is the price agreed. It is yours," Adam said.

"Listen," the old man said, "even I must have something more than the knowledge that I have learned to live. If I take that money I should have only that knowledge. The boot would no longer be mine."

"But that is the point," Adam said. "I want to pay for the boot. The boot is mine."

"No, my son," Old Jacob said. "It is not yours. It is mine. It is mine, but you may wear it. You may wear it on a loan from me to hold up your leg straight."

"But—" Adam began.

"You may wear it to hold up your leg straight in America. You may wear it to march in. You may wear it into battle. But it will still be mine. Do you understand?"

For a moment Adam had a sense of entrapment, a flicker of desperation. He could not answer the question.

"You may wear it even to die in," the old man was saying. "With the bullet in you. But the boot will still be mine. For I must have the knowledge that my boot has walked on the earth in America, through mud or dust. Do you begin to understand?"

Adam nodded. Yes, he was beginning to understand.

"Pick them up," the old man said, pointing distantly at the gold coins there. "Pick them up, for the boot is mine. I have paid for it by learning how to live."

Adam silently reached out and picked up the coins. He held them in his hand, looking at them.

So Adam had carried the two gifts from Bavaria, he thought now, watching the green shore of America glide past—the satchel with the objects of devotion, given him by his uncle, and the boot, given him by Old Jacob. He thought how the gifts had come to him in balanced and mutual inimicalness. They were like gifts in some fairy tale, each, by bad magic, canceling the efficacy of the other. He could not pray, and that boot would never walk the earth of America.

Watching the green shore yonder, he thought of the cobbler. *Poor Old Jacob,* he thought, *you paid so much for that boot, and now you have been cheated.*

No, there was no use to keep his eyes on that green shore. The boot would never walk there.

He lowered his gaze to the salt-rust and resumed the rhythm of the old chisel striking the chain. Then he was aware that someone was near him. Someone was looking down at his defenseless shoulders. Slowly, he turned his head.

A seaman was lounging on the rail, some three paces off, looking down at him—a stubby, pink-faced, scrubbed-looking man, with graying chop-whiskers, a villainously black pipe stuck in one side of his jaws and eyes as coldly gray-blue as a winter afternoon in high latitudes. He had hands very red and much too big for him, like unwieldy tools carried about to be ready for a job. One lay on the rail now, like a tool, momentarily idle, laid on a workbench. Adam recognized him as one of the two seamen to whose mercy he had been consigned by the boatswain, that morning when Meinherr Duncan rejected him.

"Ye are a ruddy fool," the seaman said now, with no heat, past the black pipe yet in his jaws.

The chisel in Adam's hand stopped in mid-air. The words the seaman had spoken hung curiously in his head, like an echo. He knew he was staring blankly at the man who had spoken them, as though he had not heard, or as though too stupid to understand. The words hung in his head like an echo of his whole life.

"A ruddy fool, I said ye are," the man repeated. And as Adam still stared at him, he said pettishly: "Ye do speak English, don't ye? I heard you speak English that day?"

Adam nodded.

"So ye want to go to America?" the sailor demanded.

Adam nodded again.

"The more fool ye," the sailor said.

But now he deigned to lift the pipe from between his jaws.

"Listen," he said, "it'll be early afternoon when we make Castle Garden. That's where we drop anchor, to ease ourselves of the first parcel of vermin.

"What?" Adam asked.

"Emigrants," the seaman said. "Two hundred and fifty stowed away down there," he said, and pointed down at the deck with his pipestem, "tighter'n pickled eels in a brine barrel. But we ease ourselves at Castle Garden. We pile 'em overside into tenders, sternforemost and arse over teakettle. That is where you'd been dropped, had it not been for that Duncan's warmhearted wish to send you home again."

The seaman pointed his pipe at Adam, severely anticipating any hopefulness.

"But no," he said, "raise up no hopes. They ticks 'em off, the vermin, and you'd ne'er make it."

The seaman fell, briefly, into thought. Then he resumed.

"Then we," he said, "go up river to our proper berth.

By then it is late. When we are tied there'll be bawling and hooting and general botheration. After the gentlemen passengers are ashore and their precious bloody traps, they'll bring the other vermin up—the ones as could not pay their own passage to the Land o' Liberty, and so signed articles for a soldier. But now they—that Duncan and that swivel-eyed beer-belly of a Dutchman—they will not be even bothering to count 'em off. They will huddle 'em off into the warm, waiting arms of some of Uncle Samuel's Marines." He stopped. "Ho, ho," he exclaimed, laughed, and then paused to relish the humor of the picture in his head.

"But listen," he resumed. "Yonder's where they'll huddle 'em off. You ought to see their faces then. All the way over they been thinking on the bounty money they get—what's left of eight hundred dollars after all the agents and crimps get theirs. They been thinking of booze or wenches or being made a sergeant or getting rich. They have not been thinking of being shot in the gut.

"But when they look down that plank to America, they all think sudden of being shot in the gut. You can see it on their faces. They will be huddling at the plank-head, clotting together thick as burgoo and bold as sheep, and you can see them turn white in the face, and they hang back a little like a fellow asking the hangman to wait just a minute please while he blows his nose, and they mill around at the head of the plank. You be ready."

35

"Ready?" Adam asked.

"Yes, my sonnywhack, you be squatting yonder by that stanchion, out of harm's way. Chipping on your chain like it was for Eternal Life. You will be of no slightest interest to no human creature. No man will give tuppence nor fish hook for you, my cock. You will be of such general interest as a sea-glin at sunset. Have your sack or parcel or whatever, hid there before. To be more natural-like when the time comes. Sneak it up before. Watch smart, now. When the agent—that bloody Duncan—has led the vermin down the plank and the vermin have been kissed and petted by a detachment of Uncle Samuel's Marines, when whatever hands are on deck are watching and laughing, or going about their business, ye up and sheer off down the plank. Like ye was one of the vermin that got forgot. Which, in a manner of speaking, ye are.

"Nobody, like as not, will stop ye. By that time the Marines will be marching off the vermin to get shot in the gut. You pretend to be hurrying to catch the Marines. But watch smart, you make a cut for it."

"Suppose I did not make a cut for it? Suppose I caught up?" Adam asked. "Up with the Marines, I mean? Would they take me?"

The man looked down at him, shaking his head in wan pity. "And Christ spilled His precious blood for such as ye," he said.

"What do you mean?"

36

The man pointed the pipe stem at the foot. "Ye are a ruddy fool," he said.

The man stood there studying the foot. "Anyway," he said, finally, "that Duncan will be there, with the Marines, and he does not love ye. I do not know why he does not love ye, but there be them as must have something to hate. He would see ye back aboard and home to mother."

He again studied the foot. "No," he said, closing the subject, "ye cut for it."

The seaman turned away and took a couple of steps. Adam scrambled to his feet and called, "Wait!"

The seaman turned.

Adam could not find words. His heart overflowed with gratitude. No, it was a sweetness deeper and stronger than gratitude, a happiness that took his breath.

"I don't know how—how—" he managed.

"How what?" the man demanded.

"To thank you," Adam said.

"For what?" the man demanded.

"For what you did."

The man studied him. "Whatever I did," he said, "I don't know why I did it."

"You don't?" Adam demanded.

"Perhaps I did know," the man said. Then he gave a quick, dry laugh. "Aye," he said, and tapped out his pipe on the rail. "Suppose I am pleased to wonder how a thing will work out. I wonder sometimes how

---

37

this thing or that thing can be done. It was only I took to wondering how a fellow in your fix could get proper ashore."

Adam took a step toward him. "You're not telling the truth," he burst out.

"What's it to you?" the man demanded. "You wanted to get ashore. To the bleeding U.S.A. That's all you want, isn't it?"

"Yes."

"Well, you may get ashore, you ruddy fool. But—" Again, he turned away, and stuck the pipe into his jaws.

Adam seized him by the arm. "But what?" he demanded.

The man took the pipe from his mouth. "Why don't you leave me alone?" he burst out, in anger.

He looked northward, up the street. It was a rather wide street, with houses three stories high, some wood, some brick, narrow and blank-faced, mean or at least unhopeful; half-cellar shops and artisan studios here and there, the signs of trade or occupation displayed, pridefully or drooping, above the rabbit-hole entrance; boxes and cans of trash set irregularly along the curb. The street seemed strangely empty. A block and a half off, a dray, drawn by two horses, entered from a side street, crossed hastily and disappeared. Its muted rattle and bang seemed portentous.

Then, again, there was silence. You had the feeling that eyes were peering at you from the cellar shops and second-story windows. It was getting toward twilight, but no lamp yet showed from any window in the block. Far off, to the northeast, black smoke hung over the city.

After the dray had passed, Adam stood and let the silence settle again, like dust. He had come quite a way since his escape from the *Elmyra*. He had escaped, he had run down the plank, he had run after the Marines and their recruits, he had then cut into a side street, he had run until breathless. He had paused, gasping, and in that moment had realized that nobody, not anybody, had tried to stop him. Nobody had even yelled after him. He had escaped, he was free, and in that moment of freedom felt completely devalued. Nobody, nobody in the world, cared what he did. He could go or come, like a leaf in the eddy of a stream, like a mote of dust in the wind. This was America.

Now in the blankness of the street, after all the other streets he had come, he stared around him and felt the same sense of devaluation. Now again, nothingness swallowed him up. His body felt like nothing. He seemed to be floating.

It must be hunger, he thought.

He reached into his coat and took out a letter. He studied the address:

> Herr Aaron Blaustein
> 5th at 39
> City of New York

He must find someone to ask. Back there, after he had cut for it from the *Elmyra* and the Marines, he had found someone to ask. The man had looked at him queerly and said: "North, get on north. Quite a way."

Then the man had studied him. "Furriner?" he demanded.

Adam nodded.

"Well, you might make it," the man said. "Keep north."

He had not found it. He would have to ask again. But there was no one.

He picked up his satchel (he had lost his parcel of clothes in his dash from the *Elmyra*), and raised his eyes northward. The smoke to the northeast was worse now, and more smoke was rising, farther east. Far off, the new smoke rolled upward, greasily convolving upon itself, coiling weightily upon itself, but somehow, at that distance, over so many roofs, seeming unreal, with no reference to human pain or loss, like a picture. The evening light laid a coppery sheen over the upper bulges of the greasy blackness. Then, far off, from the northeast, Adam heard the sound, a muffled, cottony explosion.

Then it came again, three times, evenly timed.

It could not be thunder. He decided that it must be some manufactory burning, some place where inflammables were stored. He moved on up the street, with his satchel.

The houses were meaner now. He saw a light in a

window here, another there. Now and then a human form appeared from a door, looked up and down, and soundlessly re-entered. Or moved quickly off, as soundlessly. You could not ask directions of people like that.

When he had gone four blocks he heard the shouting, very faint, again toward the northeast. Then it stopped. He went on up the street. He saw a torn newspaper lying on the cobbles, and leaned to pick it up.

The upper right half of the sheet was torn off. He began to read what remained:

> to criticize General Meade for his conduct. After all, he has won the Battle of Gettysburg. Lee and his minions of Slaveocracy have been thrown back, and Washington is saved. The Union is again saved. True, Lee is still in the field, and what might have been a crushing rout has been permitted to become an orderly withdrawal. . . .

He read on to the end. So there had been a great victory.

He walked on, holding the torn newspaper in his hand. He heard the distant shouts again. People, he thought, must be shouting for victory, and the triumph of Justice. With that thought, with the yearning to join with others in joy, a sweetness now began to grow in him, like a shy sprig of green forcing up between cobbles.

Between the houses, shadow was thickening. In the high, last light, swifts made darting patterns. Some blocks off, he saw that street lamps were being lighted. He heard, again, that muffled, cottony reverberation, to the northeast, one, two, three, four explosions, evenly timed. He thought, suddenly, that that must be artillery. Yes, how stupid not to have known!

Then he thought: *That is what my father heard.*

The Rebels must be attacking the city. That was why everything was so strange.

But, no, there had been a great victory. The paper said there had been a great victory. He stopped and peered again at the torn newspaper, reading the words. Then he tried to find a date. On the upper edge, he found:

July 10, 1863

That was five days back, he thought. Yes, today was the fifteenth, wasn't it? Perhaps Lee had turned. Lee could never be beaten, they said. But the South was far away. He knew, for he had studied the maps. And five days—even for Lee—was little time to turn, to revenge and defeat, and get here. But what could it be but the enemy?

He hurried up the street.

At the next corner, he saw it.

It hung from a lamp post, and when he first saw it, he could not imagine, as he approached, what it might be.

It hung there irrelevantly. It hung there like an empty sack, with the top tied together and the loose

43

part of the top fluffing out and falling to one side, over the tight cord. That was what it first reminded him of. His mind clung to that image as long as possible. Then he knew that it was a human form. It was the form of a man, and the loose part of the top of the sack that fluffed out and fell to one side, over the constriction of the cord, was the head, hanging pensive, quizzical, abashed.

He stared up into the face, and in the sympathy of blood beating in his head and the stoppage of his own breath, he felt the agony that had popped those eyes and darkened that face. Then, in the waning light, still staring into the face, he gradually became aware that the focus of his attention was widening from that face, like the circular ripples from the point of contact where a stone has been dropped into the water. In that widening of focus, he realized that a gull was passing over the roofs, uttering its cry. But he also realized that the clothing on the body had been more than half stripped away, slashed perhaps, and wherever the flesh was exposed it was dark. At first he thought it was the color of dried blood. But he looked downward. The drooping feet, naked, were dark brown. He looked back up at the dark face. Then he knew.

It was the face of a black man, a Negro. It was the first black man he had ever seen.

And in that moment of recognition, he realized that the sympathetic pain, felt at first when he had thought the darkness of flesh to be a mark of the agony

---

of strangulation, was now gone. With a gush of shame, even of desperation, he thought that as soon as he recognized the man as black, the deepest, instinctive blood-sympathy had begun to ebb. *Can I be that vile?* he demanded of himself. *Oh, can I be?*

To recover something, he studied the face again, he looked down at the body. He saw that the clothing had, in fact, been slashed, and that the flesh was scored with gashes. In the bad light he had not at first realized the fact. *Blood drying looks dark,* he thought, *like dark skin.*

The blood had dried, dark blood on dark skin. Then he saw that one last, slow, tumescent drop was falling from one foot. He looked at the foot. The toes had been cut off. His gaze wandered back up to the hands, tied primly before the body. He had thought —if he had thought anything—that the fingers were curled inward. Now he saw the truth. There were no fingers.

He found himself staring avidly, prayerfully, at the mutilation, hoping for something to happen in his heart. Once, as a boy, back in Bavaria, he had seen an old man stop at a little wayside shrine, fall on his knees, and stare at the sacred wounds. At that time he, a boy, had hidden behind a bush to watch. He had watched for more than an hour. At last the old man had crept forward on his knees and had risen to press his lips against the wound in the side. Adam, the boy, had wondered why. Now, he remembered that scene and thought that now, at last, after all the other answers, he had the answer. The old man had been waiting for something to happen in his heart.

He wondered if something had happened in that old man's heart.

But nothing, now, was happening in his own. Nothing but the dry, grinding shame at the fact that nothing was happening.

He went across the street and sat on the curb, staring at the body. Perhaps it would happen yet. The gull came back, higher now, screamed, and was gone into the gathering darkness. A dog came and licked the stones under the hanging feet. It could not reach the feet. He managed to get up and drive the dog away. He came back to sit down.

Three children, very dirty, frowzy-headed, and unkempt, two little girls about seven and nine dragging a naked-butted boy of some two years, came and stood to stare up at the body. He rose again, and went toward them, waving his arms, he did not know why. Did he want to ask what had happened? Or to drive them away?

In any case, they ran away, dragging the little boy between them. He returned to the curb. Down the block, he heard the children singing some song. With two other children, he could tell in the remaining light, they were dancing in a ring, dragging the little boy.

If something would only happen, he thought, he could rise and go on his way. If something would happen in his heart.

46

Then a thought came. The Rebels—they must be here, after all. That would explain everything. They had plunged through the city. Not Lee perhaps, but their great raider of cavalry. What was his name? Stuart—that was it. He thought of the Rebel cavalry riding through. They had hanged this lone black man, for a warning. They had ridden on and set those fires to the northeast. Yes, that was it, the Rebels.

He felt much better. Yes, the Rebels had done it.

He rose, picked up his satchel, and moved northward. He passed the lamplighter, on the far side of the street, a tottering old man. He suppressed the impulse to ask him what had happened. He felt like fleeing from the spot.

He looked over his shoulder and saw that the lamplighter had swung out to avoid the post where the body hung. He had not lighted that particular lamp. A little farther along, Adam again looked over his shoulder. He saw that the next lamp farther down had been lighted.

It was then that he again heard the shouting, much closer now. Perhaps it was, after all, the shout of victory.

Perhaps Stuart had been driven off.

He saw the crowd debouch into his street, northward, two blocks off. They were waving torches and shouting. He could not make out the words. He moved toward them. He passed an intersection, and saw that another crowd was approaching from the east. He continued up the street, trying to make out the words.

All at once his heart leaped, and he found himself shouting, hurrying forward. He would join those who rejoiced.

Then he saw the gleam of light on steel. Somebody was waving a musket with a fixed bayonet. He saw the staves and clubs being waved in the air. He stopped. He looked over his shoulder and saw that the other crowd was pouring into the street behind him. He was between.

The first crowd was almost upon him now. In the forefront he saw a big woman, red hair streaming, face sweaty-red under the torches, dress torn nearly down to her navel. She was waving a butcher knife and shouting. He heard the words: "Shag them niggers! Shag 'em!"

They were upon him. He was whirled around with the press of bodies. He smelled the whisky and sweat. He was part of the crowd as it swept forward and swerved into a side street, westward. It was getting dark, it was night. The torches tossed above the crowd.

The crowd was yelling and swirling, and Adam, clutching his satchel, was borne with it. In a momentary break in the press, Adam saw, in the torchlight, a gaunt high-backed hog plunging wildly ahead of the crowd. Then it had fled into shadow. The crowd filled the street—an alley rather than a street—solidly from one side to the other, but Adam, even in that light, could see that the houses on this westward street were dirty, crest-fallen, decrepit, some standing only by grace. The doors—when there were doors and not merely a gaping darkness—were shut. No window showed a light. Then Adam heard the crash, then the yell, as a door was broken in.

For a moment the pressure of bodies on his body was relieved, for, with the breaking of the door, some of the crowd had spilled into that dark interior. Then the pressure resumed and he was caught in the surge toward the stoop of the next house. That door, too, crashed, and again, momentarily, the pressure was relieved. Above the yelling of the crowd Adam heard one pure, high wail from within the house.

In the middle of that wail the tumult of the crowd suddenly ceased, as though all were, in the same second, rapt by the clear beauty of that utterance. For an instant after the cry had ended that rapt silence yet prevailed. Then came the pervasive, guttural roar, filling the street. Then a woman's yell: "Shag them niggers! Shag 'em!"

As the next door crashed, Adam found himself borne toward the right side of the street. He heard the crash of another door, and the answering yells. In the tossing torchlight he saw a body, a man's body, alive and struggling, being passed from a doorway over the heads of the crowd, sustained and rolled and thrust forward by scores of hands, like a chip in a flooded sewer. The body was sucked down into the current.

Another body was being borne aloft, then another, the last one—it was close now—being rolled in a peculiar retardation over and over. For an instant, in the flare of torches, Adam saw the black face and the whitely distended eyes. Then the face was rolled over. Then it was upon him.

Mysteriously in that press, the crowd drew back to make a little space, and the body was sucked down into the vortex. Then, before the work began, the body lay across the very toes of Adam Rosenzweig.

A woman leaned over and uttered a shrill, sustained whinnying sound, and plunged her knife into the man's thigh, not terribly deep, and with a ripping motion jerked it downward. Adam could hear the sound of the blade—it was not a big knife, really not much more than a paring knife, something snatched in haste off the kitchen table—ripping the denim of the man's trousers. The man, staring upward, uttered no sound.

"Shag them niggers!" Adam heard a yell behind him.

Turning, he saw that it was the big woman with the streaming red hair.

At her yell a dozen people, men and women, leaned or squatted or crouched over the body, trying with blade, fist, fingernail, stick, or stone to get at it. But there were too many to be really effective. They got in each other's way. They pushed and shoved. They uttered blasphemies and cursed each other. One man held up a bloody hand. Some son-of-a-bitch, he affirmed, had cut him. Folks ought, he affirmed plaintively, to take care.

But they simply wouldn't take care. They were crowding and shoving. A man got shoved so hard that he fell back into the crowd, flat on his behind, leaving for an instant that space clear, and in that instant and space, Adam looked down and saw that the man on the ground was staring directly into his eyes.

Until that instant he had stood there entranced, blood beating in his head, nausea swelling in his stomach, breath short, limbs frozen. Now, by some magic, he was, to his great surprise, leaning to claw at the shoulders of those stooped over nearest him. He had dropped his satchel and was jerking them back. He was crying, "No! No!"

He was crying, "Stop!" He would not permit this to happen in the world. He was trying to wrest a knife from a crouching man who stared up at him in impotent astonishment.

Then the man began to resist. He said that the knife was his own. He swore at Adam Rosenzweig shockingly.

But the big woman with streaming red hair and torn dress cried out, offended by injustice, "God durn it, give the little fellow a chance!"

And the man who owned the knife got a kick in the butt from one of her brogans. "Here!" she said, and thrust a knife toward Adam Rosenzweig, not her own great butcher knife but a perfectly adequate instrument; she was annoyed that the little fellow didn't even have no knife, and fair was fair and square was square, she said, and she was going to see it fair and square. She was, in fact, giving him her extra knife. "Take it!" she exhorted Adam. "Take it and cut meat!"

Adam took it. He felt the knife in his hand. The

crowd pressed around him. The nearest score were trying again to get at the man. Adam was pressed down with them, half leaning, half crouching. He caught the flash of a knife that plunged forward. The whinnying cry filled his ears, then the throaty, pervasive roar. He was gripping the haft of the knife. He felt his muscles knotting. He felt a crazy elation. He felt the need to thrust with that knife. He crouched and gripped the haft and knew that he would thrust.

It was then that the vomit came up into his throat.

He had dropped the knife. He managed to push back a little. Someone was pushing to take his advantageous place. He was caught in a side-swirl of the crowd. He was propelled toward a doorway just breached. He was in the house. The narrow hall of the house was filled with people. He found himself against a little door. The door gave under his pressure and he slipped in, into total darkness. At least it was totally dark as soon as he pushed the door closed behind him. Then he fell.

He had, he discovered, fallen down a short flight of steps. He was not hurt, for at the bottom he had come into contact with the yieldingness of a human body. But there was no grunt or exclamation. The body withdrew in the dark. Adam could hear the sound of breathing.

He stood there in the dark, clutching his satchel. He could not remember how he had recovered it.

He groped his way a couple of paces and again was

in contact with a body. This body, too, withdrew with no sound. He groped further, in the dark. He found a wall. It was an earthen wall. This was merely a dug cellar, with no masonry. Adam leaned against the wall and heard the sound of stinted breathing in the dark.

The door above was pushed open and a torch appeared. Now he could see the crouching forms, the dark faces, the glint of eyes in the torchlight. Then there was a giggle at the door, the torch was withdrawn, and the door was closed. It was fully five minutes before the door opened again. It was now opened only a few inches and left that way. The cellar was, for all practical purposes, dark. Again there was the giggle.

The next sound was water splashing down the steps. It became a steady sound. It was the only sound except, very rarely, a whispering and giggling outside the door, like the sound of children playing a joke. The bottom of the hole began to fill. It filled slowly but steadily. It was boot-top high. Then, after a long time, it was knee-high. It was over waist-high before anyone made for the door.

Whoever it was whose nerve had failed, clawed at the door and got out. The door was promptly shut—shut at least as far as it would go with the hose stuck in it. There was a roar of laughter beyond the door. There was one cry. Fully ten minutes passed before the next person made for the door. The water was now breast-high.

Five people had gone out and water was nearly to

the collarbone when Adam began to explore the wall behind him. He found that there was a kind of shelf there, the level of the earth surface on which the house was built. Instinctively he tried to clamber up, sloshing the water.

Then something brushed the side of his head. Something fumbled at his shoulder. A hand—now he knew what it was—had got him under an armpit. Another hand had him by the coat. The hands were drawing him up, in the darkness.

5

His eyes opened to a high ceiling, light beige in color, the plaster worked in an intricate design of delicate craftsmanship. He felt the downy softness of the pillow under his head. He caught the starchy, clean, sunbathed, herby smell of the sheet which lay across the jut of his chin. His eyes fell shut again, and in the hypnosis of that scent, he thought of lying on a high field, in late summer, smelling the gorse, watching the unmoving blueness of the sky. He had lain, once, in such a place. His mind probed back, trying to remember.

But suddenly his mind came wide awake: *Where am I now?*

He pushed up on an elbow, and his gaze swept the large room, the rich furnishings. The heavy blue drapes on the two tall windows were drawn so that only a little light came in. The ray of sunlight that entered the slot between the drapes on one of the windows was nearly level. He watched the motes dance in the light, and in doing so forgot, for the moment, himself. Then as his mind returned to himself, it seized on, and made logical sense of the leveling ray of light: it had to be late in the day. *A man lives in Time,* he thought. *I have seized on the concept of Time, therefore I must be a man,* he thought sardonically, staring at the leveling ray. His fancy seemed terribly amusing to him.

Then his eyes fell on his little satchel set discreetly on a chair, against the wall, beyond the door. Looking at it, he added to himself: *That is my satchel. And I must be me.* He was overcome by sadness. The sadness flowered into a strange sense of guilt. For a moment it was a guilt without reference, without crime. Unless, he thought, the sadness and the guilt came from the realization that he was himself.

Then in his mind he saw the image of the man hanging from the lamp post, in the evening light, like an empty sack, and the feelings of that episode came flooding back over him. It was, however, an image suspended, as it were, in the darkening mid-air of nothingness. He was remembering nothing before it, and nothing after it, only that, at a certain moment, the redeeming experience of sympathetic pain had been withdrawn from him. He had not been worthy of the pain. Ah, that was his guilt.

Abruptly, he sat up in the bed. His mind was in a whirl. All that he could remember was that figure hanging before his eyes. He had to know what had happened. Then the door opened.

The dark-clad figure that entered was probably not of more than average height, but a preternatural thinness made him seem tall. He was a man of late middle years, wearing an elegantly cut black silk dressing gown, with a dark-gray stock, in which was a pearl pin, not excessively large. The face was thin, the aquiline nose almost paper-thin, and skin, against the black silk, looked white as chalk. The man's hair was gray, and receding far back on a thin, elegantly domed forehead, on each side of which, on the temples, veins protruded. Even at that little distance, the nervous pulse in those veins was visible. The eyes were dark, and bright.

The man took a couple of steps toward the bed, and looked down at Adam. He spoke in German: "You are Adam Rosenzweig?"

Adam nodded.

"You speak English?" the man asked in German.

"Yes," Adam said.

"Good," the man said in English, "for I fear I have

let my German lapse somewhat." He paused, studying Adam. "It is one of the several things," he said, "which I have let lapse."

The man held a piece of paper in his hand. "I am Aaron Blaustein," he said. "I am happy to have your uncle's letter. And to have you. You fainted at my door, and the letter was in your hand. But the letter —I could scarcely read it. It had been wet. Your Negro was trying to explain when—"

Adam was not listening. He leaned forward in the bed, saying: "It was a lamp post. He was hanging on a lamp post. They had cut off his toes and—"

"Who? What?" the man demanded.

"The Negro, the Negro—I saw him. I saw the dead Negro hanging on a lamp post. I saw them kill the black men in the street. I saw it. As first I thought it was the Rebels, but—"

The man was shaking his head. "No," he said. "It was not the Rebels."

"But what—but what?" Adam was straining forward.

"It was a mob rising," the man said. "We'll talk about it later. Try to forget it now." He held out the letter. "Look," he said, "it was wet. As I was saying, your Negro was trying to explain to me, but just then you—"

"My Negro?" Adam echoed, completely baffled. He sank back into the bed.

"Yes," the man said, "the one who says he saved your life. Or maybe that makes you his, and not him yours. He was a thoroughly frightened black man. He didn't want to be separated from you, even after you'd fainted. He acted as though you were his life-assurance ticket, or something. In any case, I want you to know that he has been taken in, and provided for. Poor black devil—after what's been happening here the last days. Burned out, and tortured, and killed, and—"

"He—he saved my life?" Adam puzzled over the question.

"Pulled you out of the water, he says. In the cellar."

Adam jerked up in bed. It was coming clear. He felt himself being whirled down the street, in the crowd, with the flames of torches. "Yes," he began. "They caught me, the crowd caught me. They—"

"Yes," Aaron Blaustein said. "I know."

"I hid in a cellar," Adam said.

"He told me," Aaron Blaustein said.

"I lay there on the shelf," Adam said, "in the dark, and didn't know who it was."

Adam waited. Then: "After a while it was all over. There was no one else in the cellar. Except me, and the man beside me on the shelf. I could hear him breathing."

Adam waited again.

"There was no other sound," he said. "They had gone away. The water had stopped rising."

He fell into meditation.

"You know," he resumed, at last, "what is the strangest? It is strange to think that anybody, anybody in that crowd, would stop at the end, after it was all over, to turn off the hose."

"Yes," Aaron Blaustein said.

"I lay there, on the shelf, till a light began to come over the water, through the crack in the door. Then I heard the voice from the man in the dark, behind me, a whisper. He said, 'Do you hear anything?' I said I didn't, and the voice said, 'Let's try it.' "

"I don't think you should talk of it now," the man said.

"I slid down into the water," Adam said, ignoring him. "It was just chin-deep. I managed to get to the steps. I waited at the top for the man. When he came up I saw that he was a black man. We crept out. The black man, he led the way, not to the street but out back. I wished he had gone out by the street."

Adam stopped. He felt an enormous weariness come over him, his brain fogging, his tongue thickening. Very carefully, he let himself back to the pillow.

"You see," he said then, "that was the way the others—those others who had got out of the cellar—had gone. Or tried to go. They were still there."

The tall man in the black dressing gown came closer to the bed. "Don't talk any more," he said. "The doctor is coming any moment now. He says you are unharmed, but he wanted to come back this evening, to make sure." There was the sound of a bell, muffled. He glanced toward the door. "That must be the doctor," he said.

He went to the door, and laid his hand to the knob.

60

"Try not to worry," he said. "Try not to think. You are welcome here. I was—I am—a friend of your uncle."

He opened the door, and was gone, leaving it open for the doctor's arrival.

Adam heard steps from the hall, approaching.

He was unharmed, the doctor had affirmed, and gone. The manservant had entered, laid slippers and a robe on a stool by the bed and clothing on a chair, said that the master hoped to see him below if he was so disposed, indicated the adjoining bathroom, then run a bath, and gone. Adam bathed, then went to examine the clothes prepared for him. He put on the linen drawers, remarking the lightness of the fabric; then the undershirt. He put on the black broadcloth trousers, held high with black silk braces. He examined the white linen shirt, with gold cuff links, the collar, the blue stock, the buff waistcoat, the coat, a dark-gray coat, wool but soft and light for the season. He noticed, then, his own boots; they were his. They had been set aside, carefully dried, oiled after their soaking, and blacked.

He looked at the boot, the boot that testified to all. He wondered who, after he had fainted, had taken it from his foot. He thought of the manservant, leaning over the bed to take off the boot. He thought of that strange man staring at the foot.

For a second, a split second, a murderous rage flashed through him. If that man should come in now!

Then the rage was gone. He felt a little dizzy. He sat down in that rich room, where the gas was now lighted, and drew a black silk sock on his left foot, and pulled on the boot. He put on the right boot.

Then he rose and caught a glimpse of himself in the tall glass of the dresser. He saw, marveling, the erect figure in the elegant gray coat and gleaming linen. He saw the head held high, the black hair, damp from the bath, curling slightly off the well-shaped skull, the blue eyes bright with excitement, the fine thrust of the nose, the cleanly modeled jaw. *Why*—he thought, marveling—*why I—I'm handsome!*

He stood there and felt, in the depth of his being, possibilities richly, sweetly growing. He drew himself up even straighter, and smiled into the glass with gracious charm.

Suddenly, he put his hands over his face to blot out the sight. *I do not want to be this wicked,* he thought. *For it is wicked,* he thought.

He stood there and thought of that body hanging from the lamp post under the evening sky. He thought that he could not smile into the glass in the world where that was. He removed his hands from his face, and looked down at his left foot.

If he looked at the foot, he thought, it might help him to remember.

At dinner, across the mahogany, beyond the candles, with the manservant erect in the background, Aaron Blaustein had said: "Let us talk first of Bavaria. Tell me of your uncle. Does he still conduct his *schule?*"

"Yes," Adam had said, and so told of his uncle.

"We were boys together," Aaron Blaustein said. "He was older than I, a little. He was kind and already learned. I knew your father, Leopold, but not so well. No one knew him well. He was somewhat secretive—secretive and angry. No, brooding and—shall I say?—withdrawn. It was no surprise when he fled from Bavaria."

"He was a great man," Adam said, staring at the candles, thinking of the smell of burning tallow in that room in Bavaria, of the words when the body was laid in the earth.

Have mercy, he thought, *upon the remnant of the flock of Thy hand.*

But Aaron Blaustein was saying: "I learned that he became a poet."

Adam nodded, staring into the flame of a candle.

"I learned that he was killed at the barricades," the voice was saying, "in Berlin."

"No," Adam said absently, "but he was there. He was at Rastatt, too. At Rastatt, he was taken. He was in prison for many years. He died this spring. Back in Bavaria. He died," he added, after a slight pause, trying to make his voice dry and factual, "he died a—a *baal t'shuva.*"

Aaron Blaustein said: "Your uncle—was he happy?"
Adam nodded.

"Were you?" Aaron Blaustein asked, softly.

63

Then as Adam lifted his eyes at him, the man shook his head. "Don't answer," he said. "Please do not. I had no right to ask the question. I think I was asking it of myself, really. Repented—so he repented." He paused. "You live, and so much happens," he said.

He touched his tall, elegantly domed brow with the tips of the fingers of his right hand.

"Come," he said, "let us go into the drawing room." He stepped aside to let Adam precede him. Once there, he hesitated, then said: "No, first come with me. To my study." He led the way to a room off the back of the drawing room, a tall walnut-paneled room, lined with books. He turned to Adam. "You saw the satchel? In your room?"

"Yes."

"Did you open it?"

"No."

"Well, I did," Aaron Blaustein said. "I apologize, but it was soaking, and I feared for the contents." He indicated a massive desk. "Look," he said.

There were the contents of the satchel, carefully laid out. Aaron Blaustein picked up the prayer shawl. "The *talith*," he said, "it seems to have dried without harm. And everything except the *siddur*." He examined the pages of the prayer book. "But the book," he said, "it will be all right. Only it needs some care. One of the maids, a very clever girl, she worked on it this afternoon. She will again, tonight."

Before Adam could say anything, the man fixed his

dark, shining gaze on him and asked: "Your uncle gave you these? When you left?"

Adam nodded.

"He gave the same to me," Aaron Blaustein said, "when I left for America. Forty years ago."

He turned on his heel, abruptly, and went back into the drawing room. Adam, following, could see that the butler was settling the big crusty-looking silver tray on a low marble-topped table, with gilt legs.

As the butler served the coffee, Aaron Blaustein said: "They were a comfort to me, for some years. They were a comfort to a poor Jewish basket-peddler. Yes, for five years I tramped with a budget on my back, full of kuttle-muttle—that is what we Jew peddlers call our Yankee notions. I tramped most of Georgia and Carolina. I—"

Georgia, thought Adam, *Carolina.* He tried to see those places in his mind. He tried to see people there, white faces, black faces. He scarcely heard what Aaron Blaustein was saying, telling how he had got to be a "wagon-baron," then a "store-prince."

"Georgia, Carolina!" Adam burst out.

"Yes," the old man said studying him. "Oh, yes, it seems strange to you, doesn't it? But they treated me rather well, you know. When I was traveling around, even with a budget on my back, they might set me at the table. Even nice and proper houses. It was because they were lonely, I suppose. They wanted somebody to talk to. They knew nothing of the world.

65

They do not see the logic of the world. That's it!"

He paused, to let a secret excitement die.

"That's it," he repeated, "and that's how they got themselves into this mess, poor wretches. They got into this war because they knew nothing of the world. How the world is moving. That's why they'll be beaten—"

"Yes, yes!" Adam exclaimed, "they will be beaten." He looked down and saw that the hand holding his cup of coffee was shaking with sudden excitement. He steadied the cup with his other hand, to prevent the tiny rattling.

"Yes!" Aaron Blaustein echoed. "They'll be pushed into the sea! They'll be killed! They'll pay, they'll—"

Adam looked up to see the man's face suddenly gone white and strained, the nostrils twitching, the dark eyes flashing. Then, in that instant, he saw the control re-established. It was as though a hand had closed strongly on a sponge, had squeezed out of it suddenly all the burden of wrath and tears, had let it assume its old shape, dry and light.

Adam thought he heard the dry, quick breath of the man. Then he saw him smile, a smile sad and flickering, as he said: "It is hard to remember."

"Remember what?" Adam asked, when the man did not go on.

"All that goes into the making of any one moment we live," Aaron Blaustein said, and shrugged gently. "There are things one must try to remember. Do you know what is the hardest thing to remember?"

"No," Adam said.

"Well, I'll tell you, my son," Aaron Blaustein said. "The hardest thing to remember is that other men are men."

He leaned to set his cup down. "But that," he said, "is the only way you can be a man yourself. Can be anything."

The old man looked about the room, the great gilt mirror above the screened fireplace, the crystal chandelier where the small gas jets spread glittering light, the deep-red carpet, the rosewood, the mahogany, the great bronze of Perseus meditatively holding the head of Medusa. "Look," he said, "I am rich. I am not as rich as—as August Belmont. I am not a Sephardi. I do not have a gentile wife—yes, the daughter of the great Commodore Perry."

He stopped. He sank, for a moment, into profound thought, then said: "In fact, I have no wife."

He stopped again, then straightened up, and lifted his gaze to Adam. "But I am rich," he said. "Yes, and sometimes at night I come into this room, when the three Irish maids have gone to bed, and the English butler and the black cook, and the black cook's black helper, and the coachman, and I am alone, and I walk around this room and touch things—"

He paused, and reached out a hand to touch, tentatively, a piece of Sèvres on the mantel.

"I have to touch things to think they are real. That I'm real. I shut my eyes and I think, *Is this me?* Then I think, *No, I am a poor Jew back in Bavaria.* I have to

---

67

try to remember how everything happened. I am rich, I own land and houses and banks and railroads, but you know I still keep my supply house, where I sell goods, tinned food and cloth and things." He paused. "Only now it's wholesale, of course—and I go there every day and I put on an old black alpaca coat and I wander around among the clerks and I am like the poor old Jew in his hovel of a shop on Baxter Street. "Yes," he said, then, "every day I have to go there and put on that old coat."

He paused, and Adam again heard his breathing.

"I do not pray any more," the old man said. "But when I go there and put on that old coat, which I have had for so many years, it is, in a way, like praying."

He smiled fleetingly, and shrugged. "But I do not know precisely how," he said.

As he said that, there came the distant reverberation. Adam stared in question. Aaron Blaustein shook his head. "Merely thunder," he said. "It is building up to rain. But there was cannonading—yesterday. And this morning on Second Avenue."

Adam rose abruptly from his chair. "I heard it," he said. "I heard it yesterday, yesterday evening. I thought it was fighting with the Rebels—"

"No," Aaron Blaustein said, "the troops had arrived. And they leveled the cannon straight in the face of the mob, and fired. They fired grape and canister at a range of eight paces. I am told," he added, "that now it is generally known in the city that grape will clear a street rather thoroughly for two blocks from the muzzle. The troops did a clean job."

"Troops?" Adam asked.

"Yes, and some fresh from Gettysburg. Where they had been killing Rebels."

"But here?"

"Here," Aaron Blaustein said, "they are killing men who do not want to kill Rebels." Looking at Adam's face, puzzled and disturbed, he said: "Forgive me. I do not mean to be ironical. But if you have stopped worshiping God all you can fall back on is History. I suppose I worship History, since a man has to worship something. I suppose I am not wise enough not to let worshiping History make me ironical."

"I want to know," Adam said.

"Know what?"

"I want to know why they do not want to kill Rebels."

"I stated it badly," Aaron Blaustein said. "I should have said men who do not want to be killed by Rebels. But who are now being killed by troops trained to kill Rebels." He studied Adam. "I apologize," he said. "I pick at that business, like a scab. The simple fact is, there's a new conscription law, and the mob has risen because they don't want to be conscripted. So they have gutted conscription offices, killed all the black people they could lay hand on, burned the Colored Orphan Asylum—and would have killed the orphans but for luck—killed police, fought the troops, and looted and burned a big part of town. But—"

69

He stopped, and seemed about to turn listlessly away.

"But what?" Adam asked.

"Only that the war will be lost if there is not conscription. You see—" He stopped, to listen again to the thunder. "You see," he resumed, "the heroes are long since promoted lieutenant or general or something. Or," he added, "are dead."

He took out a cigar, cut it, and was about to put it into his mouth. Then he caught himself. "Oh," he cried in a burst of profound, excessive distress, "oh, I'm sorry! Forgive me." He proffered his pocket case. "Do have one."

"No, thank you," Adam said.

Aaron Blaustein lighted his cigar, shut his eyes and inhaled the comfort of the smoke. "And," he said, "when the heroes are dead, you have to fill the ranks some way. Even with ordinary mortals. Who much prefer to stay at home and make money and sleep with their wives."

He drew the smoke from his cigar, took a pace or two, closed his eyes, and let the smoke float from his nostrils. "Yes," he said, opening his eyes, looking down at Adam, "only conscription can save us. Conscription and—"

He paused, then took a step toward Adam. "What ship did you come on?" he demanded.

"The *Elmyra*. It is English. But we came from Bremerhaven."

"How many did they bring?"

"Many—many what?"

"You know," Aaron Blaustein replied impatiently. "Men to die for liberty," he said, and for an instant drew down the corners of his mouth, in an expression that was pain.

Für die Freiheit, für die Freiheit: the phrase rang in Adam's head, with the pain and betrayal of that morning on the deck of the *Elmyra* and, even, the shame. His gaze dropped to his left foot. He found that it, as though independent of his will, as though unattached to his body even, had withdrawn slightly, like a sick animal trying to slip under the skirt of the chair.

Then he realized that Aaron Blaustein was, also, looking down at it.

"Forgive me," the old man said. "You are the son of your father. I think I can understand why you came. And what happened. They—they discovered—"

He paused. Adam nodded, scarcely able to look at him. Then he managed. "Yes," he asid. "It was because of my father. I came to fight. But they—" He hesitated, then thrust the foot forward into full view. "They discovered my deformity."

"Was it an accident?" Aaron Blaustein demanded, with sudden firmness. "Or was it so from birth?"

"Birth," Adam said, trying to keep his eyes on that dark, shining stare.

"Birth," the old man said, "there is always something from birth. There is your fate to bear. There is yourself. There is"—and he hesitated—"even life."

71

He stiffened, and squared his shoulders, as though, despite his age and frailness, imitating a military stance. He looked down at the foot. "Even so," he said, "you would have made a better soldier than most they get. Drink-sodden Irish and pudding-bellied Plattdeutsch. Yes, those same Plattdeutsch that Napoleon pushed around like trusses of hay. Well, the Rebels push them around in the same fashion. You know what they say those Plattdeutsch are good for? Raping and running—that's what the Yankees say!"

He shrugged, resumed: "But it's the way to win since not every Yankee is interested in being a hero. It wears down the Rebels—to kill even Plattdeutsch. It takes time, energy, and powder. And there are always more Plattdeutsch."

The thunder came again, with a scurry of rain brisk on the window glass. One of the curtains bulged back into the room, billowing with wind. Aaron Blaustein went to inspect the window. He drew the curtain aside. "It's where the cobblestone came through," he said factually. "We fixed the hole with cardboard, but it has slipped."

He was kneeling, working on it.

"Cobblestone?" Adam asked.

"Yes, when they attacked the house."

"Who?"

"The mob." He drew the curtain farther aside. There were rifles stacked to one side, behind the curtain. "Some of my clerks," he said, "they came here to defend us. I didn't even have to ask them, they came with rifles. Some of them Irish, too. I guess the man they shot coming up the steps must have been Irish. That's comedy, I suppose."

He paused, then added: "They had to fire only one volley. The mob then tried an easier house."

He let the curtain drop, waited for an instant to see that his repair would hold, and came back toward Adam. "You know," he said, "it is rather refreshing to be attacked by the mob merely for being rich. Not for being a rich Jew. It makes all the trouble of coming to America seem worth while."

Suddenly he looked very tired, and the flesh of his face even chalkier. He sat down. "I really am not that bitter," he said, looking at his cigar, now dead, but not making any motion to relight it. "Most of the mob, they had come to America, too. But they had not got rich. You know, there's always a reason. That's what History is—the reason for things. That's why it can take the place of God. God being the reason for things, too. That's it—"

He paused, and gave a quick dry laugh.

"That's it," he resumed, "it's just that God is tired of taking the blame. He is going to let History take the blame for a while."

He laughed, under the glittering chandelier.

He stopped laughing. "What I said," he complained peevishly, "I don't think it is very funny."

Then his tone went factual. "Those poor devils, the

rioters," he said, "the very ones who did what they did to the black people—they are part of the reason of History. Oh, yes!"

Adam felt a faint nausea, as though his dinner had gone bad. His throat had a brassy taste, Aaron Blaustein was staring into his face, saying: "Yes, you are shocked by what you have seen. You got off your ship and stepped on the soil of America and you saw what you saw. But listen, everything is part of everything else. Did you know that?"

Adam was shaking his head, numbly.

"It is hard, my son, to know," the man was saying, in infinite pity. "But you will learn it. Only by learning it can you live. That is the only way I can live. Whatever comes out of History—out of this anguish even—will come only because everything is part of everything else. Yes, my son," and he paused, "even the good. Yes, my son, I urge you not to despair. Try —we must try—to think of the reason. Those people who did what they did to the blacks, they had a reason. People always have a reason. Ah, that is the pity. Did you know that?"

Adam stared at Aaron Blaustein and did not know anything. Far off, he saw the man's lips move, and far off, a voice was saying something.

"—had come for freedom and hope," the voice was saying, "and now would be betrayed, would be seized and shot to death for the black people. So they kill black people and—"

Adam watched the lips move. If he watched the

lips move he would not have to hear the words. But he heard them.

"—for freedom and hope, but did not get rich. That is why they were screaming, 'Down with the rich!' Because the rich have three hundred dollars, and if you have three hundred dollars you can buy out of conscription and stay home and get richer."

Aaron Blaustein laughed. Then he stopped laughing. "Yes," he said, "everybody is getting rich now. Did you know that?" He paused. "Everybody, that is, who isn't getting killed."

He rose abruptly from his chair. Adam saw the thin white fingers twist and break a dead cigar.

"But some believed," he said thickly. "Some believed. Like you. With your bad foot."

He stopped. Adam heard his breathing.

"Yes," Aaron Blaustein said, when his breath came again properly. "But the world grinds on. And people get rich. I get richer."

He stopped again.

Then resumed: "Did you ever hear of Chancellorsville?"

Adam shook his head.

"Those damned—those God-damned, pudding-bellied Plattdeutsch—they broke. It was getting dusk, and the Rebels—those God-damned Rebels—they came storming out of the woods. It was Stonewall, and those Germans broke."

He flung the twisted, crumpled cigar to the red carpet, and stared down at it.

"My son was killed," he said dully. He sat down.

He found his breath, and said: "My son was with Howard's corps. The Germans broke and let them through on the flank." He waited, then spoke again, his voice lower. "It wasn't much over two months ago. My wife could not live. Not with Stephen dead. I did not think I could live."

He looked down at the broken cigar on the red carpet. "You know," he said, and lifted his dark gaze beseechingly to Adam, "I cannot die."

He rose from the chair. He was shaking as with a chill.

"What do I care what happens now?" he demanded. "They kill in the streets. They hang the niggers. They get rich. They blaspheme and couple and fornicate. Let them all die, North and South. Oh, what do I care—" He lifted his right hand, thin, bony, white, shaking in the air, under the glitter of the great chandelier of icy crystal, in which the innumerable small jets of gas hissed.

"What do I care," he cried out, "if this land be smitten with the botch of Egypt and with those emerods that cannot be healed? Let it be blasted. Where is my son?"

He stood there, shuddering under the glitter of crystal. His hand descended slowly.

"No—no," he said. "Forgive me. I do not know what is happening to me." Very carefully, he took out his cigar case, and prepared and lighted another cigar.

He drew in the smoke, exhaled it. He inspected the

cigar. "These cigars are very expensive," he said.

"Yes," Adam said. He had to say something, for Aaron Blaustein was staring at him.

"Do you know what History is?" Aaron Blaustein demanded.

"No," Adam said.

"It is the agony people have to go through," Aaron Blaustein said, "so that things will turn out as they would have turned out anyway."

He burst out laughing, under the chandelier.

He stopped laughing.

"I don't know what is wrong with me," he said fretfully. He leaned forward, then took a step, staring down at Adam. "Do you know whose coat that was?" he asked.

Adam knew. He knew, suddenly, with cold terror.

"I see you sitting there in that coat," the old man said. He stopped, then resumed: "I am not superstitious. I do not believe in God. But I believe that God has sent you to me."

He looked searchingly down at Adam. "Do you know for what purpose?"

"No," Adam managed to say.

"To be my son," Aaron Blaustein said.

In that moment, Adam really did not see the thin old man with the chalk-white face and darkly burning eyes. It was as though his own father had appeared, not the broken man dying on the cot in the darkening room in Bavaria, but the same man magically rising beyond pain and distemper of spirit to welcome his son into his triumph. Adam's eyes filled with tears, and the black-clad figure swam in their glitter.

"Even that," Aaron Blaustein, standing there, rapt in his own dream, was saying, pointing down at Adam's boot.

Adam looked down at his boot.

"Even that is a sign," the old man was saying.

Adam stared down at the boot. *It is my boot,* he thought. *I had that boot made.*

"It is a sign that you are sent by God," the voice, far away, was saying.

Adam felt a thousand filmy strands being cast over him, binding him, netting him down. He did not think that he could breathe.

"It is a sign," the voice was saying, "that you cannot be taken from me. They will not take you for their war. You will be with me. You will be in my house. Oh, my son!" he cried out, and with that, dropped to one knee before Adam, letting the cigar fall from his fingers, reaching out to touch the boot, like something delicate, something precious.

Adam, sitting there in his sickening disorientation, stared at the cigar on the floor. He saw the red carpet about the lighted end of the cigar scorch to brown, then to black. He saw the smoke from the carpet begin to rise to mix with the pale smoke from the cigar. He saw the red winking of the blackened strands of the fabric as they were consumed and parted.

Suddenly he heard in his mind the voice of Old

Jacob back in Bavaria: . . . *wear it even to die in it.* That was what the voice in the dark of his head was saying. *With the bullet in you,* the voice was saying. *But the boot will still be mine,* the voice said.

Adam rose abruptly from the chair. He thrust his left foot forward from under the touch of the old man crouching there, and ground his boot on the cigar and the smoldering spot of the carpet.

"You want something from me," he said to the old man.

The old man, still crouching, looked up. "I want the hope that I am not to die in bitterness," he said, and hung his head, as though at a shameful admission.

"I want something from you," Adam said, surprised at the distant harshness of his voice. "Something more important."

"What is it?"

"You are rich," Adam said, and gestured around the room at marble and polished wood and gilt and glittering glass. "You are powerful. You have influence. You can do it."

"Do what, my son?"

"Do not call me your son. You have not heard what I am going to ask." He waited, and when Aaron Blaustein made no reply, he said: "I want to be in the army. You must arrange it."

Aaron Blaustein rose, weakly, and stood there.

"I can march," Adam said. "Look!" He took three strides across the room, and swung smartly to face again Aaron Blaustein, who, he discovered, was shaking his head sadly.

"No," the old man was saying, "that is beyond my power." He pointed at the boot.

"All right," Adam said, harshly, withdrawing. "I shall walk there. To Virginia. I shall be there. When my father went to the barricade, nobody looked at his foot. They handed him a musket. At Rastatt, they handed him a musket."

He came and stood angrily before the old man. "Do you think I came here to be rich?" he demanded.

"No, you did not come to be rich," Aaron Blaustein said.

"Well?" Adam demanded.

The old man meditated. "If you must go," he said slowly, "I could arrange a mission. But no one will hand you a musket. Yes—" He paused. "Yes, I could arrange a mission, a matter of—"

"I cannot go on your money," Adam cut in. "Don't you understand?"

Aaron Blaustein studied him for what seemed a long time. "My son," he said then. He stopped.

"If I may call you my son," he then said. "Let me have the word upon my tongue," he said, "even if your heart is deaf to it."

"It is not that my heart is deaf—it is that—"

Aaron Blaustein lifted his hand with sudden authority. "You shall go," he said. "I know the way for you to—"

"Not on your money," Adam cut in.

"No," the old man said. "On money you earn. But not from me. It will not be much, but you will live. And get to Virginia."

Adam leaned close, and laid his hand on the thin arm. The muscle, he felt, had withered from the bone. "Please understand," he pleaded. "Please understand why I have to go."

"I think I do," Aaron Blaustein said, slowly. "I think I understand." He paused.

"But I wonder if you—you yourself—know, really know, even now, why you must go." He shook his head. "No," he said, "for you have to go—to understand—to understand why you have to go. For"—and a flicker of excitement touched his face—"don't you know that the only way to know why you do a thing, is to do it. That is the only way, I suppose, for a man to know what he needs to know."

He turned listlessly away. He took a couple of steps. Suddenly his knees gave down, and he sat, abruptly, in a chair. His breath came with difficulty. "I am an old man," he managed after a moment, "and I do not know what I need to know."

He let his head fall against the cushioned chair back, and closed his eyes. "I only know that Stephen, my son, has gone away."

Then added: "I should have known that you, had you stayed, would not have been my son. Only by your going is that possible. For Stephen went."

Adam swung down from the big wagon and the wagon drew away.

The dust of the limestone pike whitened the grass and fennel and dock where he stood. The blossoms of the butterfly weed were a flaming orange standing sharply above the chalked-over green. A fritillary—a swallowtail, tigerishly black and gold—hung from one of the blossoms. Adam, standing with his feet in the white dust, watched its wings pulse slowly in the sunlight, opening, shutting. The afternoon sun blazed. The air was motionless. He was almost sure that, in that air without motion, he might feel on his cheek each small, measured, velvety puff from the voluptuous motion of those wings.

He heard the second wagon approaching, the dust-muted grind of the iron tires on the gravel of the pike. He looked up. The first wagon, the big one, was fifty yards past him down the pike, moving in its stately pace, the white canvas hood gleaming in the sun. The second wagon drew up, and stopped. Adam put his good foot on the hub.

"He tell you to git off?" the Negro driver asked.

"Yes," Adam replied, and swung up beside the driver.

"He likes tellen folks things," the driver said.

Adam, saying nothing, settled onto the board seat.

The driver picked up the reins, the horses moved forward. "Why he tell you to git off?" the driver asked.

"He said he wanted to think."

"Thinken," the driver said. "That 'un ain't thinken but on one thing."

Adam said nothing. He was looking down the road at the big wagon, drawing on through the lifting, languid foam, hub-high, of white dust.

"Money," the driver said. "All Ole Him ever studyen on."

The tires made their soft, steady sound on the gravel.

"Money," the driver said, "and one other thing. Tellen folks things. Do dis. Do dat."

"I didn't resent being asked to get off," Adam said. "He has a right to be alone. Some people have to be alone to think." And he added: "It's his wagon."

"Do dis, do dat," the driver mimicked. "Yeah," he said, "you know whar he come from."

"Yes," Adam said. "Carolina."

"Yeah," the driver said, "Ca-lina—but ain't nuthen but buckra."

"Buckra? What's that?"

"The kind of white folks ain't got time for nuthen but kicken niggers and ass-kissen rich folks," the driver said. "Ole Him. Trash."

Adam carefully watched the wagon ahead.

"Buckra," the man beside him said. "Yeah, that kind doan know but two words—*you black son-a-bitch* and *yassuh, cunnel.*"

"Has he ever called you that?" Adam asked.

"He ain't never called me cunnel," he said, and giggled.

"I mean the other," Adam said.

"He ain't never said it, but you kin smell it on him," the man said, then sank into a brooding silence.

Measuring his words, feeling suddenly lost and sad in his heart, watching the wagon ahead, Adam said: "You know the story. How he came here. What he did. You heard Mr. Blaustein tell us."

"Yeah, Mr. Blow-steam," the driver said. "Mr. Blow-steam—what the hell he knows? Him a rich Jew, setten in New Yawk. Me, I bin down thar. Bawn down South."

"Mr. Blaustein was down there. Some years."

"Yeah, and him rich," the driver said.

"He was very poor," Adam said. "He was a poor

peddler." He thought of Aaron Blaustein. In his mind he tried to see the young man, with a thin, pale face and dark eyes, walking down a road hot and endless, a pack on his back. A budget, he had called it. "He had a pack on his back," he added.

"Yeah, and the son-a-bitch got rich," the driver asserted bitterly, and Adam knew that the reins had been loosened to fall on the rumps of the team, and that the man was turning toward him. Resolutely, he did not turn, keeping his gaze fixed down the pike.

"You ever hear 'bout a nigger gitten rich?" the driver was demanding.

Adam felt the man's breath, he was leaning so close.

"I am not rich," Adam said, and in saying it, felt an instant of elation, of purity. He saw, in that instant, the rich room of Aaron Blaustein, and himself leaving it. Suddenly, inexplicably, he felt saved.

"But you," the driver was saying, "I bet you git rich."

"I don't think so," Adam said, soberly.

"Yeah," the driver was saying, "but the richest any nigger ever got is to git away."

Looking straight ahead, Adam saw the reins drop completely loose on the backs of the team.

"Look-a-here!" the driver was saying.

Adam looked.

The man beside him was twisting his near shoulder down, stripping the calico shirt back. "Look at this-here back," the man said.

Adam saw the old welts plaited and crisscrossing

grayly on the dark skin. He felt the cold prickle of the flesh on his own back as he stared.

"That's what I up and run off from," the man said, and pulled up the shirt, with a sharp, conclusive motion, as though he had fulfilled his part of a bargain. He picked up the reins. "Yeah, and run to New Yawk," he said.

He giggled. Or made a sound resembling a giggle. "Yeah, New Yawk," he said, giggling, "and you seen what them folks does thar. Can't tell 'bout them folks. You jes walken 'long the street—then wham, you daid. Ain't ne'er seen 'em afore. I ain't stayen in no New Yawk."

Adam swung his gaze from the road, to the trees, to the green meadows, the green swell of the hills. In a flicker of time, less than an instant, he had some sense of himself leaping from the wagon, running across a meadow, flinging himself down, face down, in the secret depth of a green thicket. Then the craziness of that vision of flight was gone, as though it had not existed at all. But he kept his eyes turned away.

"Ain't stayen in no New Yawk," the driver was saying. And again giggled. "Not this here nigger chile of the Lawd-God."

Adam kept his gaze averted, but he was not seeing the green meadows now. "That night," he said, "that night in the cellar—" His voice trailed off.

"Yeah?" the driver asked.

"When you pulled me out of the water, did you know—" His voice trailed off.

"Know what?"

"Know I was white, I mean," Adam managed.

The man seemed to be thinking. Then he said, "Yeah. Reckin so. When they open the door, and stuck the light in, it lay on yore face." He paused, ruminating. "Maybe not white, but bright-skin. One second I seen the light lay on it."

Then he made that sound that resembled a giggle. "Yeah, white," he said, "but I didn't know it was Jew-white."

"Yes," Adam said. "I am a Jew."

He turned his eyes, again, to the meadows and hills and the shadows of the groves. It was a beautiful country, he thought.

"You saved my life," he said. "I suppose you did. I can't swim. I was getting afraid, the water was so high. I might have tried to go out the door. They might have killed me."

"Mought of," the driver's voice said.

Adam turned to look at him. It was, in a way, as though this were the first time he had laid eyes on him. He saw the strong, black shoulders under the red-check calico, the long arms lying loose, forward over the knees, the strong hands, seamed and calloused, holding the reins. He looked at the face. The skin was dark brown and smooth as oiled leather. The thrust of the jawbone was strong, but the lips were heavy and low, with a piece of chewed straw hanging out one side of the mouth. The eyelids were pendulous, slightly swollen-looking, and the eyes bloodshot.

Those eyes, Adam knew, could sharpen to a quick, penetrating, assessing glance. But now, looking at that slack, somnolent face, he could scarcely believe that.

He did not know what to believe. Suddenly he felt that he knew nobody, nobody in the entire world. He felt lost in a realm of fantasies.

Then, looking at the man's face, he remembered the face of the body he had seen hanging from the lamp post. He remembered his shame when, knowing the man for what he was, his instinctive sympathy for that man's death-agony had faded. Suddenly, looking at the man now beside him, he felt, with the sweetness of water upon a parched tongue, that lost sympathy for the nameless, abused black body suspended from the lamp post.

With a gush of feeling he touched the driver's shoulder.

"I want you to know that I am grateful," Adam said. Then: "I should like to do something for you. Sometime, when it is possible."

"Yeah," the driver said, and Adam said nothing.

The wagon drew on through the heat. Secretly, Adam studied that face beside him.

He saved my life, Adam thought.

He wondered what his life was. He decided that he did not know what his life was. That was what he was going to discover. Somewhere at the end of this winding white road. At the end of muddy clay roads. Somewhere, far off, south. *Yes,* he thought, *yes,* and remembered Aaron Blaustein saying: "The only way to know why you do a thing, is to do it."

Then Adam thought: *No.* He decided that that could not be true. The belief did not come out of the action. The action came out of the belief. He listened to the soft grind of the iron tire on gravel and thought. *I am moving down this road because I believe.* He was about to try to say to himself what he believed, but his mind let go, like a tired hand. It could not hold the thought, whatever the thought had been about to be.

He sat there, staring down the white road, swaying in the retardation of that rhythm of wheel and dreamily heaving hill and heat-throbbing sky, bemused in the strangeness. He thought of the man beside him. *Do I know him?*

Then: *Does he know me?*

The first day out, Jedeen Hawksworth had, as today, said, "Git down, I can't think and you setting thar. Git on the nigger's wagon a spell."

Adam had obeyed, and, as today, had swung up beside the Negro. His mind now went back to that first day out, the moment when he had turned to the Negro and said: "I should like to know the name of the man who—who did what you did for me. That night. In the cellar. Mr. Blaustein called you Mr. Talbutt, but what is your full name?"

"Mose," the driver had said. "Mose Talbutt."

"Moses?" Adam echoed, in question.

"Naw," the driver had said. "Ain't no Jew name."

"But it—" Adam hesitated. "What I mean is," he resumed, "it must be the same name—from the Bible, I mean."

"Mought be Bible," the driver said. "But ain't Jew."

After a moment Adam asked: "I want to be your friend. We shall be traveling together for a long time. What do you want me to call you? Do you want me to call you Mose?"

"Naw," the man said.

Again after a moment, Adam said: "Yes, Mr. Talbutt."

The driver giggled. "Doan call me that—that what Ole Blow-steam called me." He giggled—or rather, made his noise like giggling. Then he mimicked Aaron Blaustein, prinking with his mouth: "Mis-ter Tal-butt, Mister Tal-butt." Then added: "Ole Blowsteam—he just sort of got hung-up some way on that *Mister* stuff. Got to prissen and pranken with hit and couldn't let go. All he wanted was to be shed of it. Shed of that *Mister* stuff. And shed of me. Lak sellen me off to that buckra." He nodded ahead to the white canvas hood of the wagon up the pike.

Looking at the big wagon ahead, Adam said: "He didn't buy you. He is paying you wages." Then added: "He is paying us the same wages."

"Dat what he say," the driver said. "You wait and see."

"That was the agreement," Adam said. "And if he doesn't pay the same—if he—"

90

"Den what?" the driver demanded. "Den what, Big 'Un—what you do?" He waited, then leaned slyly toward Adam, and said softly: "Gimme yourn, huh? To make ev'thing even?"

"I should like to believe that I would," Adam said.

Mose giggled, then fell to whistling a scarcely audible tune, a tune thin and gay.

Adam looked off across the green fields, toward the woods, where the cool comfort of shadow was. Then, turning back, he said: "What do you want me to call you?"

"You jes call me Talbutt," the driver said. "I reckin you kin git that out, huh?"

"Yes, Talbutt," Adam said. Then: "Do you know my name?"

"One of them names like Blow-steam," he said.

"Yes, Rosenzweig," Adam said. "But I have another name."

"Yeah," the driver said, "but I fergits yore other one. I hear'd hit, but I fergit."

"It is Adam," Adam said.

"Yeah."

"Do you know what Adam means?"

"Naw."

"It means, simply, man," Adam said. "In the Hebrew tongue—the language of the Jews."

"Yeah."

"But it is not a usual name for a Jew to be called. My father gave me that name because he loved mankind and wanted men to be fully man. He fought and suffered for that. He gave me that name that I might try to be a man in the knowledge that men are my brothers." He paused. "Do you see what I mean?" he demanded, softly.

The man beside him said nothing.

Adam waited.

"Will you call me Adam?" he then said. He waited, then added: "To help me be worthy of my name."

The driver looked at him sideways, up and down. His hooded, cautious, assessing gaze went, suddenly, sly. "Naw," he said, "naw. Reckin I'll call you Slew."

"Slew?"

"Yeah," the driver paused and giggled. "Yeah," he said, "fer Slew-foot."

And that was what Mose Talbutt had named him: *Slew.*

And now, ten days later, in the hot afternoon in Pennsylvania, Adam, meditating on the strangeness of the road lying white ahead, on the heavy bemused strangeness of the green fields and hills, on the strangeness of the man beside him, turned his thoughts to the strangest thing of all, the fact that he was no longer Adam Rosenzweig. He was *Slew. Slew* to Mose Talbutt. *Slew* to Jedeen Hawksworth. *Slew,* no doubt, to all the men whom he would encounter in this land to which he had come.

He lifted his eyes to look at the land. It was a land undulant and slow, like limbs drowsily outstretched, and the white road wound across it, tracing swell and fall. Over the next rise in the road the white canvas hood of Jedeen Hawksworth's wagon had just sunk from sight, and now, from that direction, the high sunburned bulge of a hay wagon was just breaking above the rise. He could not yet see the hay wagon itself, as yet hull-down, just the great gold-green hulk heaving up massively, by infinitesimal gradation, to his sight. It was as though a hill itself, a sunburned hill, were moving toward him, in the decorous, ripe magic of this land.

Then, out of the timelessness of the road, white oxen topped the rise, the wagon coming into sight now. The oxen came on, white in the white road, white dust rising sleepily about their knees, dust stirred by their strange, drag-footed, incompetent-seeming motion, the great slack folds of flesh and gray hide under their necks swinging from side to side. As they approached, their eyes seemed almost closed. Then the two wagons drew even, drew apart.

As they themselves topped the rise, Adam saw the meadow beyond stretching gently away. Near the road the cows stared without curiosity. Beyond the meadow, the green hill was swelling up, and a grove at its base swam above purple shadow. The sun was westering and the light lay in gold striation across the open.

Adam looked to the right. Here the woods came close to the road. A brook came out of the woods and ran near the road, murmuring and glinting under the leaves. The leaves of trees on the right hand were

---

lightly powdered with white dust. In the hot motionless air the leaves were like eyelids about to close. The white dust on them seemed a luxurious powder of sleep. But night—night would never come. All time had ceased, and life would drift forever in this deep-bosomed sleep that was not quite sleep.

At that instant Adam thought: *I am nearly thirty years old, and I have never lain with a woman.*

And with that thought, the sickness of desire had already seized him. He felt dizzy with the blaze of sun, the dazzle of whiteness, the insidious obscenity of green land and purple shadow.

He shut his eyes, and thought that if he had stayed in the house of Aaron Blaustein, he would have been rich, and if you are rich you can have anything, you can lie in a soft bed, in a rich room, while the afternoon light of summer filters in through drawn curtain and the gold motes dance in the beam, and you stretch forth your hand and lay it on a white, swelling breast, and nothing, nothing else, matters.

But something else did matter, he was able, finally, after the pain of deprivation had passed, to decide. He sat there on the wagon seat, ashamed, as though what had happened in his mind had been visible to the man beside him. He thought: *I am what I am. I must do what I have to do. God help me.*

7

Jedeen Hawksworth was a silent man. And if a man spoke to him, he might turn his bloodshot gaze slowly upon him, as though his eyes had strayed in that direction by accident, and fix upon the speaker a blankness of unrecognition. The words spoken would wither away in the air. The speaker's very existence would be called into question.

He was a tall, scant man, with sandy hair, thinning sadly to show freckles rusty on his large skull, a skull too big for the narrowness of shoulders or the sharpness of nose. His eyes were blue, and inclined to blinking. He had long yellowish mustaches, between which his chin jutted out, as sharply incongruous to the large round skull as the nose. His Adam's apple was so prominent that when he sat with his shoulders hunched forward—the characteristic posture on wagon seat or stump—his neck seemed jerked backward in the agony of an invisible garrot. His hands were preternaturally large, hairy, red, liver-splotched and big-veined; and their size made the wrists seem even more spindly than they actually were. It seemed strange that the nails of those raw hands should always be so carefully trimmed.

Jedeen Hawksworth wore nondescript dark trousers, tucked into cowhide boots, boots large, old, patched, and softened to a distinct familiarity with bunions, bony joints, knobbed heels, and jack-splayed toes. The lower half of Jedeen Hawksworth, in other words, seemed adapted to the dreary grind of life and the brute work of the world. He was a kind of centaur, a centaur with the animal part drearily plow-broke and spavined, but the upper half affirming some dignity and aspiration, some human hope.

For the upper half was clothed in an old frock coat, the black going rusty now but the fabric itself in good repair. Despite the weather he wore a waistcoat under the coat, with a gold watch chain swung across it— with a watch rarely consulted, and when consulted held guiltily in the cup of a big hand, for the watch was silver, not gold, and tarnished to boot. He wore a stock of blue silk, meticulously tied, stuck into the waistcoat.

That stock was by far the newest thing on Jedeen Hawksworth, and it gave the vision of him standing, only a few weeks back, in front of some smart shop of haberdashery on Broadway, staring into the window, yearning toward that scrap of blue silk displayed behind glass, feeling the mysterious, desperate compulsion grow in him to have that cloth about his own neck, wondering what price might be asked, trying to screw his courage up and force his prudence down enough to enter the door. Well, Jedeen Hawksworth had the stock now, the blue somewhat sweat-stained, and his glory was topped by a high beaver hat, rarely taken off, moving like a smokestack of a steamboat across the green land of Pennsylvania, a steamboat drifting with an idle current, the fires dead.

Even after they had made camp and eaten their supper Jedeen Hawksworth rarely removed that stock and that beaver. He would sit withdrawn, on some stone, stump, or log, with a bottle beside him, sucking at it only parsimoniously while he meditated the coming darkness or the blade of his knife which he honed on the sole of his left boot. For the knife, too, was part of him, a big pearl-handled clasp knife with a long, wickedly curved blade. With that knife he cut his meat, prepared the cud of tobacco, and kept his fingernails in genteel repair, but it served mainly as a companion to his twilight meditations. He would sit and stare at the blade as he moved it deliciously, interminably, across the leather to keep the edge that would allow him to cut a scrupulously selected hair off the back of his hand.

Adam Rosenzweig, beside him on the seat of the

big wagon, in the long sun-dazzle of early afternoon, would steal sidewise glances at the hunched shoulders and painful Adam's apple and thin jut of chin between the tobacco-stained mustaches. Or he would sit with Mose Talbutt, not too far from the campfire, for the evenings were cooling now, and when the talk with Mose fell away, would take his secret glances and catch the motion of the distant blade, as it picked up the faint gleam of firelight, and wonder what obsessed thought maintained that indrawn silence and the rhythm of the blade.

Out of that silence characteristic of Jedeen Hawksworth, and more startling because of that context, the question came. It was afternoon, an afternoon like the others they had drifted through. Adam was sitting beside Jed Hawksworth on the seat of the big wagon. He became aware that the man was no longer staring ahead over the team, up the white road, but was looking down at his, Adam's, foot. He mustered his forces to look into Jed Hawksworth's face.

The man looked at him with that blankness of unrecognition that denied existence; then, with an adept, viperish turn and thrust of his head, spat precisely between the rumps of the hind pair of horses, to splash his ambeer on the wagon tongue. Then he nodded toward the boot.

"How come?" he demanded.

"I was born with it," Adam said.

"Huh," Jed Hawksworth uttered, and turned his gaze up the pike.

98

After a moment, not to Adam, not even to himself, just putting the words out into the hot air, he said: "Slew—the Slew-foot. Yeah."

He fell into thought. Then, nodding toward the foot, but not turning his gaze—as though neither boot nor man any further merited his serious attention— he said: "Yeah, with that thing, what made you come? Was it what that Ole Jew-booger Blaustein told me?"

"What did he tell you?" Adam asked.

"Said you loved niggers. Come to set 'em free. Gonna fight." He paused. Then: "That right, huh?"

After a moment Adam replied. "I had hoped to fight," he said.

"Yeah," Jed Hawksworth said. Then: "With that thing hung on you?"

There was nothing for Adam to say. *With that thing hung on me*, he thought.

Yes, there had been a time when, even with that thing hung on him, he had dreamed of the fulfillment. But that was a long time ago. No, it was no time ago, for where he was now, what he was now, was out of Time. And the self that had once existed and had had that dream no longer existed. Only the dry, pale shell, like that discarded by a locust, existed now.

He shivered in the sunshine. He felt the sweat slide icily down under his armpits. He thought: *If I'm not careful something will happen.* He did not know what it was. But he knew it was terrible.

Not knowing what it was, only that it was terrible, he did not know what to do to prevent it.

Then, with a gasp, almost physical, of relief, he thought he knew.

"Mr. Hawksworth," he said.

"Huh?" Jed Hawksworth said, staring up at the white pike.

"I just want to say—" He did not know how to go on. He, too, stared up the white pike.

"Huh?" Jed Hawksworth said once again.

"I just want to say I honor what you did, Mr. Hawksworth." He paused, then managed to continue: "Down in Carolina. Long ago. Mr. Blaustein told me."

For a long time the man said nothing. It was as though he had not heard.

He did not even take the trouble to turn his pale bloodshot gaze on the speaker to deny the existence of the speaker or the words spoken. But after a while, eyes up the pike, he said: "Looks like Ole Blaustein better stick to running his store. Looks like he can't keep his God-durn mouth shut."

He sank into himself, staring up the pike.

Aaron Blaustein had not kept his mouth shut. He had said: "Jedeen Hawksworth was a brave man." He had continued: "You will, no doubt, not find him a pleasant man, nor a very generous one, but if you find him difficult you can remember what he did."

So now, watching Jed Hawksworth profiled against the late heat-dazzle over the green fields or against the gathering darkness of some wayside wood patch, Adam remembered what Aaron Blaustein had said.

———

"You will sympathize with Hawksworth's feelings," the old man had said. "Because you had such feelings you came a long way to fight, and what he did, long back in North Carolina, took as much courage as fighting."

Yes, Adam decided, it had taken more courage. To go, unsummoned and unannounced, into a courtroom where a black man was being tried for striking, with murderous intent, the son of his owner. Where the black man could not give testimony. Where all the hard eyes fixed on you and withered you away. Where your knees trembled and your mouth went dry of spit as you rose to say: "Your Honor—Your Honor, I ain't been asked, but I was there, and I can tell what happened. I can swear it on the Book. It was not like they say."

It had taken courage—especially for a young fellow, just twenty-five or twenty-six. And a special courage, too, Aaron Blaustein had said, because the father of young Hawksworth was a planter and slaveholder, not a big one but respectable, and would be outraged. And the mother, furthermore, was cousin to the biggest house in the region. And the plaintiff was the son of that great man, sitting there now in that courtroom, and the accused, the slave, was his property.

When the young Jedeen Hawksworth entered the courtroom, the great man hadn't stirred, Aaron Blaustein said. He had not moved even a muscle of his face. Jedeen Hawksworth's word had had no effect.

The Negro had been convicted and hanged. "For," Aaron Blaustein said, "that was back yonder—thirty years ago, almost—when the situation was worsening, when the slaveholders began to worry more. About uprisings. About Abolition."

And he had added: "About themselves, too, I suppose."

As far as Jedeen Hawksworth was concerned, the great man, the father of the plaintiff and the owner of the accused, had had to do nothing about anything. A night mob, not large but competent, took Jedeen Hawksworth out, beat him soundly, swathed him in tar and feathers, rode him on a rail and dumped him into a swamp.

How Jed had been succored, how he had made his way north, Aaron Blaustein did not know. But he had gone away, and when shortly after, Aaron Blaustein himself sold out his store and went north, not being able to stomach the "worsening of the situation," he had read in a newspaper in New York that a certain Jedeen Hawksworth was to appear at an Abolitionist meeting to "bear witness." He had got in touch with Jed, who then was working with the Abolitionists—"of the Garrisonite stripe," Aaron Blaustein said. But he hadn't worked with them long.

He had never had the knack for working with anybody, Aaron Blaustein said. "At least," Aaron Blaustein ruefully said, "he never had the knack of working with anybody in my store, my first little venture in New York. He left me."

After a few years he had dropped from Aaron Blaustein's sight, to reappear, time-abused, seedy, and arrogant, some twenty years later, in 1862, to ask credit to set up as sutler with the Army of the Potomac.

"I was in my old supply house when he came in," Aaron Blaustein said. "I was wearing my old alpaca coat, the one I mentioned to you once. It was as though the years had not passed, even if we both had got somewhat creaky and gray—I particularly, for I'm more than ten years older than he. I gave him credit."

He paused, brooding. "I guess it was because I was wearing the old alpaca coat. It reminded me of when I was poor. And when I was full of yearning and schemes. And I suppose, too, I remembered his old courage."

He paused again. Then he said, briskly: "I made no mistake, though, in giving him credit. Substantial credit. He has done rather well, it seems."

And then, after a silence: "Yes, it seems that many have done rather well, in the war."

That was how Aaron Blaustein had not kept his mouth shut, and now Adam looked at the man beside him on the wagon seat and said: "Mr. Blaustein—he told me how he admired what you did."

"He give me some credit," Jed said grudgingly, "I got to admit that. Credit in his old store, I mean. It's the only kind of credit anybody but a fool looks for." He laughed drily.

Then added: "Durn it, why oughtn't he? Him in

the credit business, and getting rich, I bet. Me—I'd been rich too, if I'd done like him. Like a durn Jew. Scrimping and starving, living like a nigger in some rat hole, living with niggers right now, I bet, and—"

"Yes," Adam said evenly. "There are two black people in his house."

"Yeah," Jed Hawksworth said, "just like I told you and—"

"Yes," Adam said. "One is the cook, the other is the cook's helper. But in addition there are the three Irish maids and the English butler, and, I think, a coachman."

Jed Hawksworth turned on him, but now the blighting unrecognition was not in his eyes. There was, instead, focused outrage. "You're lying," Jed Hawksworth said through his teeth. "It's a God-damned lie."

"I have been in his house," Adam said calmly. "It is a great house. It is on Fifth Avenue near Thirty-ninth Street."

Jed Hawksworth seemed about to protest. His lower jaw moved, ever so slightly. Or it was quivering under the mustaches? But if he had been about to speak, Adam forestalled him. "You see," he said, "the house is so grand that the mob tried to sack it. But they were fought off."

The man turned away. His narrow shoulders drooped more than before; his Adam's apple seemed more painful; between the drooping mustaches, his

chin thrust forward more sharply in its thin stubborn-
ness.

After a while, still looking up the pike, he said: "I
could of had me a plantation."

After another while, he said: "I could of built it up.
I could of reached out. My pa—he didn't know how
to manage no plantation. He didn't have no grip on
things."

After another and longer while, he said: "But I
got run out."

It was a half-mile before he spoke again, a half-
mile at a slow amble through the hot white dust. Not
looking at Adam, the man said: "You know what—
when the war's done I'm going to Carolina. I am going right back to Peacham County, North Carolina.
The Rebs are going to get the gut-grease kicked out of
'em, and they won't have a durn thing left. You will
be buying land for nothing plus gnat spit. I aim to
buy me a lot of land. Half of Peacham County, North
Carolina, and I aim to hire me a lot of Rebs to work it.
Sun to sun. And nigger drivers. Yeah, I'm gonna have
me nigger drivers to drive them Rebel sons-of-bitches,
and sun to sun."

He sank into his dream, for a minute. Then he
stirred out of it. "Yeah," he said, "and they'll take it,
them cunnels and ginnals, and such."

He waited. Then added: "Yeah, a man will take
anything, when starve-time comes."

It was as though Adam Rosenzweig were not there.

———

The wagon moved on through the white dust. It was some time before Jed Hawksworth seemed to rouse to his presence. He drew the reins. The horses stopped. "Git off," he said, "and ride with the nigger. A man's got to think. Sometimes."

It was that night they camped at the spring.

The big wagon had waited ahead. As soon as the small wagon drew up, Jed dropped down, and motioned to Adam to climb into the seat and take the reins. "Wait," Jed ordered, and stepped down into the white dust. He came around to the right, to the west side of the road, and moved into the knee-high spook-white weeds of the roadside. He walked back through the weeds, making the white dust rise around his waist, then plunged into a dry ditch, emerged, and moved toward a stone house back down the road some two hundred yards. The house was set back from the road on a shoulder of a rise, crested, far beyond, with woods—a medium-size house, two stories, solid gray stone with a slate roof, flanked by a stone barn and a big stable, or second barn, painted red. Both barns had some askew cabalistic signs at the gable. Adam wondered what they were.

He looked down at the roadside, nearer. Then he understood why they had stopped. A branch, a little creek, flowed down here, coming out of an oak grove, then bending southward along the pike. Across the stream the oaks stood back to make a glade, carpeted with grass smooth, dark green, cool-looking, inviting the touch. To the farther side of the glade a spring fell out of gray mossy rock, splashing into a little basin with a soft sound that now, in the sudden quiet of late afternoon after the grind of the wagon, came quite audibly across the little distance. The water from the basin found a channel across the glade, half the way wandering concealed from sight, through beds of cress. Ten paces or so down the pike a stone bridge, crumbling but sound, invited access, and across it a grassy track drifted off into the woods.

Jed Hawksworth came back, swung up to the seat by Adam, took the reins, drove the wagon toward the left of the pike to make the swing practical, and crossed the stone bridge. The trees, the big oaks, were widely spaced here. The wagon moved off the old track, under the great boughs, toward the glade. At the edge Jed Hawksworth drew rein, grunted, said: "Git at it."

He himself dropped off the wagon and crossed to sit on a stone near the spring. He began to read a newspaper.

Adam and Mose had finished making camp when he came back to them. "Git the tents out, too," he ordered. "We'll stay a spell. The lady at the house give her say-so." He turned away, then hesitated. By way of a grudging explanation, he added: "The Yankees are moving in. In Virginny. Looks like Old Meade is hunting a fight. We don't have to connect with 'em when they are moving in."

He gave a dry laugh, quickly hacked off.

"Yeah, it is not good business to leave your wagon and stock of goods for the Rebs for free, when the Yankees come back."

He spat, shifted his quid.

"The Yankees, durn 'em," he said, "looks like they got the habit to come back faster'n they go in."

He folded the paper, stuck it back into his pocket, and sat on his stone, honing the clasp knife. Adam went over to him. "May I look at the paper, please," he asked.

Wordlessly, the man passed it to him, and Adam withdrew a few paces and crouched to read it. Yes, Meade was in Virginia. He was hunting a battle. Adam lifted his eyes to the green woods, not really seeing, not really thinking.

He heard the voice of Mose: "Hey you, what you doen, Slew? Wishen you was down in Virginny?"

With elaborate theatricality, like a boy playing, Mose lifted an imaginary rifle and fired into the deep of the wood. *"Ker-boom!"* Mose said. *"Ker-boom! Ker-boom!"*

All at once Adam found Mose looking directly at him. The grin went off of Mose's face. Adam did not know what was taking the place of that grin. But Mose rose, abruptly, and came toward him. He stood above Adam, lax but strong, his shoulders bulging high up there in the red-check calico shirt, his face looking down with an indeterminate expression which Adam had never seen there before.

"Son," the man said, "doan you let Ole Mose rile

108

you. Doan you let him stick in yore craw. This nigger chile of the Lawd-God—he jes gitten his fun!"

And he broke into an uncontrollable laughter, jerking his head from side to side.

He stopped laughing. He leaned over and gave Adam's near shoulder a comradely whack. "Yeah, son," he said, "you git one fer Ole Mose. You git a Reb fer Ole Mose."

He turned away and went back to the other side of the cook-hearth he was rigging out of stones from the branch. He placed a stone or two, then looked up. "Yeah," he said dourly, "you kin kill 'em all fer all of me."

Adam looked off into the woods. The first shadows were beginning to gather. Deeper and deeper the woods recessed, in vault after dimming vault of shade and coolness to that inward point where shade was beginning to coalesce to darkness. Adam, looking into the depth, thought of quietness. He thought of peace. He thought of Time moving deeper and dimmer, into coolness and peace.

Then, all at once, he thought of the woods of Virginia. You moved into the woods, far off in Virginia, and what was there? Yes, what would be there?

It must have been some movement, or sudden cessation of movement, on the part of Mose that made Adam, standing there thigh-deep in the creek, soaping himself, look up. He saw Mose standing in shallower water, but, more fortunately than Adam, with at least the benefit of the drawers that some crazy modesty made him keep on, even when washing like this. Mose was, for the instant, frozen there, gape-mouthed and bug-eyed, and in the instant Adam saw why. A woman, a girl, was standing there on the bank, frozen too in her surprise, her mouth making a little *O* to shape the exclamation she was, actually, too surprised to utter. She was a large girl, wearing some kind of a long blue dress, yellow hair braided and wrapped around her head, a fat baby propped on one hip, on the other side an arm dangling to hold a flat-tish basket, heaped high with purple grapes, and behind her was a tangle of leaves, brightened to gold and translucent green by the last sunlight striking through them.

Adam, too, in that instant felt himself frozen, felt himself gape-mouthed, then with a thrill of release turned and flung himself face-downward into the water. As he struck the water, even as he made his splash, he heard the little sharp, breathless cry from the girl, the exclamation finally achieving itself from those round lips. He came up, half squatting in the water, so only his head was above surface, and looked back. The girl was gone.

But he heard the murmur of voices from the left, beyond some bushes, over near the camp. The girl must have found Jed Hawksworth sitting on his stone, and interrupted the honing of the knife. Adam came out of the water, taking from the air a sudden shiver, a sadness premonitory of autumn and night, and hurried into his clothes.

As he drew on his left boot, he thought how, the first time they had bathed at a wayside stream, he had had to force himself to walk into the water, exposing the imperfection of that naked foot.

As Adam came to the edge of the bushes that concealed the camp site, he heard Mose's voice, then the girl's, saying something he could not make out. For an instant he stood there, caught in a nameless reluctance, not fear, timidity, or shame, a sense, rather, that if he did go on into the open space where the voices were, something, what he did not know or guess, might be lost. Then he came around the bushes.

The girl, the baby now propped in her lap, was sitting on a stone a little way from Jed Hawksworth, nearer the spring. The basket was at her feet, and she was eating grapes, holding a bunch up in her left hand, away from the baby's clutch. She plucked and ate the grapes one at a time. For an instant, she would hold a grape up and, even though saying something, brush it with an appraising, drowsily appreciative glance, as though she already felt the rounded, juice-swollen bulb break deliciously in her mouth. Her skin was very clear, her cheeks pink, her neck, with its latitudinal creases, as though the skin was plumped a little too much with the gentle softness within, very white. Now and then a little juice might run out of the corner of her lips, and her tongue would slip out, as pink and innocent as a child's, to wipe it back in where it belonged. Now and then she jiggled her right leg to reassure the baby. When she did this, the skirt fluttered and waved, ever so slightly, above the toe of her right shoe. The toe of the shoe looked sturdy, dusty, scuffed. The hand that held up the bunch of grapes was sunburned and strong.

Jed Hawksworth was eating grapes, too. His knife was stuck in the ground before him. Mose was squatting on his hams, decorously apart, eating grapes. He would put six or seven into his mouth at one time, then spit seeds and skin out, with a soft *plop*, letting them fall to the ground between his parted knees.

For a moment, feeling unseen, invisible, Adam stood there. Then Jed jerked a thumb in his direction. "That's Slew," Jed Hawksworth said.

"I'm pleased to meet you, Mr. Slew," the girl said, and bobbed her head politely at him.

Adam bowed, not finding words, and stood there. She leaned, picked up the basket of grapes, and held it out to him. He took a bunch, and standing there, began to eat. She said that they had more grapes than they could use, that the grapes were doing fine this year, that her husband being in bed and help hard to get she didn't even have time to pick grapes for jelly and preserves like she ought. She said they could get all they wanted off the arbor, up near the well house.

The baby began to stir and whimper. Turning herself slightly on the stone, in a token gesture of decency, she released her left breast and began to nurse the baby. She jiggled the baby while he sucked. One of the baby's feet gave a little rhythmic kick, over and over. Now and then, he made a little sigh, or grunt. The girl's breast was large and full and extraordinarily white, almost bluish, with a delicate, vinelike tracery of blue veins.

While the baby sucked, and its foot wagged, she talked. She didn't have many people to talk to, she said. Her husband was feeling too bad to be much company. His wound wouldn't heal, she said. He had been shot by the Rebels, back in the spring, fighting down in Virginia. You couldn't get proper help to work the farm, she said. And to take care of the baby and her husband. She just did the best she could. Her husband was German, she said. He had come over a long time back though, ten, twelve years. He was some older, but he was a good husband. And a good farmer, too. He had been a schoolteacher in Germany, she added pridefully.

"Slew here," Jed Hawksworth said, then corrected himself, in satirical politeness. "Mr. Slew here," he said, "he is a German. That right, Slew?"

"I come from Bavaria," Adam said.

"He is a Jew-German," Mose said.

"Come over here to set the niggers free," Jed Hawksworth said.

The girl was looking curiously at him, Adam discovered. He looked down at the bunch of grapes he held, picked one studiously and ate it, with eyes lowered.

Then he heard her voice, with its strange, slightly thickened accent, not like the other voices he had heard in America, and he knew that somewhere in it was the echo of German. He heard the voice saying: "I think there's worse things a man could be doing, no?"

Adam heard Mose giggle.

He ate another grape, studiously, not yet looking up. Nobody spoke. When Adam looked up, the other men were eating grapes, quietly, as though alone. The girl was holding the baby, but she was looking away absently, her blue eyes darkening, her face shaded by some sadness. Now and then, the baby made his little sighing, grunting sounds, but she did not look down at him. She sat there, on the stone, with her body white and cloudy-soft under the faded blue dress, and with the sadness naked on her face.

Suddenly she got up, switched the baby to her hip, and buttoned her dress with a sharp, precise motion, as though repudiating something. "I got to go," she said. "I got to get back and take care of him. He might wake up—my husband, I mean."

Mose had risen and gone to the small wagon. He came back and held out something to the baby. The girl looked at it, then at him, with question.

"Candy," he said. "Mo-lasses candy. Ain't gonna colic him."

The baby was reaching for it. She let him take it. "Thank you," she said.

"Good night," she said, and turned away.

Jed Hawksworth managed to say something by way of thanks for the grapes.

"Gute Nacht," Adam said.

She looked back at him. He hadn't meant to say it. It just happened. He was flushing, he knew.

"Gute Nacht," she said.

When the girl had gone, Mose turned to Jed Hawksworth. "That candy," he said, "it weren't none of yores. If'n that's that you thinken. It was mine. I brang it from New Yawk."

Jed sat on the stone, again honing the knife on the side of the boot, looked at Mose for a time, not speaking. Then he said: "I ne'er said a word."

He tested the blade on a hair on the back of his left hand. Absorbed in that process, he was saying: "I ne'er said a single word, not about it. Nor nothing."

The next evening the girl came back, again wearing the blue dress, again bringing the fat baby, propped on a hip, and a basket of grapes. Again, they ate grapes, and the girl talked. Her name was Goetz, she said, Maran Goetz. At least that was her born name. Her name was German, but her people had been here a long time. This land had been her grandfather's. But now she was Mrs. Meyerhof. She hadn't been married but three years. Then the war came. It looked like the war came before they really got settled in, she said.

She paused, then added irrelevantly that her husband's name was Hans. The baby's name was Hans too. He—the husband—was not better today. The wound wouldn't stop running. He just lay there, getting weaker, and didn't seem to take an interest.

When she got up, she turned to Adam. "Mr. Slew—" she began. Mose giggled.

"My name," Adam said, "it isn't Slew."

He waited an instant for the question to form on her face. "My friends call me Slew," he said evenly, and then thrust his left foot forward a little, and waited until he was sure her eyes had fixed comprehendingly upon it. "They call me that," he said, "because of my foot."

With no haste, then, he withdrew his foot and stood straight and calm on it. He looked her straight in the face. It was a round, soft face, gently blunted in its contours, the cheeks pink with sun and strong blood. He saw the downy yellow hair on her upper lip, like peach fuzz. He saw a little moisture that caught in it and glistened. Her eyes were blue, darkening with puzzlement. He realized, all at once, that that face was the face of a little girl—say ten or twelve years old—a simple, plump little girl who didn't understand something. And perhaps never would, he added to himself. And with that he felt a sadness for her come sweet in his breast.

"My name," he said, and hesitated. He was aware, without looking around, of the eyes of the men on him, and anger and elation blazed up together in him. "My real name," he said, "if you want to know it, is Adam Rosenzweig."

116

He heard Mose stir behind him. "'At's tellen 'em," he heard the voice of Mose say. Then he heard Mose snicker.

"I'm glad you told me," the girl said. "I'm glad to know you by your right name."

Adam waited an instant, expecting some stir, some sound, behind him. None came, so he said: "But I had interrupted you. You were about to say something."

"Yes," she said. The baby stirred, and she shifted it to the other hip, and jiggled it a moment. Its round yellow-fuzzed head bobbed comically, then, with abandoned truthfulness, flopped over against her breast. Adam could see that the lid of the one eye visible to him was drooping. The baby was about to go to sleep. The baby's name, he remembered with sudden precision, was Hans—Hans, like the father.

The girl was saying: "—and you speak German. Maybe if you would come talk to my husband—you being from the old country not long back—maybe he would take an interest. If you would be so kind, no?"

He said, yes, he would be glad to come, but what time?

Tomorrow evening, she said, but well before sun. She could do her milking while he talked with her husband. She went away, up the grassy slope toward the stone house and big purple-shadowed maple trees and big barns, carrying the baby like a soft ill-wrapped parcel, and as she moved she leaned her body, inside the faded blue dress, to one side, against the cant of

---

117

the slope and the weight of the baby. He watched her up the slope.

Mose was murmuring something. Adam turned toward him. Mose was squatting on his hams, looking up the slope. "Sawf and juicy," he murmured, "sawf and juicy."

Adam felt the hatred rise in his stomach, like bile.

"Well a-fore sun," Mose murmured now, mimicking the girl's voice, still squatting on his hams, skewing his glance sidewise up at Adam, "yeah—well a-fore sun."

Adam turned away.

Mose was saying, "Yeah, son—and you give it one poke fer Ole Mose."

And he added, murmuring: "Sawf and juicy."

Over to one side, sitting on his stone, Jed Hawksworth looked up from honing his knife. "Listen," he said dispassionately to Mose, "that's a white woman you talking about. Did you know that?"

Mose, squatting there, said nothing. He seemed enormously interested in an acorn cap there on the ground between his knees.

"Yeah," Jed Hawksworth said, "and if it was some places and some folks and you talk that way about a white lady, they'd cut yore black tongue out and throw it to the hogs." He looked down at the knife in his hand, curiously.

Mose stared down at the old acorn cap.

"Hell," Jed Hawksworth said, absently, as though to himself, "one time and I might of done it myself."

He snapped the blade of his knife shut and stared down at it. "But not now," he said. "Looks like now I don't give a durn."

Mose lifted his head.

Jed Hawksworth was staring at him. "Go on and say it," he commanded, almost in a whisper, an angry, husky, vibrant whisper. "Yeah, say it."

Mose stared back at the man. A slow, sleepy grin grew on his face. "Sawf and juicy," he whispered throatily, watching the face of Jedeen Hawksworth.

Adam walked away, toward the woods, quickly.

Adam could not really talk with Hans Meyerhof. He was, clearly, a dying man. Under the single sheet the body was nothing more than a heap of bones, lying almost as starkly obvious as they would lie in the earth, if a spade, some years from now, broke open the coffin. Adam sometimes had the crazy feeling that he was staring right through the sheet, through, in fact, the last shrivelings of flesh and wrapping of fever-dry skin, to see those bones slack and calm in their last repose.

The flesh of the face had shriveled away and the skin drawn tight and transparent. Life showed only in the eyes, and then only sporadically—large blue eyes that now and then glittered with astonishing brilliance, as though some great excitement, some commanding thought, were taking hold. Then they would grow filmed with gray, like the eye of a sick chicken when the lid draws over it.

But even when the eyes glittered, the cause, Adam came to feel, was not in anything that had passed between them, only some fluctuation of the fever or the transitory flicker of some old event in that fading brain.

A few facts, however, Adam managed to get from him. He was from Westphalia, the son of peasants. But he had managed to get an education and had become, as his wife had boasted, a teacher. In the famine year 1846, he had got mixed up with the revolutionary movement among the peasants. He had wound up at Rastatt.

"Rastatt?" Adam had demanded. He heard the word, which did not seem his own voice, come like a croak. He felt the word come into his throat, shape itself there, bulge his larynx, and break forth, like phlegm. No, it was not like a croak. It was as though the creature that would croak had bulged his throat and then broken forth, croaker and croak in one. He felt a chill, a disorientation. He felt as though his life were curving backward on itself, had veered out of the dimension of Time. He felt as though, again, he sat beside a dying father, a father who had handled a musket at Rastatt but who, in dying—dying with a rifle ball in him taken in another war and another place—would not repudiate the old truth.

The chill, the sense of disorientation, passed into a breathless and grateful joy. He was surprised, in that instant paralyzed, into a bliss. What had been thought lost returned to him.

———

"Ja," the voice said from the bed, "Rastatt."

It was a voice weak, dry, distant, a voice not out of Time, but in Time, marked by Time. Adam looked at the man's face. The moment of bliss was gone. He had to live in Time. He had only what he had to live by, and with.

"At Rastatt," Adam asked, leaning toward the bed, "did you know a man named Rosenzweig?"

The man seemed to be thinking. At least, over his gaze what seemed the gray glaze of abstraction was growing.

"Rosenzweig—Leopold Rosenzweig?" Adam asked. He leaned closer. He was in Time. What had happened had happened. He was not sitting by the side of his father's bed. But if that man had seen his father he might now know—know in a deeper and fuller way, a way more essentially involving his own being —that his father had actually stood at Rastatt, had fought and had suffered. Entering into the pathos of that far time and place, he felt that he might be, somehow, freed from a burden.

"Leopold—Leopold Rosenzweig?" he repeated urgently, leaning, his voice sinking to a whisper.

The man's gaze moved creakily toward him. He felt that he could almost hear the painful little creak of tendons of the dry neck, and how the eyes, as they turned, would grind with tiny grittiness in the sockets.

"No," the man said.

The man's head turned away. The eyes fixed on the

ceiling. "There were so many," the dry, distant voice said.

"But—but—" Adam began. He was about to say, he was yearning to say: *But he was my father.*

But the eyes of the man were filming grayly over. Adam felt that a gray film was coming down over all the past and what it had meant, cutting it off from the present. He was left alone with the present, and he did not know what it meant. Hans Meyerhof might know what the present meant. But his eyes were closed now. The room, Adam suddenly realized, was full of the smell of the wound.

Adam rose softly and went out of the room, finding his way down the unfamiliar hall, through a kitchen, out into the yard. The door of the stone barn was open. Two cows, brown cows, were drinking from a stone trough near the door. That was where she would be. He went to the barn, and entered.

He stood there a moment, watching her milk. Apparently she did not know he was there. Her left knee was swung toward him, so that she might lean comfortably from her stool toward her work. The blue dress was drawn up nearly to the knee, showing the vertical upward thrust of her ankle from the scuffed shoe set solidly on the dungy straw. The hands moved in a precise, strong rhythm. For a moment the two streams of milk made a metallic ringing on the bottom of the pail, one ringing counterpointed against the other, *ting—ting*, the stroke of one hand balanced against the other. She must have just begun on this cow, for the pail must be nearly empty to make that sound. But the sound quickly gave way to the muffled purr of a stream thrusting solidly into the milk already in the pail, one purr balanced against the other, the sound becoming more and more muffled as the body of liquid rose.

Her head was dropped forward against the side of the animal in a posture of fatigue, or despair, belying the steady motion of the competent hands. Adam looked down at the back of her neck. Some wisps of blond hair curled damply there, like tendrils. The neck looked unfended, given in surrender, offering itself, in exhaustion, almost a voluptuous exhaustion, to the stroke.

"Your husband—" Adam began.

She gave a little start, jerking her head up.

"I'm sorry I frightened you," he said.

"You didn't," she said. "It's just that I—" She stopped. Then: "It's just I didn't expect you."

"Your husband—he's asleep."

"Yes," she said. Her eyes darkened. "I don't worry about him so much when he's asleep. It's when he just lies with his eyes open, looking out the way they do."

"Yes," he said.

She turned back to her task. Her head leaned forward again, but now without that abandoned droop, as though some pride, or rectitude, forbade when his eyes were upon her.

He looked farther into the gloom of the barn. He saw straps, buckets, scythes, cradles, coils of rope, a length of trace chain, and other such tools and gear hanging from pegs or nails in the posts. There were three more cows, standing farther in the shadow, heads down, jaws moving slow, soundless, remorseless.

"I would like to help you," he said.

She looked up again. She wiped some tendrils of loose, damp hair back from her forehead. "I don't mind saying there's something to do," she admitted.

"I would be happy," he said.

She looked at him appraisingly, dubiously, as though about to revise her implied acceptance.

"I want to do something," he said. "That is what I want."

"You can take that milk to the house," she agreed, nodding toward a couple of pails to one side. "You'll see the crocks in the kitchen. Pour it in the crocks. Look at Hans—I mean the baby. The cradle is in the kitchen. Then—I mean if you really want to—you can pump water in the trough. The windmill is broke. When things are this way, it looks like everything begins to break. It looks like they got a spite in 'em to know when to break. And then—you can come on back here and—"

In this way the routine began. Every afternoon he would go up to the stone house on the hill, feeling the eyes fixed on his back as he moved away from the camp. He could feel them all the way. When he entered the door of the house, he always had to suppress the impulse to put a hand out to prop himself while he caught breath. It was as though he had reached safety by only a hair.

He would talk with Hans Meyerhof—or sit there in the silence while the eyes stared up, or the wax-colored lids dropped to screen the man into the dark secrecy which was all that was left of Hans Meyerhof, who had stood at Rastatt. Then, after a time, as though some ritual penance for an unspecified crime had at last been performed, Adam would leave the faintly sweet scent of that room, and go out into the light of afternoon.

The rays of light would now be stretching out, over the woods that created the hill to the west, back of the house. The shadow of trees would be creeping down the slope toward the house. A cow lowed near the barn. Far away, on the next farm, a dog was barking, dutifully, wearily, punctuating the absolute stillness that, like the clarity of this late light, seemed to revoke distance and time. Then Adam would move toward the barn. Or perhaps into the lot, or even down to a field, to take up some predetermined task.

He learned to mend a wall. He helped the old man from the village, the only person to be found for hire, cut and haul winter wood. He forked fodder. He learned to handle a corn knife. Then, at dusk, he would go down the hill to the camp, to meet the eyes. Now and then the girl would send crullers or pie down to the camp. When Adam laid the offering before the men, they looked at him wordlessly. As they ate it they would move their jaws in a slow assessing fashion, trying to discriminate, as it were, some delicacy of flavor.

Dusk came earlier and earlier now. Waking at night, Adam thought that the stars were sharper and higher than before. He would lie awake, listening to the owls call in the oak woods.

One afternoon Adam left the house and moved hurriedly toward the barn. He entered the door, into the gloom, where the girl was milking. The girl was looking up at him, the apprehension stiffening on her face.

"You better go—go to him," Adam was saying.

But she had already risen, letting the pail fall over, and had pushed past him, out the door. He turned and watched her moving toward the house. She was running now.

He turned again into the gloom of the barn. With a kind of stealth he moved to the cow she had been milking and stared stupidly down at the spot where the spilled milk soaked the dungy straw. Then he leaned over and picked up the pail. He set it to one side, with excessive care, as though trying to right a wrong.

He sat down on a cask, and held his head in his hands, waiting. He did not know what he was waiting for.

After some time she came back. He raised his head in question.

"He's all right," she said. "What I mean is, he's quiet now."

"I don't know what happened," he said.

"He ought not to of moved like that," she said. She picked up the pail he had set aside, and inspected it. "It's got dirty," she said.

He started to say that he would go get another, but she continued: "I had to give him the stuff—the laudanum."

"I don't know what happened," he said. "He seemed like before. Perhaps more awake—more interested. He asked me why I had come to America. I told him. It was his asking that made me do it." He stopped.

"Do what?" she demanded.

"I asked him where he was when he was wounded. What battle, I mean, and he turned toward me. He tried to push himself up. He ordered me to get out. You would have thought he was trying to scream. But his voice was so weak, and—"

"I should have told you!" she cried desperately.

She turned the bucket in her hands.

"It was Chancellorsville," she said dully. "Hans—he was with General Howard's corps. I guess that's what Hans said you call it—a corps."

"Yes—corps," Adam said, nodding.

"They got surprised," she said. "The Rebels came out of the woods, and surprised 'em. That Jackson—he came. Hans said it was the fault of the generals and those people. They ought to have had somebody watching out. It wasn't their own fault that Hans and those men got surprised, and had to run. But they tried to fight. Hans said they tried to fight. A lot of 'em did fight. They'd get together and try to stop the Rebels. Hans was a sergeant and he got some together to stop the Rebels. That's how he got shot— trying to stop the Rebels. Oh, it's not fair," she said, looking down at the bucket she was gripping hard by the rim.

He saw there were tears in her eyes. "What's not fair?" he asked.

"What they say," she said.

"What?"

"That it was the fault of the Germans. All those soldiers Hans was with were Germans. The companies and regiments. And now people say the Germans are cowards. That they always run away. That they let the Rebels win at Chancellorsville. All the newspapers say it. Hans would make me read the newspapers out loud to him, and he would lie there on the bed, and I would see his hands gripping hard and his face get whiter and his eyes stare. But he'd make me read every word, out loud, how the Germans were cowards. And one time he began cursing them, the people who said that, and tried to push himself up and his wound broke—"

She dropped the bucket. She looked stupidly down at it, then at her empty hands.

"Oh, it's not fair," she wailed, "what they say!" She uttered a dry, choking sob. "He came all this way—

over the ocean—and he wanted to do what was right —nobody made him join the army, he just did because he thought it was right—and he fought and he tried to stop the Rebels and people call him a coward and—they call all the Germans cowards and—"

The tears came in a flood. She took a step toward him, groping. Her head was against his chest, and her hands hung on to his coat. Her hair was in his face. He was aware of the smell of her hair, like cut hay in the field, in the sun. He became aware that he was patting her shoulder. It seemed to be the only thing he could do, while her sobs came, and now and then she broke the sobs to say how it wasn't fair—oh, it wasn't fair!—and he was going to die.

She kept saying that he was going to die. Then she stopped saying it, and clung to his coat. He could hear her breathing. Then she withdrew from him; she turned and moved away from him, moving unsteadily toward the house. He stood there watching her. He could not move. He had the feeling that he might stand there forever watching her withdraw toward that shadowy house.

She had reached the back stoop. She stood there a moment, not touching hand to the door. She had turned and was staring at him. She was coming back toward him, almost running. His heart gave a great leap.

She was before him, staring into his face. He felt naked under her eyes.

Then she was saying: "Listen—listen!" She was

saying: "He is going to die. He is going to die and leave me, but oh—"

She could not finish.

Then she did finish. She said: "But oh—he did right. He did what was right!"

She had turned and fled from him.

On the way down the hill, he stopped well before he got to the edge of the grove. He sat on an outcropping of gray stone, and looked back up the slope. The house, the barns, the long slope—all were in shadow now, with the sky red above the woods, and the woods growing darker and casting their darkness down the slope. He looked at the house again. He saw a light appear at a window. She had lighted the lamp in the kitchen. She would be bending over the cradle. He thought of the hovering whiteness of her body in the big, shadowy kitchen, like a cloud.

He drew his eyes away, and stared at the ground at his feet. He thought: *He is going to die.*

That thought in his head was like some bright object dimly gleaming in the darkness. He shut his eyes, his physical eyes, as though to shut out that dim gleam. But the gleam was there.

He rose and went down to the camp.

The men looked at him, Mose from the fire where he was frying meat, Jed Hawksworth from the stone where he sat, holding but not reading a newspaper. The man on the stone rattled the paper. "Meade," he said, "he is not going to git his fight." He paused.

Then: "If'n he really was hankering fer one. Them Yankees." He meditated.

Then: "Looks like they gonna let this durn war last till Hell is froze over."

Mose, with elaborate care, shook the skillet a little, then looked over at him. "Ain't hurten you none," he said. "Naw," he said softly, "the longer they fights, the more you kin sell 'em."

Jed Hawksworth stared at him for a long moment. Then he got up from the stone. "It ain't me made 'em start killing each other off," he said.

"I ne'er said 'twas," Mose said.

But the man did not seem to be listening. He was sunk in thought. After a time he lifted his head and walked over to the fire. "We're pulling out," he said. "Tomorrow morning. That is," he said, bowing elaborately toward Adam, "if you give yore kind permission."

Mose giggled.

"That is," Jed Hawksworth said, "if you done finished yore business, and ain't decided to settle down and be a farmer in a big rock house."

"Sawf and juicy," Mose murmured, and gently shook the skillet.

Adam stood there, in the shade of the trees and felt stripped naked, as though by an icy blast.

131

Adam thought, *If they had not said it.* He looked up
the road at the big wagon where Jed Hawksworth
would be sitting alone, with chin sharply outthrust
from between the mustaches and with neck at that
painful, garroted angle. If Jedeen Hawksworth had
not said what he had said. Then Adam stole a look at
the figure beside him. If Mose Talbutt had not said
what he had said. Had not giggled. What had he
said? The words came into Adam's mind—no, into
his very ears, as though at this moment the Negro
beside him were murmuring, over and over, in his
thick, insidious, furry voice: *Sawf and juicy.*

Yes, Adam decided in a candor that was like physical pain, if two days ago Jedeen Hawksworth had not said it about the rock house, if Mose Talbutt had not giggled and said what he had said, now he, Adam, might not be on this wagon, moving south. He might have stayed at the farm, have been the hired hand sleeping in the attic of the house where a man was soon to die. He would have lain in the dark, waiting.

If it had not been for Jedeen Hawksworth and Mose Talbutt he might have been able to stay there. He might have been able to deny to himself every motive that made him stay. But Jedeen Hawksworth and Mose Talbutt had known all the time, watching and grinning. They had understood his every motion, penetrated every self-deception. Dully, he asked himself if virtue was possible only in the shame of discovery, in the terror of accusation. He asked if there is such a thing as virtue in the last private darkness of the soul.

But then, in a distress of deprivation he demanded: *What harm to have stayed?*

And he answered: *None.*

None, for nothing was his fault.

He had not blundered and let the Rebels burst unhindered from the woods. He had not fired the shot that hit Hans Meyerhof. He had not set up corruption in the wound. Nothing was his fault.

What harm if he had stayed to carry the milk, mend the wall, cut the wood? No, no—it was evil to leave that girl alone, to let her head sag in weariness against the flank of a cow, to breathe the odor of the wound, to weep at night in the dark house.

His mind, with a flash of liberation, leaped past the death of Hans Meyerhof. It had happened. He, Adam Rosenzweig, was reaching out his hand to the girl and her blue eyes were fixed on him and her lower lip glistened and trembled. Then, in the very midst of that breathless fantasy, he asked himself if he knew why he was here on this dusty white road, moving southward through late sunshine. Was it because he would never have had the courage to reach out a hand to her? What would she have had to say to Adam Rosenzweig, Jew from Bavaria, with a bad foot?

Was that why he was on this road, he sadly asked himself, because he had known that he would never have the courage to reach out? Whatever else had impelled him, or drawn him—had it withered away, leaving only this? Was it only because he lacked the courage to live that he might have the courage to die?

Well, he thought, others had traveled this road and some had traveled it in virtue. Some had believed. The son of Aaron Blaustein had believed.

But what did Aaron Blaustein believe now, alone in his rich house? Hans Meyerhof had believed. But what did he believe now, lying on his bed and staring upward? What did Stephen Blaustein believe, hidden in the earth of Virginia?

Adam listened to the soft grind of the wheels on

stone, muffled by dust. He thought of a dark forest, far to the south, where Lee crouched like a beast, hurt perhaps but full of coldly exalted ferocity and patient in cunning, waiting in the darkness of Virginia, like a cave.

They had passed through the clean village, and gone out a road marked BALTIMORE. Then the wagon ahead had stopped. There was a stream there, and a few trees. For a moment Adam had the crazy thought that Maran Meyerhof would be sitting there, the fat baby on her hip, the basket of grapes at her feet. He felt a terror that everything was to begin again. But it passed. He wished now he had had the courage to tell her good-bye. That might have ended something. But what could he have said?

What could it matter, he thought. A woman with a stone house and two barns and two hundred acres of land—some man would come to take care of her. He, Adam Rosenzweig, had robbed her of nothing. He wondered if, years from now, she would ever remember him.

When they had made camp, Jed said: "Want to know why we're stopping so early? Well, I just thought I'd step over and see the slaughter pen."

Adam looked at him in question.

"Yeah," Jed said, nodding toward the hills, "yonder's where they done it."

Adam looked at the blunted gently swelling crests, to the southwest.

"Yeah," Jed said, "that's where they kicked the be-Jesus out of Ginnal Lee. That is Gettysburg, where they fought it."

He turned his gaze back to the hills, peering at them. "I just had me a hankering to take a squint." He continued to stare, and then repeated, as though to himself: "Yeah, I just had me a hankering."

He turned with sudden briskness to Adam. "You aim to come?" he asked.

Adam nodded. He could not take his gaze from the hills.

"You coming?" Jed asked Mose.

"Today's a lot better'n two months back," Mose said, and grinned.

"It was more than two months," Jed said.

Yes, Adam calculated, it was a good deal more than two months since he had cut out, down the plank of the *Elmyra,* and found himself in America, in those blank, silent streets, lost, unpursued, and devalued.

The gate of the cemetery was a formidable brick structure, some twenty-five feet high, squarish, squat, pierced by an archway, on each side of the arch four narrow windows in two tiers, the windows of the top tier arched. The glass of the windows was, of course, shattered, but the structure itself had sustained little damage.

Beyond the gate were the headstones, simple slabs for the most part, some leaning a little this way and that, as time and the sagging of sod had prescribed. Such were the marks of time and peace in the plot.

But here and there the earth was rawly scored. Some of the stones were flattened, and not by time. Some were broken off, or lay shattered on the ground, and the exposed edges of fracture showed white as bone. Toward one corner of the plot a considerable area of earth, some three hundred square feet, had been rooted up, it seemed, and the hole then rawly refilled. There were no headstones showing now in that area, where the pattern of the rows would have dictated their presence.

"Them folks what was laying over there," Jed Hawksworth said, "they just got blowed out of the ground."

"Lak Jedgmint Day," Mose said. "Bet it sounded like Jedgmint. Bet they was bug-eye surprised to find a fawse alarm."

Jed had stopped, was peering at the new-scarred sign by the cemetery gate. "Huh," he grunted, "huh," with a sound like an incipient laugh. "Yeah," he said, and began to read the words:

"ALL PERSONS FOUND USING FIREARMS IN THESE GROUNDS
WILL BE PROSECUTED WITH THE UTMOST VIGOR
OF THE LAW"

"Prosecuted," Jed repeated, with a whispering relish. "Huh."

"Who gonna pros-cute 'em?" Mose demanded. "Going *ker-boom, ker-boom, ker-boom!*" With his imaginary weapon he swept the landscape. He stopped, and grinned. He giggled with a secret joke. Then he could keep it no longer.

"Listen," he said, "I tell you who pros-cute 'em. They pros-cute one t'other. They pros-cute one t'other to death. De death sentence—dat's what! They pros-cute, aw-right. *Ker-boom.*"

Adam saw a broken wheel against the brick of the cemetery gate. It was a heavy wheel, sturdily bound with iron, the wheel of a gun or caisson. But one third of it had been randomly wrenched away. The splintered butts of spokes stuck from the chunky hub. The iron of the tire was twisted back and pointed upward. It had begun to rust, Adam noticed. Somebody had propped a ramrod against the cemetery gate. It waited there tidily like a broom some housewife had propped when called away from her task.

Why hadn't it been knocked down, Adam asked himself. He thought of the rammer waiting thus, year after year, the butt sinking by infinite gradation into the turf, the metal flaking away.

Adam looked north, toward the village. He saw the roofs, the white spire among the calm trees. The trees, now, were taking on the color of autumn. He heard the movement of the two men behind him, approaching. He turned, and moved on.

He stopped and saw, westward, beyond a stone

wall near at hand, the land falling away into a shallow valley, rising beyond to a low ridge sprigged with orchards and clumps of timber. The light was falling toward him across the crest of the distant ridge, leveling out.

"Yeah, son," a voice said, and Adam turned.

"Yeah, son," the voice repeated, "that's where they come from."

Then Adam saw them.

Not far away, back from the stone wall, three men sat on the ground. Adam moved toward them. One was a fat man, propped against what remained of the trunk of a small tree, the main part having been snapped, or hacked, off some seven feet above the ground. The fat man was very fat. He sat with his legs spread out before him, bulging the black breeches, and his belly bulged out and dropped in the space between his legs. In front of the belly, a stone jug was set. A length of rope was looped in the handle.

Adam looked at him in question.

"The Rebs," the fat man said, nodding westward. "That's where they come from."

Jedeen Hawksworth, followed by the Negro, came up. "Good evening, good sirs," the fat man said. He lifted his face in a muddy, sweaty, dust-streaked jolly grin. It was not hot now, but the sweat of his face seemed in constant supply, exuding steadily from the massive flesh-heat within.

"How-de-do," Jed said.

———

139

The fat man wiped his face with a handkerchief as big as a towel and much the color of plowed loam. He shoved his black felt hat back and wiped the handkerchief across his brow. He twinkled his small eyes, recessed in the red folds of flesh, picked up his jug, uncorked it, and said: "Hot work, friend."

He was about to drink—had, in fact, dropped his lower lip and laid the nipple of the jug on that ample cushion—when he suffered an access of courtesy. "Your pardon, kind sirs," he said, as soon as he got the jug off his lip. "Won't you, kind sirs, take a snort?"

He passed the jug to Jed Hawksworth, who thanked him, did some damage, and coughed in tribute. Jed passed the jug to Adam. For an instant Adam stood there in embarrassment, then said, no, no thanks.

The fat man wagged a finger about the size and shape of a respectable sausage. "Fudge," said the fat man, "oh, fie. No harm in it. It will increase the outgiving flow of blood to the cranium, the healthful flow of urine to the bladder, and the cheerful flow of conversation to your lips. It will, in fact, mollify the pangs of encroaching age and—"

The face went redder than ever, lard seemed to spring more liberally upon it, and the mouth emitted a shattering belch.

"What I mean is, take a snort," the fat man said, when he had recovered himself.

"No thanks, sir," Adam said, "but I thank you very much," and passed the jug toward Mose.

Adam was aware that the hand of Mose had, with alacrity, moved toward the jug. But it had stopped before making contact. Adam saw that the gaze of the fat man's little jolly eyes were no longer jolly. The gaze was sharpening, whittling down to a point, and when that point was reached, the lips in that fat, ruddy, jolly face were going to move and say something. The men beyond the fat man, a pale thin young man sitting hunched over, and a man of nondescript, nonprosperous middle age, were staring too. They stared at the face of the fat man, then at the hand of Mose Talbutt poised in the air, then back at the face of the fat man. Jedeen Hawksworth, Adam noticed, was staring at the black hand hung in the air.

Then Jedeen Hawksworth turned toward the fat man. "That's fine booze," he said firmly, "yes, sir! And I'm sure you want my nigger to have him a snort. Yeah, give the nigger a snort right here where they kicked the be-Jesus out of Ginnal Lee. Les have us a nigger drink to kicking the be-Jesus out of Ginnal Lee. Hell, don't a nigger git just as thirsty as a white man?"

The eyes in the fat man's face wavered toward the face of Jed Hawksworth. "Sure," the fat man said, and turned to watch the black hand take the loop of rope. With an expression that Adam could not read, the man watched Mose lift the jug, drink slowly, lower the jug and pass it back to Adam, who, in turn, passed it back to the owner. Adam wondered, flickeringly, why Mose had done that—passed the jug to him.

But Mose was saying, "Much obleeged," politely to the fat man. Then he wiped his mouth with the back of his hand.

The fat man had the jug almost to his own lips. But it stopped. A faint cloud seemed to pass over his expectation. "Here," he said, nodding to the middle-aged man beyond him, "your turn. Have some."

The middle-aged man took the jug, drew a quid of tobacco from his jaw to balance it on a kneecap, and after a moment drank. But, Adam observed, he had surreptitiously wiped the nipple of the jug on the sleeve of his coat.

The fat man was making a gesture westward, saying: "Yes, sir, they come right across yonder. Three times them Rebels essay to knock us off these hills. That last day they come—a man can see 'em coming —ten thousand, fifteen thousand, marching across that valley. It was Pickett and his—"

"And Pettigrew—him too," the nondescript man amended.

"And Pettigrew—General J. Johnston Pettigrew of North Carolina, and his division"—the fat man graciously acknowledged the correction—"ah, they came too, with the red flags of treason, battle, and rapine. It was shot and shell. See this very tree under which I repose myself. It is sawed off by Minié balls. Fifteen, twenty thousand Rebels—they are coming.

"They broke in here. Over that wall—behold, they

come! But our covenant, it is with the hills. Jehovah reacheth out His hand."

The fat man stretched forth his arm in a gesture of command, and lifted his head.

When he had belched, he resumed: "They could not push us off. I say now unto you—"

The middle-aged man gave a discreet cough. "Push who off?" he asked.

With untarnished dignity the fat man turned his gaze from the scene of carnage to the nondescript middle-aged man. "And where, pray," he demanded, "were you and your filthy, unprecious, pox-plagued carcass on that day?"

"Under the bed," the nondescript man replied without hesitation. He snickered. Then, with innocence, asked: "And where was you?"

"If it is not immodest of me to affirm it," the fat man said, "I was—"

He paused, lifted the jug, and drank.

"Was where?" the nondescript one demanded, leaning forward like a terrier on a leash.

"I was," the fat man affirmed, "where the Lord of Hosts, in His infinite wisdom, had called me."

"Yeah, and where was that, Mr. Mordacai Sulgrave?"

"Doctor, if you please," the fat man corrected.

"Well, Doc, where was that where you was?"

"I was under the bed," the fat man, in unclouded ease, replied. He stretched forth his hand, again in his gesture of authority, to still any untoward response. "And may I say," he added, "that there were five blankets, four quilts, and two feather tickings on that bed, that I occupied the space nearest the wall, and that the Lord in His wisdom had seen fit to place my spouse and wife of my bosom on the outside. Selah!"

The nondescript man again snickered.

"It is not for mortal to question the wisdom of the Most High," Dr. Sulgrave reproved.

"I aim to leave the Most High out of it," the nondescript man said. "But I aim to say that you never seen nuthen."

"I have it from reliable sources," Dr. Sulgrave said. "Am I, thus far, correct, Mr. Hankins?"

He bowed toward the pale young man, but before that young man could summon strength to reply, Dr. Sulgrave remarked to the strangers: "Mr. Hankins here—Sull Hankins—he lay here and endured bombardment and assault. Right, Sull?"

The young man weakly nodded. Adam noticed that his left sleeve was pinned to his coat, a fact not previously plain in the young man's hunched position.

"Sull has felt the iron fist of battle," Dr. Sulgrave said.

"It looked like the air was full of cook-stoves and hot plow-points," the young man said. "We laid on the ground and them things come flying over."

The nondescript man looked at Mose. "Where was you when they fit Gettysburg?" he asked.

_____

144

Mose looked at him, then let his gaze stray off over the empty valley, westward, toward the far ridge. For a moment, it seemed as though he had really forgotten the question. Then he said: "New Yawk."

The man said: "Looks like you'd a-been here. They was fighting over you niggers. Looks like you might of give a hand. You look stout."

"I got a bad back," Mose said, after a moment.

"Yeah," the nondescript man said, "and lots of fellers have wished they had 'em a bad back. And lots of 'em did. Have bad backs, I mean. Mighty bad backs that come on 'em all of a sudden, and they was laying on 'em and looking straight up at the sky. But they wasn't seeing nothing. They is laying right now under this ground thick as potatoes in a rich man's potato hill."

The fat man swept his right arm in an embracing gesture. "Aye," he said, "all this precinct is but a great potato hill of heroism and holiness. Except," he said, pausing to amend himself, "for such Rebels as are here interred. But let us speak not of them. I consider it a privilege that I am to assist in removing the bodies of our righteous sons from their present low associations and cramped precincts and adjust them in a—"

Jed Hawksworth took a step forward. "You mean," he said, pointing to a spade lying on the autumn grass, "you mean you're digging 'em up?"

"Exhume, exhume, sir," the fat man waved a finger in protest. "It is a word of more tone and dignity. But

---

to answer your query, the Governor of our state proposes a great cemetery on this hallowed spot, a shrine of patriotism. The fallen are to be reshuffled—rearranged, I mean—"

He paused to cough, refresh himself, and cough again.

"Rearranged," he continued, "more appropriately. By states, I believe. As for me, I am not to do the actual labor. My friend here"—and he indicated the nondescript man—"has done the actual digging. But today is merely exploratory. To take, you might say, a sampling. Determine condition. My role will be supervisory. I am employed by a friend—who will contract with our great Commonwealth of Pennsylvania. My past experience with the dead will, no doubt, prove invaluable and—"

"He had plenty," the nondescript man said. "He was a doc."

"I am not referring to my years as a physician. Nor as a minister of the gospel. I refer to my experience as an embalmer."

"He quit doctoring," the nondescript man said, "because too many folks died. They got the habit. Quit embalming because all of a sudden they quit dying. If he had just hung on to his doctoring and mixed it with his embalming he would of been rich and no need to take up preaching. Now he quit preaching because—"

"You vex me, varlet," the fat man said. "I have tried many things, it is true, and usually with no mean success. The sage of Concord says that the proper American tries many things, storekeeping, farming, schoolteaching and so on. And though my roster of occupations is different, I offer myself as that Emersonian American. I am a man of parts and—"

"Yeah, and if you'd kept 'em in yore pants they wouldn't of got you out of the preaching business," the nondescript man said.

"I freely acknowledge a certain proneness to temptation contingent upon a robust constitution and attractive personality. But I left the ministry of my own free will, sir. Patriotic motives, gentlemen." He turned to the group. "You see, there is a great need for embalmers with our troops. Even in winter, with exposure and disease, business is not slack. I mean, there is a grave need. Ha-ha."

He paused, looked at the unsmiling faces and said: "Wit is the salt of human life. But the dog saltest not his meat."

"It is a joke," the nondescript man explained judiciously. "He made a joke."

"Yassuh," Mose said, and laughed briefly.

The fat man bent his gaze upon him. "Thank you," he said. "But to proceed. When a gallant lad dies, even of locked bowels in winter quarters, the loved ones want the body of the beloved. The body must be prepared for transport. Ergo. For example, I have a friend in the profession who travels with the troops. A perambulatory embalming establishment. I considered returning to that profession as an act of patriotic service. Very good thing my friend has made of it, too."

The nondescript man gave his snicker.

Dr. Sulgrave looked pityingly at him. "Poor simple soul," he said, "he does not know the complexity of life. If a man does a good deed and in so doing prospers, does it not prove merely that his faculties are working in harmony and under Divine sanction? But I decided to give up the wealth and the opportunity for patriotic service which would be mine should I enter the business of perambulatory embalming. I am called to a more comprehensive task. As I was about to say, I regard all my past life as merely a Heaven-ordained apprenticeship for this sacred—"

Adam had gone back around the tree. He was not listening now. Quietly he had come around beyond the spot where the young man crouched. The young man was not listening either. He was rolling a piece of straw between the thumb and forefinger, back and forth, and was staring down at it in marked absorption. Adam crouched quietly beside him. The young man did not seem to sense his presence. Adam put a hand out as though to touch the young man's arm, or pluck his sleeve, but he withdrew it, waiting for recognition.

Finally, very softly, almost whispering, he said: "You—you were here?"

Slowly, the young man turned his gaze upon him. He looked at him from a great distance. Then he moved his left shoulder. The empty sleeve stirred flaccidly, ever so little.

"You think I got this bit off by a bear?" the pale young man demanded, with no expression, or heat.

The young man had returned his gaze to the revolving straw between his thumb and forefinger. Adam hung his head and looked at the straw. It rolled back and forth.

The fat man had heaved to his feet, with some help from the tree behind him. Puffing from the exertion, he looked down at the jug. "Git the jug," he said to the nondescript man. Then to Jed Hawksworth: "If you will kindly step this way, I'll show you the condition."

Adam saw him, followed by the others, move toward a pile of earth, southward along the stone wall. The pale young man rose and followed. The fat man was now gesturing down, beyond the pile of earth. Adam knew what they were looking at. He knew that he would have to look at it.

He approached, and looked.

"He ain't as bad off as one might presume," Dr. Sulgrave was saying. "Our gallant troops have the Christian practice of laying something over the face of the deceased. If something is handy. A cap or a piece of shirt, or blanket."

"It keeps the dirt off yore face," the nondescript man explained.

"His face is in right good shape," Dr. Sulgrave said judiciously, "considering what he has been through. But it drains good here. And besides, the weather has been favorable, not too wet."

The young man had been staring down into the shallow hole. Now he turned away and began to study the stone wall.

"With careful handling—" Dr. Sulgrave was saying. But he stopped, and reached for the jug.

Adam stood beside the young man. The young man's attention was now fixed on one point of the wall. Then he stirred in his bemusement. "Thar it is," he said.

"What?" Adam asked.

"That durn rock." He nodded toward a large stone at the base of the wall. It looked like any one of a dozen to be seen from the spot. Adam turned in question to the young man.

"I knowed I'd find it. I'd a-knowed it in the dark." But the young man did not seem to be talking to Adam.

"I had me long enough to git acquainted with it," the young man said. He turned abruptly to Adam, and stared at him. "I was laying right there"—and he pointed at the ground—"looking at that durn rock. All that time they was throwing them cook-stoves at us. I studied that rock. I sure got me an acquaintance with that rock." He stopped.

Adam saw that his face was sweating.

Then, after his pause in which Adam could hear his breath, the young man said: "It looked like it give me something to do. Studying that rock." He paused again.

Then resumed: "Till Pettigrew come. Them Pettigrew bastards from North Carolina."

"North Ca-lina?" Jed Hawksworth demanded. He had been in the act of drinking from the jug, but now he held it chest-high, turning from Dr. Sulgrave to the young man by the wall. "You say North Ca-lina?" he demanded.

"Yeah," the young man said. "Them bastards. They hit right along here. I was behind that wall and I seen 'em coming. When they stopped throwing them cook-stoves I peeked over the wall. They was down in the valley, marching at us. Pickett and them Virginians yonder"—he pointed his finger weakly to the left—"and them North Carolina bastards down here. They was angling up the rise. They marched into the canister. A bastard would get hit and fall, but they'd close up and come on. By God, I'll say this fer 'em, them bastards would close up and come on. They come marching. They held their line. They durn near held it clean."

Jed Hawksworth absently passed the jug back to Dr. Sulgrave. He came to stand by the young man, and looked over the wall down the slope, across the valley. "They come all that way across?" he said.

"Them as made it," the young man said. "And too God-durn many made it, you ask me." He moved his left shoulder and the sleeve stirred, like an idle flag in some slight movement of air, quickly spent.

"They stopped just once," he said. "To give the volley. Then they come on. But not marching now. It was double-time. Hell, it was running, and they give their fool yell. They was carrying steel. They come piling over the wall."

He stopped, seemed to draw into himself.

Dr. Sulgrave lowered the jug from his lips, and said: "Gentlemen, if you will kindly step this way, I can show you one."

"One what?" Jed Hawksworth demanded.

"One of those persons whom"—he paused for a belch—"whom our friend here terms them bastards from North Carolina. Alas, he has his excuse for rancor."

Dr. Sulgrave stood at one end of another pile of earth and again looked down. Jed Hawksworth came to the other end of the pile. Adam approached, and the others.

"To judge from his rags," Dr. Sulgrave said, looking down, "he might be any disreputable mendicant. But observe, gentlemen. On his belt buckle you will find *CSA*. Now the man just at his feet—whom, by the way, we have again covered, as we shall this one —his trousers were supported by a piece of rope. To such straits is treason—"

"Well, he wore 'em up here, didn't he?" Jed Hawksworth, in sudden anger, demanded. "His trousers, I mean. Didn't he wear 'em up here? All the way?"

"Yes, indeed," the fat man agreed blandly, "he was quite properly clothed. But you will observe that a jacket covers the face of this citizen of North Carolina. That was an act of chivalry to a fallen foe. I have, by

the way, examined the face. It is not in good condition. I advise that you leave the fabric undisturbed."

Dr. Sulgrave drank, and stood there by the pile of
earth, swaying slightly.

The pale young man stared down at the jacket in
the hole. "Could be," he said.

"Be what?" Adam asked.

"Be the one I got," the young man said. "I got me
one when they come over the wall." He fell into
thought. "Yeah," he said, "but then it could be the
son-of-a-bitch who—" He paused and fingered the
empty sleeve.

Dr. Sulgrave had stopped his swaying. His eyes
were distended and he stared at nothing. All at once
he collapsed across the pile of earth. The nondescript
man was trying to roll him over.

"Drove his head nigh into the ground," the nondescript man said. "Help me roll him."

Mose helped roll him.

"Durn, we ain't got no water," the nondescript man
complained. "We can't bring him round." He held the
sleeper's head on his lap. The sleeper began to snore.

"The son-of-a-bitch is breathing," Jed Hawksworth
said contemptuously. As he stood there and stared
down at the man, the contempt faded from his face.
Something else was there, rising, spreading, man-
tling from an inner depth—rage or pain. He turned
on his heel, and went to stare over the stone wall,
across the valley. It was sunset.

The nondescript man looked down at the lardy

face, the small eyes closed in the folds of flesh, the big lips painfully puffing with each raucous exhalation. "Old Mordecai," the man said, "he ain't a bad man. He just never had no luck."

"Ain't gonna have no luck now," the pale young man said, "digging up folks here, and no permit."

"Says he has, but I bet he ain't," the nondescript man said.

"We ain't gonna have no luck, either," the young man said. "We'll be in jail fer coming along."

"Somebody had to come along," the nondescript man said. "Suppose he was laying here like this all night, and nobody here." He looked up at Adam, defensively. "He warn't so bad. That time he was doctoring round here—he saved Sull's life. Ain't that right, Sull?"

The young man nodded. "That's what they tell me," he said.

"Sull, here," the nondescript man explained, "he wasn't nothing but a boy and he had a swelled throat. Would a-died if the doc here"—he nodded down to indicate the fallen form—"if he hadn't sucked the pus out. With a tube."

The form stirred slightly, and the lips emitted a sigh.

"Ain't every man will suck out pus," the nondescript man said. "It will kill you, you git it in you."

"He would suck pus out if it was in a jug," the pale young man said.

"He saved yore life, Sull," the nondescript man said in mild reproof.

Jed Hawksworth had turned from the valley and was regarding them. Beyond them Mose was squatting at the head of the trench. With a stick he was in the act of raising the jacket from the face of the dead Carolinian there.

"Mose," Jed Hawksworth suddenly said.

"Yassuh," Mose said.

"Take your black son-of-a-bitching hands off that man," he said.

Mose jerked back.

Sitting in the shadow, some twenty feet from the fire where Adam and Jed Hawksworth sat, Mose lifted his face above his army mess-pan. He had been eating, but now he had stopped. With the last bit of food yet unswallowed, puffing one cheek and actually visible between the lax lips, he sat there.

"Mr. Hawksworth," he now said, softly.

Jed gave no sign of having heard. He had finished eating and was sitting cross-legged, staring into the fire, holding the blade of his knife against the sole of his left boot, but without motion. It had not moved in a long time.

"Mr. Hawksworth," Mose repeated, the syllables still sad and soft, but more audible.

Jed turned toward him. He stared at him across the distance. "Yeah," he said, with no expression.

"Mr. Hawksworth," Mose said, "all this time I bin

with you, you ain't done nuthen. You ain't done nuthen fer me, ner nuthen agin me. Not till this evenen."

Jed Hawksworth withdrew his gaze from the man. With care, he began again to move the knife blade on the sole of the boot.

"Mr. Hawksworth," Mose said, very softly, "you done sumthen this evenen. You done it of a sudden."

Jed Hawksworth paid no attention. The knife moved on the leather.

"Mr. Hawksworth," Mose said, soft and sad, "no man ain't a-callen me no black son-of-a-bitch."

Jed Hawksworth turned his gaze slowly to Mose Talbutt. Then he looked back to the fire, and fell into a study. "I done it," he said, after a moment.

"Mr. Hawksworth," Mose said. "I don't want you doen it agin."

The man staring into the fire did not shift his posture, his eyes still on the fire. But he said: "Anything you don't like around here, there is the big road."

He waited, then added: "It runs both ways. You can pick the way to go."

Mose said nothing. He looked down into his mess-pan. He found there one last morsel of bread. He ran it around the edge, where some grease was congealing, and raised it meditatively to his mouth. After a little, he got up and went to lie under the wagon, where some canvas was arranged to make a sort of tent. There he was completely withdrawn from sight.

After a while the knife in Jed Hawksworth's hand

began to move, more deliciously now, on the leather of the boot sole. After a while, staring into the fire, he said: "They run me out of North Ca-lina."

Adam said nothing. He felt the weight of night on the strange land behind his back.

"Maybe they done me a favor," Jed said, staring into the fire.

Adam felt the weight of night and sadness at his back. It pressed upon him.

"If they hadn't drove me out," Jed Hawksworth said, staring into the fire, "I might of been marching up that hill. I might of been a captain or a cunnel, marching up that hill. I might of been laying up there now, and some black bastard poking a stick at some blanket or something laying on my face."

He paused.

Then: "Yeah, maybe they saved my life. Driving me out."

"Mr. Hawksworth," Adam said, "I told you I respect what you did. I know why you did it and why they drove you out."

The man swung his gaze away from the fire, and upon Adam. "You don't know a God-damned thing," he said.

Jed Hawksworth waited, staring into the fire; then said: "Maybe I don't know neither. Know why. Not for a long time. Maybe I thought I was just a nigger-lover like they said."

The knife moved on the leather of the sole. Even in the silence, it made no sound. Then a cricket chirped, feebly, beyond the firelight. It chirped several times, then stopped. Jed Hawksworth, sitting there with his silk stock at his throat and his beaver on his head, stared into the fire. The knife had stopped now.

"My ma," Jed Hawksworth said, "she was kin to the high muck-a-mucks. She was first cousin to Johnston F. Harris. Cunnel Johnston F. Harris. The *F* was for Flaccus." He stopped, then gave a sharp, bitten-off laugh.

"My pa would of kissed the ass of Cunnel Johnston F. Harris," he said.

The cricket made its sound, stopped.

"Yes, sir, Johnston F.," Jed Hawksworth mimicked. "Yes, sir, Johnston F., you are right. You are right as buttons, Johnston F." He stopped. Then, mimicking: "Now, gentlemen, as my cousin Cunnel Harris says— Johnston F. says—"

Again he bit off his laugh.

"That day," he said, and stopped.

He sat there heavily, staring into the fire, with no apparent inclination to resume. His narrow shoulders seemed to have hunched lower, under the black broadcloth.

But, in the end, he said: "Yeah, that day."

"That day," he said, resuming, "they was standing in front of the court house, Cunnel Johnston F. and all them. I was standing there. My pa come up. He said to Johnston F., 'Cousin, I want to shake your hand.' Then he turned around to all them folks and said: 'Gentlemen, Cunnel Harris here, he is prepared to offer up fifteen hundred dollars' worth of prime field-hand meat to maintain order. Fifteen hundred dollars gone up in smoke. If they convict. And they will convict. Cunnel Harris here has declared that he will not accept remuneration for seeing justice done. He will not accept compensation from the State of North Carolina if the state condemns and executes that black son-of-a-bitch. He says he will not accept hard-earned money from the taxpayers of this state. I submit, gentlemen, that Cunnel Johnston F. Harris is a patriot. I say three cheers for Cunnel Harris!' "

He stopped, hunched forward, sinking more deeply into himself, and the past.

Adam watched him. Then he asked: "Did they?"

Jed Hawksworth looked at him.

"Did they cheer, I mean?" Adam asked.

"Some," the man said. He paused, looked into the fire. "Not too many," he said. "But always there's some bastards will start cheering. But them as didn't cheer. You know why?"

Adam shook his head.

"I'll tell you," the man said. "It was just one thing. It was because they was too ashamed."

"Ashamed?" Adam repeated. He felt a faint, painful stir of hope, even of joy, deep in him.

"Yeah," the man said. "If they didn't cheer it was for the plain and simple fact that they was ashamed to be seeing my pa ass-kiss Cunnel Johnston F. Harris in public. It made 'em so ashamed they couldn't cheer."

That small stir deep in Adam Rosenzweig, whatever that stir had been, was gone. Or was it? Was it simply too painful to recognize that it was yet there?"

Jed Hawksworth moved on his stone. He swung full at Adam, and leaned. "Listen," he commanded.

An excitement was making his eyes glitter. His lips worked for a second before he spoke. "Listen," he repeated, "it wasn't any cheering made me do it. Made me go in there and speak for the nigger. You know what it was?"

Adam was caught by the glitter of eye, the tight twitching of the thin lips. He could not stop staring at the face.

"Damn it, don't you know?" the man demanded.

All Adam could do was shake his head.

"Damn it, ain't you enough of a man to know?" the man was demanding, almost desperately.

When Adam did not answer he said: "It was knowing that them as didn't cheer, just couldn't because they was too ashamed. To see my pa. See him do it in public."

The man turned his gaze back into the fire. "That was what made me do it," he said. He waited. Then added: "Because I hated them for being ashamed for my pa." He waited again.

Then: "And because I hated my pa for making me ashamed of him."

They had sat there a long time before Jed Hawksworth spoke again. Then he said: "You live yore years and time it looks like you never know who to thank. And what for. Maybe I ought to thank them men who didn't cheer. It was them not cheering made me ashamed to be the son of my pa. It was them not cheering made me go in that courthouse. It was them not cheering kept me from laying back yonder on that hill, tonight. Dead in the ground. I might of been kilt charging up that hill with Pettigrew."

He laughed, bit it off, rose, and went into the shelter he had for himself under the big wagon. He had to take his beaver off before he crept under.

Adam sat and stared into the fire. He knew that soon he would rise and prepare to wrap himself in his blankets and sleep. But now he stared into the red coals, and heard the crickets in the dry grass behind him, and thought of his own father—of Leopold Rosenzweig dead in a mean room in Bavaria. He thought of the words spoken over his father's body when it was lowered into the earth. The words had asked peace for all the dead.

Adam sat there and thought of the living, who did not have peace.

Standing in the shelter of the tent—a rejected hospital tent on which the rain now dripped, no longer drumming—Adam watched his own hands touch the objects on the improvised counter of boards laid across two beef barrels. There was, of course, no real need to rearrange everything. A quarter inch this way or that for the hardbake, or the toffee, or the barley sugar, or the sardines, or the bitters, or the condensed milk, or the stationery, or the needles— what could it mean? Adam watched his own hands make the caressing, anxious movement that, when rain falls and nobody comes, and ruin draws close like a cat rubbing against the ankles, has been the ritual of stall vendors, forever.

He recognized the gesture. He knew its meaning. He had seen a dry, old, yellowing hand reach out, with that painful solicitude, to touch, to rearrange, to shift aimlessly, some object worth a pfennig. Back in Bavaria he had seen that gesture, and at that sight his heart had always died within him. On such occasions he had not had the courage to look at the face above the hand, whatever face it might be.

Now the face was his own. He wondered what expression, as he made that gesture, was on his face. He wondered if it wore the old anxiety, or the old, taut stoicism. But there was no need, he remembered, for his hand to reach out, for his face to show concern or stoicism. It was nothing to him if rain fell and nobody came. Then why was he assuming the role—the gesture and the suffering? What was he expiating? Or was he now taking the role—the gesture and the suffering—because it was the only way to affirm his history and identity in the torpid, befogged loneliness of this land.

This was Virginia.

He looked out of the tent at the company street. The rain dripped on the freezing loblolly of the street. Beyond that misty gray of the rain, he saw the stretching hutment, low diminutive log cabins, chinked with mud, with doorways a man would have to crouch to get through, with roofs of tenting laid over boughs or boards from hardtack boxes, or fence rails, with

163

cranky chimneys of sticks and dried mud. The chimney of the hut across from him was surmounted by a beef barrel with ends knocked out. In this heavy air, however, that device did not seem to help. The smoke from that chimney rose as sluggishly as smoke from any other, and hung as sadly in the drizzle, creeping back down along the sopping canvas of the roof.

Over the door was a board with large, inept lettering: HOME SWEET HOME. This was the hut of Simms Purdew, the hero.

The men were huddled in those lairs. Adam knew the names of some. He knew the faces of all, hairy or shaven, old or young, fat or thin, suffering or hardened, sad or gay, good or bad. When they stood about his tent, chaffing each other, exchanging their obscenities, cursing command or weather, he had studied their faces. He had had the need to understand what life lurked behind the mask of flesh, behind the oath, the banter, the sadness. Once covertly looking at Simms Purdew, the only man in the world whom he hated, he had seen the heavy, slack, bestubbled jaw open and close to emit the cruel, obscene banter, and had seen the pale-blue eyes go watery with whisky and merriment, and suddenly he was not seeing the face of that vile creature. He was seeing, somehow, the face of a young boy, the boy Simms Purdew must once have been, a boy with sorrel hair, and blue eyes dancing with gaiety, and the boy mouth grinning trustfully among the freckles.

In that moment of vision Adam heard the voice

within himself saying: *I must not hate him, I must not hate him or I shall die.*

His heart suddenly opened to joy.

He thought that if once, only once, he could talk with Simms Purdew, something about his own life, and all life, would be clear and simple. If Simms Purdew would turn to him and say: "Adam, you know when I was a boy, it was a funny thing happened. Lemme tell you now—"

If only Simms Purdew could do that, whatever the thing he remembered and told. It would be a sign for the untellable, and he, Adam, would understand.

Now, Adam, in the gray light of afternoon, stared across at the hut opposite his tent, and thought of Simms Purdew lying in there in the gloom, snoring on his bunk, with the fumes of whisky choking the air. He saw the sign above the door of the hut: HOME SWEET HOME. He saw the figure of a man in a poncho coming up the company street, with an armful of wood.

It was Pullen James, the campmate of Simms Purdew. He carried the wood, carried the water, did the cooking, cleaning and mending, and occasionally got a kick in the butt for his pains. Adam watched the moisture flow from the poncho. It gave the rubberized fabric a dull gleam, like metal. Pullen James humbly lowered his head, pushed aside the hardtack-box door of the hut, and was gone from sight.

Adam stared at the door and remembered that

Simms Purdew had been awarded the Medal of Honor for gallantry at Antietam.

The street was again empty. The drizzle was slacking off now, but the light was grayer. With enormous interest, Adam watched his hands as they touched and shifted the objects on the board directly before him. Into the emptiness of the street, and his spirit, moved a form.

The form was swathed in an army blanket, much patched, fastened at the neck with a cord. From under the shapeless huddle of blanket the feet moved in the mud. The feet wore army shoes, in obvious disrepair. The head was wrapped in a turban and on top of the turban rode a great hamper across which a piece of poncho had been flung. The gray face stared straight ahead in the drizzle. Moisture ran down the cheeks, gathered at the tip of the nose, and at the chin. The figure was close enough now for him to see the nose twitching to dislodge the drop clinging there. The figure stopped and one hand was perilously freed from the hamper to scratch the nose. Then the figure moved on.

This was one of the Irish women who had built their own huts down near the river. They did washing. Adam recognized this one. He recognized her because she was the one who, in a winter twilight, on the edge of camp, had once stopped him and reached down her hand to touch his fly. "Slice o' mutton, bhoy?" she had queried in her soft guttural. "Slice o' mutton?"

Her name was Mollie. They called her Mollie the Mutton, and laughed. Looking down the street after her, Adam saw that she had again stopped and again removed one hand from the basket. He could not make out, but he knew that again she was scratching her nose. Mollie the Mutton was scratching her nose.

The words ran crazily in his head: *Mollie the Mutton is scratching her nose in the rain.*

Then the words fell into a pattern:

Mollie the Mutton is scratching her nose,
Scratching her nose in the rain.
Mollie the Mutton is scratching her nose in the rain.

The pattern would not stop. It came again and again. He felt trapped in that pattern, in the repetition.

Suddenly, he thought he might weep. "What's the matter with me?" he demanded out loud. He looked wildly around, at the now empty street, at the mud, at the rain. "Oh, what's the matter with me?" he demanded.

When he had stored his stock in the great oak chest, locked the two big hasps and secured the additional chain, tied the fly of the tent, and picked up the cash box, he moved up the darkening street. He would consign the cash box into the hands of Jed Hawksworth, then stand by while his employer checked the contents and the list of items sold. Then he—

Then what? He did not know. His mind closed on that prospect, as though fog had descended to blot out a valley.

Far off, in the dusk, he heard voices singing, muffled but strong. In one of the huts a group of men were huddled together, singing. He stopped. He strained to hear. He heard the words:

> "Rock of Ages, cleft for me,
>   Let me hide myself in Thee!
>   Let the water and the blood
>   From Thy riven side . . ."

He thought: *I am a Jew from Bavaria.*

He was standing there, he thought, in Virginia, in the thickening dusk, in a costly greatcoat that had belonged to another Jew. That other Jew, a young man too, had left that greatcoat behind, in a rich house, and marched away. He had crossed the river which now, beyond the woods yonder, was sliding darkly under the mist. He had plunged into the dark woods beyond. He had died there.

What had that man, that other young Jew, felt as he stood in the twilight and heard other men, far away, singing together?

Adam thought of the hutments, regiment after regiment, row after row, the thousands of huts, stretching away into the night. He thought of the men, the

———

168

nameless thousands, huddling in them. He thought of Simms Purdew snoring on his bunk while Pullen James crouched by the hearth, skirmishing an under-shirt for lice, and a wet log sizzled. He thought of Simms Purdew, who once had risen at the edge of a cornfield, a maniacal scream on his lips, and swung a clubbed musket like a flail to beat down the swirl of Rebel bayonets about him.

He thought of Simms Purdew rising up, fearless in glory. He felt the sweetness of pity flood through him, veining his very flesh. Those men, lying in the huts, they did not know. They did not know who they were or know their own worth. In the pity for them his loneliness was gone.

Then he thought of Aaron Blaustein standing in his rich house saying: "God is tired of taking the blame. He is going to let History take the blame for a while."

He thought of the old man laughing under the glitter of the great chandelier.

He thought: *Only in my heart can I make the world hang together.*

Adam rose from the crouch necessary to enter the hut. He saw Mose squatting by the hearth, breaking up hardtack into a pan. A pot was boiling on the coals. "Done give Ole Buckra all his money?" Mose asked softly.

Adam nodded.

"Yeah," Mose murmured, "yeah. And look what he done give us."

Adam looked at the pot. "What is it?" he asked.

"Chicken," Mose said, and theatrically licked his lips. "Gre't big fat chicken, yeah." He licked his lips again.

Then: "Yeah. A chicken with six tits and a tail lak a corkscrew. And hit squealed for slop." Mose giggled. "Fooled you, huh? It is the same ole same, tell me hit's name. It is sowbelly with tits on. It is salt po'k. It is salt po'k and skippers. That po'k, it was so full of skippers it would jump and run and not come when you say, 'Hoo-pig.' Had to put my foot on it to hole it down while I cut it up fer the lob-scuse."

He dumped the pan of crumbled hardtack into the boiling pot of lobscouse. "Good ole lob-scuse," he mumbled, and stirred the pot. He stopped stirring and looked over his shoulder. "Know what Ole Buckra et tonight?" he demanded. "Know what I had to fix fer Ole Him?"

Adam shook his head.

"Chicken," Mose said. "It wuz shore-Gawd the fus chicken on the Rapidan since 'sixty-two. It wuz a real live chicken. I kissed hit. I patted hits little curly head. Then I wrung hit's neck. I plucked hit. I gutted hit. I thought mebbe he give us the innerds fer soup. Naw. I thought mebbe he give us the feet fer soup. Naw. Thought mebbe he gives us a how-de-do. Naw, he did'n say nuthen, jes set thar and et the whole durn chicken. He sop up the gravy with biscuits. Made me make him biscuits." He paused.

"But I burned 'em some," he said. "Jes enough."

Adam was looking at the slush lamp.

"You Jew-folks ain't supposed to eat no pig, that right?" Mose asked.

Adam nodded.

"Why doan you tell him you won't take no more salt po'k?"

The flame of the slush lamp was weak.

"Now if'n I was a Jew-man, I tell you I'd—"

"I don't care what I eat," Adam said listlessly, watching the lamp.

"Wal, I keers what I eat, and if'n I—"

"The lamp is about to go out," Adam said, not really hearing the voice of the crouching man.

"You knows whar is the grease can," Mose said. "And you ain't crippled."

Adam looked down at him. He was crouching with face averted, stirring the pot of lobscouse. "I didn't mean, Talbutt, that you should get it," Adam said quietly. "I didn't mean to disturb your work. I just happened to mention the fact. I happened to be looking at the lamp."

Adam moved beyond the hearth and found the tin with grease-waste from the cooking. He lowered the sardine can hung on wire that constituted the slush lamp. It was nearly empty of grease. He filled it, then found a rag for a new wick. He took a spill from the pile of them on the board shelf above the hearth, and lighted the lamp.

Mose looked up. "I didn' mean nuthen special when I said that about was you cripple."

"I don't mind," Adam said.

"It is jes a way of talken," Mose said. He returned to stirring the pot. After a moment, not looking up, he said, "That-air lamp, hit ain't much good. Ole Buckra oughta give us candles. Me, I'm gonna need candles for studyen."

"For what?" Adam, lost in his abstraction, asked.

"You is like him," Mose said.

"Like who?"

"Like Ole Buckra. Doan think no nigger oughta be a-studyen. But me, I'm gonna study, no matter. Some fellers—some sodjers in Company C—they teachen. They teachen what niggers will come and learn. They teach late in the af-noon. I ast Ole Him could I go."

"What did he say?"

"He said naw. He said it his time. He said what did I need to study. He said I could ketch gray-backs outa my wool without knowen how to spell 'em. I tole him then I'm goen anyway."

"What did he say?"

"You know how he look?" Mose asked. "Well, he set thar at that table picken his teeth. He stopped picken and give me that-air look. Lak I warn't thar. Never said a word. I put the dishes on the shelf and walked out."

Adam looked around the hut. He looked at the stools made cunningly of boards. At the two bunks made of stout log lengths and springy saplings under the mattresses of blanket sewed together and stuffed

with straw. At the smooth mud plaster of the chimney. He remembered how they had built the hut,
back in December. Jedeen Hawksworth had said to
him: "I'm going to be by myself. The nigger is fixing
me a place. He can fix one for you." He had paused,
then added: "Unless you're such an all-fired nigger-
lover you want to bunk up with one."

He, Adam, had stood for a moment in thought. Then
he had said, quietly, that he thought he might share
with Mose.

Now he looked down at Mose, stirring the lobscouse.

"You know whut," Mose said, not turning from the
pot. "Now is lak afore. Afore I run off. Down thar"
—he gestured southward with the big wooden spoon
—"they put you in jail for teachen a nigger."

Adam was looking curiously at the objects by
which life was lived. He saw his little satchel on a
shelf, unopened since the day, back in the house of
Aaron Blaustein, when the dried shawl, phylacteries, and prayer book had been replaced in it.

After a moment, Adam said: "Talbutt."

"Yassuh."

"Talbutt," Adam said, "I can teach you to read. I
can teach you every night."

The huts of Jed and his two men were about fifty
yards apart, conveniently situated just south of the
first regiment of the brigade, west of the second. The
huts clung to the sheltering edge of a patch of

thicket and second growth timber that lay southward toward the river. The timber had been spared from soldiers marauding for firewood simply because the owner had established himself as a Unionist, a claim fairly well substantiated by the fact that the Confederates had burned his big house in their movement northward after Chancellorsville. Now he lived in what had been slave quarters, ate food from the Federal commissary, and drank likker from a brigadier's private locker.

To the north of the two huts lay the regiment to which Jed Hawksworth had originally been accredited sutler, and for which he now, very profitably, ran the store. But when the army had bogged down in winter quarters on the bank of the Rapidan, luck favored Jed Hawksworth. The supplies of the sutler of the second regiment in the brigade had been lost when Meade pulled back in the fall, and the sutler, to compound his ill fortune, died of pneumonia. Jed had seen his chance. He had already struck up an acquaintance with the burned-out Unionist and had flattered his taste in whisky. He had seen the daughter—a sad, dispirited girl, but with good bust and eyes. He knew that the reputation of General Barton was well grounded in fact and that the General could scarcely have had time to complete his dispositions for the cold season. He contrived an excuse to present the girl.

So Jed Hawksworth got the post as sutler of the second regiment. Rather, he procured it for his good friend, a very fine ambitious young man who had come to America to fight for freedom but had been turned down by the army.

It had, of course, cost him $150 tactfully transferred to the pocket of the lieutenant colonel of the second regiment, who had evinced some tendency to suspect the relation between Jed Hawksworth and his young friend, and had made some references to army regulations.

The appointment had also cost Jed Hawksworth considerable time devoted to the Unionist who owned the wood lot. But a three-day drenching in high proof had somewhat blunted the sensibilities of the father. They were so blunted, in fact, that he never had to confront the fait accompli which would have been clearly before his eyes if he had chosen to open them. But he did not so choose, and so had no need to seek comfort in the reflection that if his daughter had been debauched, she had been debauched by an officer of general rank.

The unoffended father moved through the season in his rhythm of elation and nausea, in a world of delusion and fictions and self-justification, and only once or twice woke toward dawn to wonder desperately what would happen when spring came and Meade pushed over the Rapidan, and he would be left here alone.

Meanwhile, Jed Hawksworth prospered. He sat in his hut at night, by the light of three army candles set in sardine tins on the hardtack-box table, and did his accounts. He would do them over and over, gnawed by a superstitious anxiety that he had made some fantastic error in his own favor. But, strangely enough, the only errors he ever made were against himself, and once or twice such errors were of peculiarly substantial proportion. Then, upon discovering the error against himself and setting it right, after checking and rechecking, after being convinced that the figures were correct beyond all dispute, he had, on each occasion, fallen prey to a dismal dread for which he could find no focus.

He would pace the little cage of the cabin, listening to wind in the timber or rain on the canvas, until, suddenly, he could not bear to turn his back to the low door yonder. He knew that no stranger could surprise him; it wasn't that. He had long since put stout boards under the canvas of his roof. He had long since made a door of beams cleated heavily together, and barred with two beams dropped into iron sockets set in the wall. He was not afraid of being robbed. If that had been his fear, he would have taken down the two cavalry pistols that hung on the wall, and inspected the priming. But empty-handed he would sit and stare at the ironbound door. Nothing could come through, nothing short of a shot from a Parrott gun. But the cold flutter in his stomach would not go away. Nor the tightening constriction across his brow.

After a while he would count the money all over again. He would put it into the capacious money belt, take off his outer garments, buckle on the belt, bank the fire, blow out all the candles but one, crawl into his bunk, and enter the next phase of his misery. He would, no doubt, fall asleep. But then the dreams began. Before he closed his eyes he always knew that he would dream of himself lying in a grave, dead but yet not dead, or rather, dead in a death which was an eternal stifling, with a moldy jacket or piece of blanket across his face. And somebody, giggling in the dark, would be prying at the fabric with a stick.

Every night as he lay down he knew that he would wake gasping, and that, in the end, he would rise and hunt the bottle. For he had taken to drink, struggle as he might against it. And he had taken to all sorts of medicine, bitters and pills and emulsions. He would have fits of voracious hunger, then days when nothing would stay on his stomach. He began to think much of his childhood. This was painful, because he could not decide what his memories meant.

Jed Hawksworth began to find the society of his two helpers almost unendurable. He knew that his intuition about them had been correct, that in their diverse ways they were efficient, and that he had a grip on them in some way not easy to duplicate. He had, too, the superstitious conviction that if he lost them his prosperity would vanish, like fairy gold. But he could not bear them.

He could not bear the quietness, the competence, the courtesy, the self-effacement of Adam Rosenzweig. He felt some need to break that evenness of surface, to make Adam Rosenzweig cry out in some deep inner despair. And one night when Adam handed him the cash, he said: "Hey wait. What you running off for? We might have trouble in the checking."

Adam had stood there, pale and erect, waiting for the slow, grinding process to wear itself out. "All right," Jed had said, finally. Adam had said good night, and bowed to go through the low doorway. "You think you're so durn smart," Jed Hawksworth had then said, in a grating whisper.

Adam had straightened up, turning. "What did you say, Mr. Hawksworth?" he had asked. He really had not understood.

The man stared at him a long minute, then said: "Nothing. I didn't say nothing." And had turned away to the fire.

Silently, Adam had gone.

Every night thereafter, without being asked, Adam had stood there, pale and calm, while Jed checked the cash box and the accounts. The man, actually, was not checking them at all. He was making the motions, but something, he did not know what, was gnawing at the back of his mind. All the while he would be casting sidewise glances at Adam, and waiting for a familiar pain to grow in himself. At last, having completed the charade, he would say: "Yeah, I reckin it's all right." Then would add, grimly: "This time."

"Good night, sir," Adam would say, and go.

But one night Jed said: "Wait." Then he said: "How you making out with the nigger?"

"We get along very well," Adam said.

"Yeah," Jed said, "the nigger tells me you all have a high old time over yonder. Says you're teaching him to read."

"Yes," Adam said.

The man studied him with grim interest. "What makes you such a durn nigger-lover?" he demanded, finally.

Adam stood there a moment. He felt himself sinking into a mire, a morass. He felt, literally, the physical impossibility of speech. Then, with an effort, he said: "I don't think I love them any more or any less than I love other people. I don't know that I love any people. It is only that I think they—the black men, I mean—ought to be free."

"Free," Jed Hawksworth echoed. He gave a sour smile that pulled down the corners of his thin mouth, under the long, stained mustaches. "You don't know a God-damn thing," he said. His breathing was audible in the hut.

He thrust his face out at Adam, the small eyes peering, the thin mouth working, the chin outthrust between the mustaches. "Listen," he demanded bitterly, "what do you know? About anything?"

As Adam stared at him, he shoved one of the candles aside so sharply that it fell off the sardine can and, still burning, dropped to the floor. "Answer me, you fool!" Jed Hawksworth cried out. "Stop looking at that fool candle, and answer me!"

Staring, Adam could not answer.

Jed Hawksworth rose abruptly. His breath was sharper than before. "Do you think I'm free?" he demanded. "Do you think I am? Do you think anybody is—is free?"

His right hand was clutching feebly at his shirt front, as though, if strength permitted, it would tear it loose. The breath was raucous. Painfully, he lowered himself back to his stool, still peering at Adam's face. "Free," he said again, not loud now, putting the word forth and then drawing his lips back from it, as though it had an evil taste.

Then he began to laugh. It was a thin, gasping laugh that continued for half a minute. Then it stopped.

Adam could hear the wind in the trees, in the dark outside.

"Looks like sometimes of an evening, you'd want to sit and talk to a white man," Jed Hawksworth said. "Like gentlemen." He paused, seemed to conquer some need to go on.

"I should like to sit with you, sir," Adam said, "whenever you wish."

The man said nothing, staring at him. Adam was again aware of the night wind in the trees.

"Go on," the man was saying dully. "Go on and get out. Get back to your black son-of-a-bitch of a friend."

Adam went directly to his hut, entered, said good evening, and sat on a stool by the fire. A pot boiled there. Mose was at the table, copying letters from the letter-cards Adam had made for him. He was now working on the small letters. He finished the alphabet and passed his sheet over to Adam. "How dat?" he asked. "How dat fer dis nigger chile of de Lawd-A-Mighty?"

Adam looked at the crabbed, cranky letters. He was aware of some small, painful strain in his own right forefinger, as though he were pushing down too hard. He looked up to see the man bowed humbly forward, the blunt, dark face outthrust, the bloodshot eyes fixed on him in naked appeal.

"How dat?" Mose was asking, in almost a whisper, pleading.

"Fine," Adam said, and shivered at the falsity of the tone. "Just fine," he repeated, and tried to put heartiness into the tone, to keep from betraying what, suddenly and inexplicably, he felt—the hopelessness, the aimlessness, and, in his very guts, the revulsion. If only those eyes had not worn that naked appeal. If only—

If only what?

"Listen," he said, "I want to ask you something." Before Mose, surprised by the sudden cold intensity of the voice, at which Adam himself was surprised, could answer, Adam went on: "Has he—has Mr. Hawksworth again spoken insultingly to you? I mean, has he called you a name you find offensive?"

"Huh?" Mose grunted in question. Then a sort of

grin twitched at his face. "You mean, call me a black son-of-a-bitch?" he asked.

"Yes," Adam said. "Yes, a black son-of-a-bitch." He heard his voice enunciating the syllables with excessive precision. He became aware that Mose was studying him from behind some thicket of assessment and distrust.

Then Mose grinned again. "Naw," he said softly, "and he ain't gonna. Ain't no man. Not again. He know he ain't gonna."

He stopped. He was hunched forward on his stool, knees spread, big shoulders forward, elbows out, above each knee a hand, with fingers spread, slowly working back and forth on the bunched muscle under the cloth.

"But," Mose said, "dat ain't sayen he doan wanna. He wanna call me a black son-of-a-bitch. You see hit builden up in 'um. His ole mouf, hit start to work, then he can't hole it no longer. It bust out. He say, 'You—you—' "

Mose laughed softly. "Yeah," he said, "you know what he wanna say. But he doan do it. He doan finish. He jes look at me."

Adam turned away. He looked down at the letters Mose had so painfully drawn on the sheet of paper. He forced himself to look at them. He forced himself to say: "These letters, Talbutt, they're fine. They really are."

But Mose, not listening, was looking at Adam, saying softly: "What you ast me that fer? About him callen me a black son-a-bitch?" He waited. Then, more softly: "What make you gotta know?"

At first Adam didn't answer, staring at Mose. Then he said: "It's simply that I wondered."

"Listen," Mose was saying, "listen here. Me, I'm gonna tell you every night. So you won't never have to wonder no more. You won't never have to wonder."

And he did. Every night, at some moment, always a different moment in the course of time, Mose would tell him. It got so Adam would wait, counting the minutes, dreading the moment to come when Mose would tell him and giggle.

One night Adam thought Mose had forgotten, or had decided to give up the game. They had gone to bed. The fire had died down. Adam was almost asleep. Then he heard the voice from the other bunk across the hut. "Ole Him," the voice said, "he ain't called me no black son-of-a-bitch today."

Then Adam heard the soft, furry giggle in the dark.

The season broke. The evening began later, and the twilight lengthened. In the twilight the drift of air from the land beyond the camp carried a saddening sweetness from undisturbed earth, mixed with the smell of woodsmoke. The word was that Grant, who had taken Vicksburg, had been appointed to Supreme Command, with the rank of Lieutenant General. He might even set up headquarters with the Army of the Potomac.

It was this news that gave the excuse for the shindig—for the singing and dancing, for Simms Purdew to revolve, in his frenzy of drunken hoots, about the bonfire, for Company C to put a half-dozen wadded greenbacks in the bottom of a washtub, cover the bills with some twenty inches of flour, and encourage five Negroes, with hands tied behind their backs, to risk suffocation in rooting for the wealth. Adam sat on a cracker box in the shadow of the sutler tent, and watched. Mose crouched beside him, squatting on his heels. They watched Simms Purdew, who now revolved, hooting, about the tub where the Negroes rooted in the flour and batted heads.

"Wisht I had me a dollar," Mose said. He was staring at the scene. "But not a-doen that fer it." He paused. "Not fer no man's dollar," he said.

Now and then Simms Purdew would interrupt his rapt whirling dance around the tub to seize a jug from one of the soldiers and take a long drag; or to lean and put a monstrous ham of a hand on the head of one of the rooting Negroes and drive it into the depth of flour. When the hand was removed, the victim would come up coughing and exploding flour in all directions, and Simms Purdew would leap, give a hoot even more maniacal than common, and resume the dance. He would shut his eyes; a peculiar rapt expression would come over his face; and he would toss his big head, which was garlanded in sweat-soaked, fire-glinting sorrel ringlets, like a child's.

Adam stared at him. "He's going to hurt one of them," he said.

"He hurt them Rebs," Mose said. "No tellen how many he done hurt. Kilt 'em daid."

They were silent, watching.

Then Adam said: "Somebody ought to stop him."

"Who gonna stop him?" Mose demanded. "Somebody try stop him, he kill 'em daid. Lak he kilt them Rebs. In that cawn field at 'Tietam, lak they say. Did'n even shoot. Naw, he stood up thar and whop 'em down with his gun—wham!"

Squatting there, Mose made the motions of wielding a clubbed musket. "Wham! Wham!" he uttered in a raucous whisper. "Wham! Wham! Wham!"

His eyes were shining.

After a moment, he said: "They give him a medal. Fer killen Rebs."

Simms Purdew was wheeling in the dance, hooting. They watched him.

"Wisht I had me a medal," Mose said.

Simms Purdew had stopped whooping and whirling. He had leaned over and taken one of the rooting Negroes up by the heels and hoisted him high. The giant stood there with a great innocent, moony grin on his sweat-shining face, and held the Negro by the heels, high up but not so high that the head did not remain beneath the surface of the flour. The head jerked and jerked. Blasts and geysers of flour erupted as the buried mouth tried, apparently, to scream. Now and then the head would manage to break surface, puff, and gasp air before being again submerged.

Adam stared at the scene. He was in the grip of a

sickening fear. He did not know what he was afraid of. But the fear, the tenseness, was building up inside him.

Then suddenly Simms Purdew roared. He shook the Negro's heels and roared with irresistible mirth. He threw back the beautiful sorrel-ringleted baby-head and uttered the magnificent and infectious mirth.

Adam found himself on his feet. He found himself running toward the tub, toward Simms Purdew. But he did not get there. He had not, in fact, made four strides before the arms descended over him, crushing him, and the voice, in a raucous, vibrant whisper, was saying: "Gawd-A-Mighty—you'll git kilt—him, you mess with him and he kill you—he kill you, Slew!"

Adam struggled against the crushing embrace. "Let me go!" he cried, or tried to cry, with what breath was left him.

"Slew—Slew—" The voice was pleading now. "You git yoreself kilt, Slew—"

Adam had twisted in the embrace. "Let me go!" he cried.

"Naw—naw, Slew—you durn fool!"

Adam had managed to get an arm free. It was his left arm. He clenched his fist and struck at the face of Mose Talbutt. The position was awkward and his left arm was not as strong as his right, but he struck as hard as he could. He hit the cheek of Mose and Mose looked down at him with a look surprised, grievous, and profound.

Adam's fist again hit the face. The face flinched a little. The head shook a little from side to side, irritably as when a man tries to get rid of a fly, or is outraged because he cannot remember something important. Mose Talbutt seemed to be trying to remember something important, or trying to think of something to say appropriate to the occasion. His face was curdled with the effort.

"Let me go!" Adam cried, and struck again.

The arms fell from him.

"Yeah," Mose Talbutt said. "Look!" He nodded his head toward the tub.

Simms Purdew had wearied of the sport. With sad indifference he had simply released the heels of the fellow and let him fall, like a half-full sack of potatoes, and moved off into the compulsion of his dance, whirling and hooting. The fellow rolled out of the tub and lay on his side, puffing flour and uttering small whimpers. A soldier stooped over him and cut the ropes on his wrists. The fellow sat up and wiped at his face, swiping off the flour, clumsily. His lips, Adam could see, were open, and he puffed painfully through them. But his teeth were clenched. He clenched something between his teeth.

With his right hand the fellow took the thing from between his teeth. It was, clearly, not something you could simply spit out and be done with it. The fellow held it up, still puffing and wheezing. Beneath the streaks of flour the face was grinning. It was a wan, sickly, distorted, flour-streaked grin, but a grin.

The thing the hand held up—not wadded now—was a greenback.

Adam retreated to his cracker box in the shadow of the tent, and sat there. Mose came and again crouched beside him. The soldiers around the tub were cheering now. They were cheering the victor who held up the greenback. The cheering got wilder and wilder. The Negro kept grinning. Despite his wheezes, he was grinning.

The other Negroes, crouching around the tub, those with hands yet tied and poverty yet unrelieved, stared at him out of the flour-streaked faces. They were grinning, too.

Suddenly the cheering stopped. A soldier turned abruptly toward the crouching men by the tub. "God durn it," he exclaimed to them, "what you grinning at? You ain't got any money. You won't git rich, squatting there grinning. Git at it!"

The Negroes got at it.

Adam and Mose, in the shadow of the tent, watched the last phase of the shindig. They saw Simms Purdew wheel and hoot. They saw the Negroes root in the tub, and saw one come up with a greenback in his mouth. But nobody cheered now. They saw the soldiers squat around the fire and pass the jug. They saw the Negro who had been suspended by his heels now lying over to one side, coughing and coughing. They saw Simms Purdew pause now and then to push a head into the tub.

After a time, Adam, staring at the tub, from which a head, relieved of the hand of Simms Purdew, had just risen, said: "I'm sorry I did what I did."

"You was a durn fool," Mose said. "He'd a-kilt you."

"I mean, I'm sorry I hit you."

"Did'n hurt none," Mose said. "Not to mention on."

"I swear, Mose," Adams said, "I didn't even know I was hitting you. It was just—just I couldn't bear it. Bear what was happening—happening out there." He nodded toward the tub.

"Bear," Mose said. He squatted there and grinned. "Bear," he said again. "Lots of things you better git so you kin bear." He turned his head and was grinning up at Adam.

Then he looked at the tub. Simms Purdew was pushing a head into the flour, Mose giggled. "Yeah, and you jes set thar," he said. "You make a move, you durn fool, and I'll grab you again. Yeah," he said, and giggled, "you up and git yore fool self kilt, who gonna teach me my letters?"

He giggled again.

After a while it began to rain. Adam saw the first drops of rain fall on the fire, the drops coming out of the dark air to glitter, sudden in the light, before descending to the flame. Some of the men began to seek cover. But not Simms Purdew. He wheeled and spun in a more devout frenzy, hooting, drunker and drunker.

All at once Simms Purdew was sitting on the

ground. He sat in the middle of the company street, rain plastering his hair, and sang, bellowed rather:

> "Soon with angels I'll be marching,
> Sacred laurels on my brow.
> I am bleeding for Abe Lincoln—
> Oh, who'll take care of mother now?"

Adam waited, watching. The rain was coming down harder. Four men approached the singer, who now wept with emotion, and picked him up, one stout fellow to each quarter, and carried him, still singing and weeping, away.

Mose got up. "I'm gitten wet," he said. "I'm goen."

Adam said nothing.

"You comen?" Mose demanded.

"No, not yet," Adam said.

"Durn fool," Mose said, and moved off through the rain.

Adam sat there a little longer. He stared at the empty street, the glitter of rain as it plunged down at the fire. Then the fire began to sag. Adam felt the wet creeping down his collar, soaking into the cloth over his shoulders.

The spring drew on.

Adam, closing the flap of the sutler tent, saw the men sitting outside their huts, on boxes, or chunks of wood, or squatting on their heels in that farmerish feat of equilibrium and endurance. It was still light enough to play cards. Or mumblety-peg. Or even marbles. In front of one hut the men were playing marbles, on hands and knees like boys. Adam walked down the company street, carrying his cash box, breathing the sweet air.

When he entered the hut, he saw Jed Hawksworth hunched over the table. In the candlelight the man's face was drawn and white, with lurid streaks. On the table before him a newspaper was spread out. He stared at Adam, but said nothing. Adam set the cash box on the table. "Here it is, sir," he said, and waited.

The man did not give it a glance. He did not take his eyes from Adam, as he thrust the paper out at him. "Read it," he said, pointing to a spot down the page. Adam read the heading:

IMPORTANT FINANCIER IS DEAD

Without reading farther, he knew. He knew that Aaron Blaustein was dead. He felt, all at once, lost. He forced himself to read on, to read the details which came like something long known.

Aaron Blaustein had died of a heart attack. He had not been well for some time, since the death of his son, his only child, at Chancellorsville, and the subsequent suicide of his wife. Yes, even that fact, Adam felt he had known, but now that he saw it in the grubby print of the gray paper, he felt an access of guilt. As though he had given her the rope, blade, or bottle. No, he said to himself, with no comfort, it was not that guilt, but the guilt of having, from the first, refused the knowledge. Rapt in his own dreams, he had refused the knowledge.

He forced himself to read on. The poor peddler had risen to great wealth. The sum of his fortune was not yet certain but it was great. The disentangling of the estate would require some time. There was a will, but it was outdated, having been drawn before the death of the son and wife. No near kin were known to exist, at least in this country. Mr. Blaustein had important holdings in railways, for example—

"You know why I'm showing you that?" Jed Hawksworth's voice cut in.

Adam looked at him.

"It's so you'll quit this durn loafing around," the man said. "I had credit with that ole Jew, a heap of credit. No telling what they'll do now. Make a man pay up of a sudden. Not give him no credit." He rose from the table, and struck the top with a fist that made the candles dance. "You got to get down and grub, you hear? If'n I go bankrupt then what the hell happens? Yeah, to you? You think of that. You and that nigger."

Jed Hawksworth sat down. He stared at the box, with little recognition. After a moment he said, not loud: "Please go. I wish you'd go."

Adam went out into the night. He moved off to the edge of the woods, aimlessly. A little westward he sat down on a fallen log. He felt weak. He asked himself: *Did I always think that when the time came I could go back? Could go back and be his son?*

His mind stopped. He felt the discomfort, like a stricture he had to break before his mind could go on.

It went on: *Could go back and be rich?*

Yes, he thought, a part of him had always assumed that one day he could go back and be rich. He hung his head in the shadow of the trees. He waited to feel better. Better with that admission.

But he did not. He felt worse. He suddenly remembered how he had felt when, upon his flight from the *Elmyra,* nobody had pursued him, nobody had even shouted. He felt again that sense of total devaluation, that sense of sad ghostliness. Yes, he decided, it was only the existence of Aaron Blaustein that had made him feel real, had made him know who he was.

Now he was alone.

He lifted his face up to the sky. It was pricked with the million stars of the beautiful night. He looked up and wondered how you can be alone and yet not alone. He wondered how you could be worth nothing, and yet be worth something.

He thought: *I must find that out. If I am to live.*

He was thinking those words when he heard the noise. Startled he turned and saw the shadowy figure. It came closer, and leaned.

"Slice o' mutton, bhoy?" the voice whispered. "Want a slice o' mutton?"

"No," Adam said. "Please, no."

193

"You sitten all alone, bhoy," she said, and sat down on the log, not very near him.

After a moment she said: "Four bits. Ain't but four bits."

He said nothing.

She said: "Ain't every colleen got what Mollie by the Grace of the Hivinly Father's got. It is a rare privilege I would share. I tell you, young man—"

"I want to sit here," Adam said.

"Rest you aisy," she said.

She grew so quiet he actually forgot she was there. Then he became aware of her breathing. He cautiously stole a look at her. By the shimmering whiteness of her face he could tell that she was looking upward.

After a little, he said, "Mollie."

"Yes?"

"Where were you born?" he said.

After a while, she said: "Cloyne."

"Where is that?"

"I'm Irish," she said. "It is Ireland."

"Was it beautiful there?" he asked.

For an instant, she was so quiet he thought she had not heard the question.

Then she leaped up. She was leaning at him under the dark trees.

"You son-of-a-bitch!" she said, her voice shaking with rage. "You louse-bit son-of-a-bitch of a fool. I was about to give it to ye. For nothing, you fool. I swear it—I swear by the sweet wounds of Our Lord."

She was striking at him. He was surprised at how

feeble was the blow that found his brow, and the other that grazed his shoulder. She struck him again, but somehow he could not move.

"—and now—not for a million dollars," she was saying, "not for a million dollars would I give it to ye, you fool."

She drew back from him.

"I wouldn't," she gasped, "by the sweet wounds of Our Lord, I swear it!"

She had turned and fled into the woods, blundering and heaving into the dark brush, like an old cow night-startled from her ground.

10

One evening, toward sunset, Adam walked into the open fields to the north. At least, fields had once been there. Now the fences were gone, rails and stakes long since burned in campfires, broken in the attempt to pry a caisson wheel from the mud, used as supports for the roof of a hut. But brush, or a heavier growth of weeds showed, here and there, the old patterns of demarcation, and under foot the parallel corrugations of old plowing, sinking now into the level of earth, told where rows had, long ago, run. How long ago? Adam asked himself that. Only three years, he decided. It might have been fifty, he thought, staring across the fields at the charred ruin of a house fallen between two tall stone chimneys.

He moved toward the ruin. There had once been an approach, too modest to be called an avenue, lined with trees. Now there were stumps, and grass had grown over the old lane. Three or four trees yet stood near the ruin. They, however, were blackened. They put forth no leaf.

He looked westward across the land. The late light washed toward him from the reddening sky. He thought of the grass coming back over the fields, the weeds coming back. The land was beautiful in the light, glimmering with that pale new green. To the north a patch of woodland showed the red mist of leafing oak, the gold of maple. He sat on a stump by the ruined lane, and let his heart be at peace. He wondered how he would feel when he was old. Would he move in a peace like this?

He wondered how this land would be when it was old.

He rose and walked toward the camp. He had just crossed a track of rutted earth when, looking westward, he saw a body of horsemen approaching. The hooves made no sound on the soft earth. But when they were still some distance he could hear the soft creaking of leather. He stood by the road facing northward and waited, while the mounts footed soberly past him.

Three men rode in front, silent, eyes fixed ahead but seemingly seeing nothing, all thought turned inward from the dimming land. Next came a lone horseman, young, heroic, gauntleted fist on hip, yellow hair, worn long, showing from beneath the cant of the cavalryman's black hat. He was, Adam could see, a captain. The captain did not see Adam. He did not seem to see anything. His eyes were fixed ahead, and in that pose of heroic solitude, or indifference, he drew steadily away.

Next came the guidon-bearer, riding on the left side of the track, supporting upright the staff, set in a kind of cup, or fewter, attached to the right stirrup. The guidon hung listless, scarcely stirred by the motion. But once, in an unexpected shift of air, it lifted, displaying for an instant its swallowtail shape and a glint of red.

Then, in pairs, troopers moved past, erect, faces blank and eyes veiled, the only sign of life the faint motion of hips absorbing the motion of the mount into the portentous immobility of the human torso. They slipped by in their visionary silence, the hooves sound-less. But the leather creaked. Now and then one of the beasts snorted softly.

The troop moved off, in that evenly paced, remorse-less process, and the leveling rays of sunset fell calmly on their backs.

The last pair of troopers had moved a few rods down the track before Adam realized what he had seen. Then he saw, in the fresh memory more sharply than he had in fact, the figure of the second of the three men riding in front, a smallish, lumpish, bearded man between two gold-gleaming warriors, a man who, despite his lumpishness, sat his mount well, a man with a hat pulled low on his brow, no insignia on his coat. The coat was unbuttoned and hung without tidiness. Adam realized that he had seen, under that unbuttoned coat, a gold sash bound over the incipient paunch of middle-age.

He watched the horsemen dwindle into distance. Then he turned and walked toward the camp. It was not the camp it had been. Even now, in the hour of ease, there would be fewer games of euchre and bluff and mumblety-peg. More men would sit brooding over the sheet of letter paper. Some would wander aside, alone, looking at the sky. At the end of the company street a wretch would be standing with arms outstretched and lashed to a beam supported by his shoulders. He would stand there, swaying, sweat on his face, a trace of bile down his chin and on his tunic. He would stare at the westering sun. He would not be released until sundown. He would not be slow again at reveille.

Somewhere men would be singing together, not in a hut now, but in the open air, without shame:

> Rock of Ages, cleft for me,
> Let me hide myself in Thee.

Somewhere men would be praying. There were men who believed in God. There were men who believed in Justice.

Adam said to himself: *I must remember that.*

Men said: "It won't be long now."

They said: "Ole Grant—he didn't come here for fun."

They said: "Yeah, we'll be crossing over."

They said: "Wonder if that ole elephant has growed."

"That elephant," a man said, a bearded middle-aged corporal leaning against the edge of the counter, "I wonder if he has growed."

"You'll find out 'fore long, Sug," a private said. "He's waiting yander." He gestured south.

"That elephant," another man said, "he don't never stop growing. I seen him three times. He gets bigger ever-time."

"I don't never want to see no elephant bigger than Chancellorsville," the first man said, glumly.

The corporal turned to another soldier. "Son," he said, "you ain't never seen the elephant, have you?"

The youth, shamefaced, said nothing. But another man said: "Naw. Jes come last fall. Conscripted." The man spat, put his foot on the spot, then added: "Ain't seen nothing."

The youth turned to the corporal. "Mister—" he asked. But he didn't go on.

"Huh?" the corporal demanded.

"I mean—" the youth again hesitated. "I mean what did you think about?"

"Nothing," the corporal said.

"Nothing?"

"Nothing much." The corporal set down his cup of cider. He turned to Adam. "Slew," he said, "this here

---

200

cider ain't a thing but swamp water and cat pee, and you know it." He didn't wait for an answer. He simply drained the cup, and turned back to the youth.

"You didn't think nothing?" the youth demanded.

"Like I told you," the corporal said patiently, "I don't think nothing. All I did, the first time and evertime, was see clear as day the soap suds in a bowl my ma was washing my hair in. I must of been six or seven years old. I must of opened my eyes. If I hadn't opened my eyes I could not of got soap in 'em to make 'em smart and water. Now ever-time hell starts popping, soon as that first gun goes off, right at first I see them soap suds. Clear as day. I don't think nothing. I don't feel nothing. Then—"

He looked into the dry cup, then set it upside down on the counter.

"Then," he continued, "you git so durn busy you don't care. Them Rebs got a talent for making you take yore mind off yore personal consarns. All you got time to know is yore mouth is awful dry."

The youth looked southward, down the company street.

"Yeah, son," the corporal said, "that's the direction. Ginnal Grant is going to take you in that direction. But I hope to God he has more sense than that Ginnal Hooker. Hooker, he taken us right in the Wilderness, and they hit us in the woods. Yeah, I was at Chancellorsville, and it was a God-A-Mighty big elephant. Yeah, if Grant takes us in there it'll be Chancellorsville all over. All that brush and scrub oak and

---

201

blight pine and you can't see yore hand afore yore face. Hell, going in them woods after Ginnal Lee—it is like crawling in a cave at night to wrassle a bear and it the bear's cave."

The corporal shrugged and walked away. The other men followed. But the youth lingered, saying nothing. Then he, too, walked away, pensive and slow.

That evening, after he had closed the tent and delivered the cash box, Adam went down to the river. It was not a big stream, just seven or eight rods across there, but apparently too deep for fording. The far bank was grassy, with willows here and there. You expected to see cattle standing knee-deep in the mirror-quiet stream, under the new-leafed willows, and the meadow beyond demurely aglow with evening light. But nothing was there, no sign of life.

Then Adam heard a stir by a willow to one side. A soldier rose from the bank where he had been sitting. He came to stand beside Adam. "Nice evening," he said.

"Yes," Adam said.

They stood there a moment, wordless, looking across the river. Then the man gestured toward the southwest. There, distant, was an eminence, rocky and wooded. "Clark's Mountain," the man said.

"Yes," Adam said.

"Bet Ginnal Lee's up there right this minute," the man said. "Up there with his durn ole spyglass watching."

Adam stared at the mountain.

"Looking right down our throat," the man said.

Adam said nothing.

"You know what they say?" the man demanded. Then without waiting, continued: "They say if Ole Lee gets a man's face down here square in his spyglass, that man has lost his odds. His chances is used up. He may git acrost the Rapidan when we moves. But he won't git back."

He paused.

"That's what they say," he said.

He fell silent. They stood there, side by side, watching dusk gather over the land.

"But me, I don't believe it," he said.

After a while the man said: "Good night," and was gone.

Across the river, the fields beyond the willows were empty, except for a few clumps of scrub timber. But Adam looked to the southeast. There, distantly, the clumps seemed to run together. There the darkness of woods hugged the land. There in that darkness, Stephen Blaustein had found the elephant.

What else had he found?

That very evening, coming back into the area of the second regiment, Adam saw a group gathering at the edge of the parade. In the distance he saw men moving hurriedly in that direction. Two other men, far off, were running. A man overtook Adam, recognized him, and turning, said: "You don't hurry, you won't see it."

"See what?" Adam asked.

"See Mollie gitten it," the man said.

"Getting what?"

"Ten on the bare doup," the man said. "The Mutton—they caught her giving a ride, and Colonel Bills, he had ordered—" The man stopped. "Hell," he burst out, "I ain't gonna miss it!"

The man broke into a run.

Adam resolutely turned his gaze from the running man and resumed his course. He took six or seven paces, then stopped. He heard, far off, the sound of singing. That was to the north. He heard, far off, a burst of laughter. That was to his left, to the west. He felt the cold twitch in his gut. He felt the cold twitch spread.

Am I not going, he thought, *because I am a coward?*

He took a step on his old track.

He stopped. He demanded of himself: *A coward about what?*

He wondered if he was too cowardly to face pain. Cowardly in that last exquisite cowardice of flinching from all pain because he appropriated all pain to himself?

He wondered if that was true. Yes, but even in that thought he knew that it was not all. He knew, with sadness, that he was afraid to face himself as he would be if he stood there, staring at the victim. No, it was worse. He knew that he was afraid to think of the eyes of the other men on his face, as he stood there. All was true.

With that, he had no choice. He had turned toward the west. He had to go and face whatever was there.

There was no laughter there now. There was no sound of any kind. When finally he came up to the group it was so still he could hear his own breath.

The woman was on her knees, leaning forward over a length of log. A stick had been laid across the back of the knees and tied at each end to a stob. With that, the woman wouldn't be able to rise, or heave about. Adam saw that the stockings had worked down below the woman's knees. They were old wool stockings, torn and mended, torn again. They were twisted laxly on the skinny legs. The old army brogans on the feet looked too big. They were turned pigeon-toed, inward.

"Got a big doup," a man whispered, "fer them legs."
Nobody answered.

The woman's clothing had been drawn forward, some of it falling over the back of the head. To each side of the woman, and forward, beyond her shoulders, a soldier squatted. Each soldier had a firm grip on one of the woman's wrists.

A lieutenant, very correct, stood beyond the ends of the log. A private stood by him, the lash in hand.

Adam found himself staring at the woman's shoes. He thought that if he kept his eyes firmly fixed on the shoes he would be all right. But the pain of staring at the shoes was too great. If they had not been turned inward, pigeon-toed, it would not have been so bad. No, he couldn't bear to look at the shoes.

He carefully looked at the faces of other men. They were all staring at the woman, some avid and intense, some with schooled detachment, some with idiotic grin and wet lips. They were all different, the faces, but the eyes of all were fixed there where he, Adam Rosenzweig, did not dare to look.

Suddenly, he heard the whizz and slash of the thongs. It seemed that he had to wait forever for the cry. He thought he would suffocate before the cry came. But it came.

With the cry he stood there, eyes closed, and thought that only if you had some kind of fantastic innocence could you have power to look at the world.

He opened his eyes and looked at the faces of the men. They were staring, waiting. They all, he thought, had an innocence that could never be his. They had an innocence that was deeper than any crime they could ever commit.

Then he heard the lash again, and again his eyes, against all his will, were closed.

"Diggety-dawg," a man whispered, "got meat that time."

He had not looked. He had almost been able to close his ears against the scream.

Then he heard a voice, not far, say, "God durn you —what you doing here?"

He opened his eyes. He was full of panic.

But the angry demand had not been addressed to him. It was addressed to Mose Talbutt. Mose stood at the edge of the ring, and into his gaping face was thrust the red, challenging face of a burly soldier.

All at once the soldier seized Mose by the shoulder, swinging him saying: "Git—git, you God-durn nig!"

Mose was pulling back, uncertain but holding his ground. "I got as much right—" he began.

"Right!" the burly soldier exclaimed. "You ain't got no right— A God-durn nig standing here and that woman white—you—"

"Let him be," a stolid-looking man said. "She ain't nothing but a pore old broke-down parcel of Irish clap."

"You ought to know," somebody said, and snickered.

"Well, she's white," the burly soldier was saying, but the lash fell again. He swung to the sound but too late to see the lash find flesh. He swung back to Mose with the double grievance shrill in his voice: "God-durn you, you nig—you—"

"Listen, Latham," another soldier said, "you haven't any right here. And I haven't either. We're just a bunch of foul-minded and debased and—"

The lash was falling. But, this time, the burly soldier did not notice his deprivation. He had leaped at the other soldier, saying: "You God-durn nigger-lover!" and had slugged him, then grappled with him.

The crowd fell silently aside, let the struggle roll

back beyond them, and closed again. The fighters rolled on the ground, and struck and gouged, groaning and whimpering. But no one paid any attention. The lash was about to fall.

Adam was staring at the face of Mose Talbutt. He saw the distended eyes. He saw the lips twitching at the corners of the mouth. He saw the hunch and shiver when the lash found its mark, and the sudden new glitter of eye.

He stood there and hated Mose Talbutt.

He thought: *I have no right to hate anyone.*

When he came into the hut it was late. He hoped that the man would be asleep, and so began to undress without lighting the slush lamp.

But there was the voice: "Dat you?"

"Yes," Adam said, and lighted the lamp.

The man was watching him, withholding speech, Adam knew, waiting.

"Ole Him," the man in the bunk finally said, "he come."

"Yes," Adam said. He did not look.

"Come," Mose said, "but did'n call me you-know-what."

Adam said nothing, giving enormous attention to buttons.

"But that whuppen tonight," the man on the bunk said, "you know what?"

When Adam did not answer, the man went on. "Hit give Ole Him a idea. Say I gotta take in wash. Wash

---

fer sodjers and take him the money. Say he gotta have more money."

"Well," Adam said. He felt an icy satisfaction growing in him, a vindication which he could not name. "Well," he repeated, "it's his time you're on, isn't it?"

Carefully he hung up his jacket, inspected it, blew out the lamp, got into his bunk, and closed his eyes.

After a while the voice came from the dark. "But I ain't gonna," the voice said. "Not take in no wash. No matter who time it is. One thing I ain't doen."

"It's between you and him," Adam said. "And please don't talk."

He lay there, trying not to think, trying to keep his eyes closed and know nothing, nothing in that world which he could not bear to look at.

But, after a time, the voice came.

"That doup," the voice said, soft in the dark, "it shore was a big doup."

"My God," Adam burst out, "can't you shut your mouth?"

He did not believe it was his own voice.

There was, for a moment, silence. Then a giggle. Then the other voice from across the hut.

"I mean a big doup fer a woman her size," the voice was saying, gently musing. "Nigh big as the doup on that-air woman you had in the rock house. Back in Pennsy-vanie. But then, that-air Pennsy-vanie woman, she was bigger built, there was more to her and—"

Adam Rosenzweig lay there and tried to know nothing in the world.

———

The heavy rains which had made a morass of the parade and now flooded the lowland by the river had abated. Steam now rose from the fields. You could see it rising in the bright sun. May was upon them. A wheel could roll without foundering.

The tent sections that formed the roofs of the huts were being stripped and rolled. The huts looked obscenely, pitifully exposed. Some men had the need to visit violence or defilement on the place that had been a shelter, and sometimes a pride. Here and there, against all regulations of sanitation, a man would relieve himself in his abandoned hut. Sometimes, having done so, the man would stand brooding, in sad puzzlement because he did not understand his own action.

Sergeants counted out the paper cartridges. Corporals checked cartridge boxes on the belts of their wards, and the percussion-cap boxes. Some men sat alone, meditatively honing the bayonet. Field rations were issued, cooked, stored in knapsacks. Men speculated whether they would go downstream or up for the crossing. If down, they would be heading for the Wilderness.

All sutlers were ordered out of camp. They were to be moving the next morning. That would be May 1. Some had already pulled out, their wagons caught in the weighty, ominous drift of traffic around the camp. The big wagon of Jedeen Hawksworth, and the small wagon, ready loaded, were parked in the edge of the timber. The horses were tethered farther in.

Mose Talbutt and Adam had tried to do one last reading lesson, sitting in the door of the hut. But Adam had said: "I'm sorry, Mose. I can't keep my mind on it. I don't know what's the matter with me."

He had risen, had walked away into the body of the camp. After a moment he was aware that Mose was by his side. He was coming too, he said.

It was full dark when, in their aimless, wordless drift from one company street to another, they came to the brigade hospital tent. Lights showed bright at the little annex at the far end. Men clustered there, looking in. "Patrol come in," a man said. "Had a scrape at a ford upriver."

"Don't belong here," another man said, "but this is fer as they made it."

Adam peered into the tent. A Negro lay on a table, under the lamps, naked to the waist, and a surgeon bent over him. The man's skin, slick with sweat, gleamed like black metal in the light. Near the door of the tent a lieutenant, booted and with the crossed sabers of the cavalry on his tunic, sat on a stool and leaned weakly back against a tent pole. His left arm, the upper part and shoulder, was enormous with the white bandages, and the slashed sleeve of his tunic was fastened with a pin to prevent flapping.

The assistant to the surgeon kept telling him he ought to lie down. The lieutenant said he couldn't, he wasn't really hurt.

———

211

The lieutenant was talking. Apparently, he could not stop talking. Recurringly he interrupted himself to ask if the black son-of-a-bitch was going to die. He would carefully point to the Negro cavalryman lying on the table, as though to be sure all knew to whom he referred. The surgeon's assistant said that the man would live if the bleeding could be stopped.

"The son-of-a-bitch is going to die," the lieutenant affirmed. "He is going to die just to spite me. He saved my life just to spite me, and now he is going to die to spite me."

The lieutenant kept saying that the man was going to die. He could not stop talking. As he talked, he kept fondling, as though with infinite love, the bandage on his left arm.

He kept saying that he had never wanted a black commission. He said he had taken it because it was the only way he could get a commission. He had been refused three times, so he took the examination for a black commission, and now the son-of-a-bitch saved his life.

He, the lieutenant, had been hit, he said, just as they were about to make the ford. They had run into the big Reb patrol and had had to cut for it. He had been knocked off his horse right at the bank. The son-of-a-bitch—oh, the God-damned black son-of-a-bitch —he had turned in the water, half over, and come back and jumped off and picked him up. They had got back across the ford. Then that black son-of-a-bitch, he had got hit too. But he had never said a word when he was hit. He hadn't even grunted. The lieutenant swore he didn't even guess the black son-of-a-bitch was hit. The fellow had just held him with one arm, and leaned over, and given the horse the spur, with the bullets flying. The Rebs hadn't followed.

"Is he going to live?" the lieutenant demanded. "Is the black-son-of-a-bitch going to live?" His voice was high and querulous.

"You better lie down," the assistant said. "I order you to lie down."

The son-of-a-bitch was going to die, the lieutenant affirmed. He hadn't even known the son-of-a-bitch was hit. Not till the blood began soaking down into him. The blood had kept coming down over him and he thought it was his own blood. He had thought he himself was the one bleeding to death. Till the son-of-a-bitch let him slip and fall, fall off the horse, and he cursed him for it. Then the black son-of-a-bitch himself had just slipped from his horse and lain on the ground.

Now he was going to die. To spite him.

"Lie down," the assistant said.

The lieutenant rose and wavered on his feet. God damn it, he demanded, who the hell wanted to command a tribe of kinky-wooled cannibals with graybacks in the wool and grease on the chin? He stood there, pale and sweating, wavering. He demanded of all present if he had ever asked any nig to save his life. Then he stopped wavering. His eyes fixed on the face of Mose.

Mose, however, had never even looked at him. He was paying no attention to him. He had never taken his gaze from the man on the table who was silent as stone and from whom the blood would not stop coming.

The lieutenant fixed his gaze on Mose. The discourtesy of Mose inflamed his grievance.

"You—you black son-of-a-bitch," the lieutenant demanded of Mose, "look here—did I ever ask you or any other black son-of-a-bitch to save—"

Mose had turned toward him. Mose stared at the wounded lieutenant. He seemed suddenly and totally bemused by that pale, sweating face.

"You—you"—the lieutenant was whispering now— "why, you—you're Mose, Mose Crawfurd! Yes, and—"

He stared at Mose. The lips of the Negro were moving, but gave no sound. It was clear that they were trying to utter a certain sound, but could not. They could make the shape of the sound, but not the sound. The sound the lips could not make was *no*.

"Yes," the lieutenant said, "and you ran off and—"

"Son," a voice said.

Adam wheeled to the voice. It was the voice of Jedeen Hawksworth. Jed took a step toward the lieutenant. "Listen, son," he was saying, "you're hurt bad. You better set down. This nigger—he's my nigger. Been with me three years. Name of Talbutt. Run off from North Carolina."

The lieutenant was wavering on his feet, fondling the bandage.

Jed turned to Mose. "Get on back. What the hell you doing over here, anyway?"

"Yassuh," Mose said, and was gone like a shadow.

The surgeon came, touched the lieutenant on the right shoulder. Then when the lieutenant turned, the surgeon slowly shook his head.

The lieutenant sat down on the stool, suddenly, heavily, and began to cry. Between sobs, he declared that he had never asked any nig to save his life.

Jedeen Hawksworth had gone. For a full minute Adam watched the man weep. He could not take his eyes from the sight.

Then he wandered off. He wandered toward the woods, and entered. He tried to pray. He actually got down on his knees. But he could not utter a word. He did not know what word to utter to be sure that he himself would never have such occasion to sit on a stool, under lanterns, and weep obscenely, while men stared at him.

There was, in the end, only one place to go. But how could he lie in the dark in the same room where that man would be lying with his shame? With a shame compounded by the fact that it was Jedeen Hawksworth who had saved him from the consequences of that shame? He thought of himself lying in the hut while the shame rose, in the dark, like a fog.

But there was nowhere else to go. Nowhere else in the world. So he turned, and entered.

And Jed Hawksworth was saying: "—and God durn it, I let you off about that washing just because we was going to move soon. But right now I'm serving notice on you, what I says goes and—"

Mose was standing there in front of the cold hearth, naked except for his drawers. He had, clearly, been getting ready for bed when Jed Hawksworth came in. His garments were heaped on a stool by his bunk.

"—and any more back talk and you'll find yourself setting on a coffin, and you won't be able to see them twelve rifles pointing at you, for you'll have a blindfold on, but you can hear the click when them Enfields come on cock. A deserter, huh?"

The Negro looked numbly, wistfully, at him. His shoulders dropped. Across the black skin of his shoulders and back, the welts of the old flogging showed pale and emphatic in the lamplight. Once or twice his lips worked, as though about to frame words. But no sound came.

"Yeah," Jed Hawksworth said, "they ought to of let you desert to get rid of you, you worthless black son-of-a-bitch. Yeah—" He looked down at the drawers.

"Yeah," he said, with a sudden gleam in the eye, "you never would take off them drawers. Naw, not even in washing yoreself. Well, if you wouldn't take 'em off, there must of been a reason. But like a fool nigger, you didn't reckin anybody could figure that out. Well, I been figgering it out. I know what them Yankees do to the likes of you."

Jed Hawksworth's right hand flicked out on the long spidery arm, two fingers hooked into the band of the old gray drawers, the hand jerked back, the button snapped off and flew across the room. The drawers, released by the fingers, fell.

On the man's right thigh, puckering and crinkling crudely up from the dark slickness of skin, was the brand. It was a big W.

With a slow, painful surprise, the man looked down at the mark on his own flesh, as though he had just discovered it, and knew that it would swell mortally.

"You know what that is?" Jed Hawksworth demanded, turning on Adam. "Reckin that's one letter your prize scholar can read. W—W for worthless! That's what the Yankees put on 'em. Put on a soldier that ain't worth a damn."

Jed Hawksworth gave his quick hack of a laugh, then stopped.

"Yeah," he said, turning avidly back to the Negro, pointing at him, "and them welts on your back. I bet no overseer ever laid 'em on. I bet they was Yankee-laid, too."

"No!" Mose Talbutt burst out. Now he made the sound. His lips worked, and words came out: "No—I swear to God-A-Mighty—I swear—"

He stopped. Jed Hawksworth was grinning sourly at him from his distance of disbelief, shaking his head.

Then he said: "Git on to bed. I want you both up and out and hitched by first light. I want to be moving. You hear?"

The grin was gone from his face. A wretched inwardness was growing there.

"Ain't gonna be taking in nothing now," he resumed. "Won't have nothing but expense now. Till we can get back with the army. And you two now—you got to save money. Naw, we got to find something to do. To git you to do. A-fore we all go bankrupt. A-fore I am ruint. A-fore I—"

He was not looking at Mose now. Nor at Adam. The words trailed off. Then almost soundlessly Jedeen Hawksworth moved to the doorway, leaned over, and was gone.

Very slowly Adam managed to turn and face Mose Talbutt. The man stood there, shoulders hunched, clutching the waistband of the drawers, holding them decorously in place.

"It ain't true," he said, through dry lips.

Adam's gaze dropped down to the location of the W, as though he could see it through the cloth. The man's gaze followed Adam's, then returned, desperately, to Adam's face.

"Naw," he said, "naw. I mean my back. Them whelps—they warn't Yankee-laid. It was down in Georgia."

He sat down on a stool, clutching the drawers. It was a warm night, almost like summer, but he was shivering.

Adam looked down at him. He felt unutterably tired.

Mose looked up at him. "You gotta believe me," he burst out, "you gotta!"

"Let's go to bed," Adam said, turning away. "Let's try to sleep."

"You gotta believe me!" Mose cried out, the cry torn out of him.

Adam looked down at him. "I believe you," he managed to say.

He began to undress. He got ready for bed. Not once did he look at the man on the stool. But he heard the breathing.

He got into his bunk, and stared up at the roof of canvas. In the morning, by the first gray light, they would strip it, and roll it. He thought of the hut empty, open to sky and weather, night and day, like a body from which life has fled. No, like a bone case from which flesh has sunk away, lying lost on the wide land. His idle gaze fell on the little satchel, on a shelf near the chimney, near the slush lamp that yet burned. He wished that he could pray. Well, he had tried that, he thought grimly. He closed his eyes.

"It wasn't my fault," the voice of Mose Talbutt— Mose Crawfurd—was saying.

Adam said nothing.

"Me," the voice was saying, "I wanted to fight."

"Let's don't talk," Adam said, not opening his eyes. He heard the thinness of his own voice. Something seemed to be stopping his throat.

Then he heard motion. Then the puff of breath as the slush lamp was blown out. He waited for the small creaking of the other bunk. But it did not come. Then he heard the breath in the dark. He must still be sitting on the stool, Adam thought. He wished that he could stop listening to that breath. Then, again, he heard the voice.

"Me," the voice said in the dark, "I could of fought as good as any of 'em."

"Please don't talk," Adam said. With the constriction in his throat he had to make an effort for the syllables.

There was silence for a little.

Then: "I could of learned to ride me a hoss. Good as any. I could of learned to fight. Even if they did'n pay no nigger but half what they pay a sodjer what is white. I'd a-fought for half-pay. But naw—they taken me off from learning to fight."

Then: "They taken most of us. Us colored."

Then: "Fer diggen."

Then: "Diggen fer them big privies. Then putten dirt back in when them privies was nigh full. Diggen up stumps. Diggen up rock. Diggen for roads. Diggen in the rain. Diggen in the snow. Diggen."

Then: "All a nigger good fer. Diggen."

"Please don't talk," Adam heard his own distant voice saying.

But then: "I could of fought."

For a time Adam heard the sound of breathing in the dark.

———

"Talbutt," Adam said.

"Crawfurd—hit's Crawfurd," the voice said.

"Crawfurd," Adam said.

"Yeah?" the voice replied.

"That night you saved me—when you pulled me out of the water," Adam asked, "why did you do it?"

There was, for the moment, no answer. Adam lay there, feeling the constriction in his throat, waiting.

Then he heard the voice: "If'n you tried to climb up—if'n you got to clawen and couldn't make it—and maken a racket—then all them folks might of tried to climb up thar."

Then after a silence: "An that shelf, hit warn't room fer but two. Two at the mostest. Did'n aim to have to fight 'em all off."

Then: "I figgered I'd git you up quiet."

Adam found himself sweating. After a while, hearing his own voice pale and distant, he said: "Was that it? Was that all?"

There was a long wait.

Then the voice of Mose: "What you so all-fired got to know fer?"

"I don't know," Adam said. He lay there, hearing his own heart, and did not know.

"Lots of things a man doan know," the voice said.

There was, again, silence.

Then: "That feller tonight. That feller layen thar with the blood comen out. It could of been me."

"Please," Adam said, "let's not talk. Any more."

But then: "I durn nigh wished it was me. I watched

him layen and bleeden, and I durn nigh wished it. It wasn't hurten him. Not much, nohow. Not lak whuppen. Not lak that hot iron laid to you. Not lak diggen in the snow. Not lak treated lak a dawg. Not lak—"

Adam heard a massive stirring, a heaving in the dark. "Be quiet," he said.

Then, he heard, throatily: "God damn it—Jesus-God damn it—I would'n keer, not if 'twas me. Layen thar bleeden—oh, you gotta believe it, you gotta—"

Adam leaped from his bunk. "Damn you," he cried into the darkness, toward the spot in the dark where he felt Mose—Mose Crawfurd—must be: "God damn you," he cried, "how many times do I have to tell you to be quiet? Haven't you done enough already? I tell you I cannot bear it."

Adam was shaken by a feeling he could not name. Then he took command of himself. "Get to bed," he said hoarsely.

He heard the breath of the man in the dark, low and grating. Then he heard a furtive minimal sound, a sense of movement rather than sound. Then, the sound as the man, with prodigious caution, was letting himself down on his bunk.

Then the voice said: "Slew—Slew—"

"Yes," Adam said.

"Slew," the voice said, from a distance it seemed, "you gotta believe me, Slew. I'd ruther be layen thar bleeden. Layen thar and the blood comen out—God durn it, Slew, I swear—I swear—"

"Shut up!" Adam cried into the darkness. "Shut

222

up, and get to bed, you—you—" His breath would not come. Then, with a sweet rush, his breath came, and a joy filled his being, as though in the darkness nobody were there, as though he himself were about to fill all the dark and be, for the first time, totally himself.

"You—yes, you—" he cried, "—you—you black son-of-a-bitch!"

He stood there and panted in the dark.

Adam stood there for a little longer. Then, with a sense of massive calm, he moved to his own bunk and lay down. He had to move with great care because the calm was, for all its massiveness, balanced like a great boulder on the verge of an abyss. He knew that. He composed himself carefully, and stared up into the dark.

For a time there was quiet, absolute quiet. After the quiet came the sound of breath, scrupulously controlled breathing. Somewhat after that the moaning began.

The moans were very soft, scarcely more than a throaty, heavy breath. They began to fall into a sort of rhythm. In that rhythm, after his first terror at the sound, Adam began to slip downward into sleep. Soon he would be asleep, he thought. He thought of bleeding. He thought of bleeding while you slipped deeper and darker to sleep.

Sinking into that depth, he could, at last, think: *I have done what I have done. I must live with what I have done. Until he forgives me.*

223

When he woke up it was still pitch black. He lay there without thought. Then he thought of himself lying, in darkness, on the shelf of earth beside the nameless man who had drawn him from the rising water. He thought of what that man, Mose Talbutt— Mose Crawfurd—had told him, why he had drawn him up from the water. His sadness enveloped him. He felt again, as he had felt on his unhindered flight from the *Elmyra,* and upon learning of the death of Aaron Blaustein, devalued. He felt his identity draining away. Was no man, in his simple humanity, more to any other man than a stir or voice, a sloshing in the dark?

Then he thought that that nameless man on the shelf, reaching out in the dark to that sound, had had, after all, a choice. He could more easily, and safely, have slipped a knife into a throat than drawn a man up to safety.

With that thought, Adam Rosenzweig felt better. He felt, somehow, restored, however little, to hope.

Then he thought that for himself drawn up in the blind lottery of that cellar to the shelf others had not been drawn up.

He closed his eyes and he saw again, as in the dawn light in the backyard when he had crept from the house in New York, the bodies of those who had not been drawn up. It was all a blind lottery. Like your life. He lay there and thought of the price of his life. Others had paid the price of his life. Then he told himself that that was not logical. It was completely illogical.

He lay there thinking how little is the difference between being lost and being saved.

He was, all at once, aware of the stillness of the darkness. There was no sound of moaning now. He listened intently. He thought of the man over there finally falling asleep, falling asleep after all the things that had been his life—the hot sun and the cotton row, the lash, the digging of latrines, the smell of flesh as the branding iron bit in, the laughter of the mob in the house above as water rose in the dark cellar, Jedeen Hawksworth's voice saying, "Take your black son-of-a-bitching hands off him," off the dead Confederate from North Carolina who had brought his pants, well tied with rope, up the long slope at Gettysburg.

He felt a wave of tenderness, touched with envy, for Mose Crawfurd. Let him sleep. He needed no forgiveness, not for anything. He had done nothing. History needed forgiveness.

He thought of Mose Crawfurd's suffering that night, his moaning in the dark. But now he slept. Tomorrow he would be himself. He thought of the giggle, the secretly hugged joke always lurking there but never told, the irony of his watchfulness. Yes, tomorrow Mose Talbutt—Mose Crawfurd—would again be himself, secure in himself and his secret knowledge, beyond blame or pity because totally himself. Mose

Crawfurd had, somehow, conquered History. He had escaped from History. He was outside History. He was sleeping like a child.

Adam Rosenzweig thought: *When he wakes, he will forgive me.*

With that thought Adam Rosenzweig felt that now he himself might sleep.

And did.

When he next awoke, the hut was still pitch dark, but he had the sense that it was nearing dawn. He listened for some sound in the dark, but there was none. He again felt that sense of peace in the fact that the man slept.

He tried to hear the breath of the sleeping man. He strained to hear it. But there was none.

Then all at once, with an icy shiver, he thought: *He is dead. He has killed himself. He has lain in the dark and cut his own throat.*

For a moment, he could not move. He did not have the courage. Then he managed it. He got up, fumbling for matches, hoarsely calling: "Talbutt—Talbutt—Crawfurd—"

There was no answer.

11

As Adam approached the hut, dawn had scarcely begun, but there was enough light for him to distinguish the darker square that was the open doorway. He leaned over to enter the low opening, then stopped, crouching there. He heard his own breath. In that moment that was all in the whole world he could hear.

Then some bird, back in the dark woods, made its first peevish note. The world was there. The world was beginning again. So he entered.

Inside, in the pitch dark, he straightened up. He waited again, then summoned his will to move. He put forth his hand in the dark and took a tentative step, then another. On the second step, his foot touched something.

Without stooping to grope with his hands he knew what it was. He stood there in the dark, and breathed, and knew what it was. Then he found his way to the table, and his fingers found matches. He lighted a match, saw a candle, and lighted it. He forced himself to turn.

The body lay on the back, the head toward the door. A candlestick was yet clutched in the right hand. An extinguished candle lay on the floor, near one of the beams that had held the door. Adam stared at the beam, and wondered what had led Jedeen Hawksworth to lift the beam from the iron brackets, what wheedling, what whining, what plea, what subtlety. He thought of Mose Crawfurd crouching in the dark, the bludgeon in his grip, grinning as he made the calculated whine.

He wondered, suddenly, what arrogance, idiocy, confidence, or contempt had prompted Jed Hawksworth to open that door to the one man in the world he had humiliated past all manhood to this last justification of manhood.

No, he decided, coldly, it had not been like that. This was only a dream he, Adam Rosenzweig, was having of how it had happened. What had actually happened was, no doubt, simple, as simple as a knock on the door, the word that something—it wouldn't matter what—was wrong with the horses. That would have done it.

He looked at the body. The underwear had been ripped loose around the waist. He saw the marks of a heavy band at the waist as into white cold tallow. For a moment he could not understand. Then he decided it was the mark of a money belt. But would a man be wearing his money belt in bed, safe behind the double-barred door? Then he knew that that was exactly what Jedeen Hawksworth would have to do, relishing the discomfort, clinging to the sensation that disturbed sleep, finding reality only in that combination of pain and gratification.

Now Mose Crawfurd, fleeing somewhere in the dawn world, had the belt. He had, somehow, known that the belt was there. Adam stood there and stared at the mark left on the white flesh of the exposed belly, and thought of the sly, sad game of spying that must have gone on, month by month, between Mose Crawfurd and Jedeen Hawksworth, the one spying for the money belt, the other for the branded *W*, each for the other's shame.

Well, the game was over.

With that thought, Adam shook as at a cold gust. What had been a charade, a dream, a drama, the logical working out of a story told long ago, was suddenly real. And nothing was over. Everything was just beginning. And Adam Rosenzweig stood there in the hut, with a body most horribly dead, and dawn was near.

He shook with fear. Standing there in his fear, he had, all at once, the irrelevant vision of armies moving, moving at night, blindly and massively, choking the land, shaking it, men, horses, caissons, wagons and artillery, and far off there was the sound of battle, and flame in the dark. He thought, somehow, of all that vast passage of foot, hoof, and wheel over his own body, treading him, Adam Rosenzweig, deeper and deeper into the earth so that he could hear nothing, see nothing, be nothing.

He found that he was holding his breath. He did not know how long he had been holding his breath. He thought that he was going to faint.

Then, like a voice, he heard his mind working: *They will accuse me. They will hold me. Who will care what will happen to me. Innocent or guilty, who will care?*

Again he had the vision of a host moving in the dark.

He looked down quite calmly at the body of Jedeen Hawksworth.

Then he thought: *Who cares about anything?*

All at once he began to do what seemed the simple and foreordained thing. Whatever there was to think about he would think about later. Whatever that was, he would have all his life to think about it. But now he moved with great strength and deftness. With pride he observed that strength and deftness. He got the body into the woods, dragging it. He buried it, and got a length of fallen tree trunk over the spot. He hitched the horses to the big, ready-loaded wagon, put the personal possessions of Jedeen Hawksworth aboard, and drove the wagon down an abandoned lane in the woods. Deep enough in, he unhitched the horses and tethered them, individually, to trees, knotting the halters loosely enough to be sure that they could eventually jerk free. He came back, stripped the canvas off the huts, rolled it, and stowed it on the smaller wagon.

He went back into the now unroofed hut that he had shared with Mose Crawfurd, and collected his things—the satchel his uncle had given him long back in Bavaria, his bundle of clothes, his blankets, a stool, a lantern. As he stood to cast his eyes about in a last survey, his glance fell on the table. There was nothing there.

What had been there?

Suddenly, he knew. He knew that the evening before, when he had risen to break off the lesson with Mose and wander out into the camp, the alphabet cards he had made for his pupil had been there. Now they were gone.

He stared at the spot.

So Mose Talbutt—Mose Crawfurd—on his way to do the deed that all his life had been leading toward, had paused in the dark hut to reach out and take away with him those cards which, evening after evening, he had pored over, like a child. Adam stood there and his mind leaped forward to an image of Mose Crawfurd crouching in some shadowy undefined spot, ready to start up with guilty fear at any sound, leaning by a single candle flame while his big hand gripped a pencil and copied a letter from a card. Seeing that image, he felt an unmanning constriction in his chest. Something too complicated, too terrible, for him to give a name to was in him, was in the world. And he could not move.

Then, not far off, he heard the first bugle. Then another, then another, another and another. Farther and farther away, sweeter and sweeter over the land, the notes broke forth, then faded, in the silvering dawn light. Adam stood in the middle of the unroofed and ravaged hut, like the pen of an animal and not a human habitation, and heard the bugles, and lifted up his face to the dawn sky. His eyes, he discovered, were wet with tears.

"I don't understand things," he said aloud. "I don't understand anything. Oh, God, I want to understand."

But the constriction in his chest was gone.

It was full light, and past, by the time he got out beyond the camp to the main road. Progress through the camp had been slow enough. Now, company by company, troops were falling in. Men rushed about, seemingly with no purpose. Here and there an officer with the gold of his rank gleaming in the fresh light, sat a restive horse, watching sleepily, uttering no sound. But from those points where the formations were accreting, the yelped orders of sergeants and lieutenants broke, rising and falling, filling the bright air with hysteria and outrage.

In company street after company street now, the formations had assumed solidity, like blocks of hewn stone set in swirling water.

The road itself, Adam realized as soon as he had broken past the hutment of the Ninth Vermont, was packed. The traffic, he noticed, with surprise, was moving on the left—a system which, for some reason of their own, the soldiers must have set up for the occasion.

Thus the inbound traffic was on the side of the road away from him—an interminable line of supply wagons, ammunition trains, new ambulances with paint brightly untried and canvas white as snow. Beyond that movement he could see field after field filled with parked wagons mathematically disposed, waiting to be sucked into that movement southeastward. Meanwhile in the interstices of that as yet unbroken mathematical pattern, there was the same swirl and angry formication as in the camp behind him. Men were putting mules into harness. From these fields rose a nervous ululation, no word distinguishable in that confused distance. Above that area some last blue wisps of smoke from newly abandoned cork fires yet hung, raveling slowly into the brightness of air.

Reluctantly, sadly, he brought his gaze to rest on the flow of traffic nearer him, the outbound traffic, that movement which he would soon join—all the nondescript traffic of the hangers-on moving northwestward; the hooded wagons of sutlers; carts, light four wheelers; here and there a local peddler with a pushcart; washerwomen with bundle on head—not somebody's laundry now but their own miserable possessions; small adventurers with, no doubt, a pack of greasy cards in pocket and a dilapidated valise in hand; the blank, undefinable, faceless ones whose purposes must have always been indecipherable and who now moved with the great mass, empty-handed as at birth or carrying some grotesquerie like a painted chamber pot, a carved clock, a large simpering portrait in oil of a child that could never have sprung from the loins of the carrier, or the Holy Bible in a size large enough for the pulpit.

A great boot had, as it were, kicked over the winter camp like an ant hill, and the life was seething desperately forth.

Adam averted his eyes from that sight. For a last time he looked back at the camp. He heard the distance-thinned yelping of orders. He saw ranks already formed, standing. He caught the flash of sun on steel. Ah, there were the ones elected to know the grandeur of truth. To see the elephant. To be redeemed from all that triviality they had been, and yet were. For a moment his heart was sore and swollen with glory.

But he knew what was for him, Adam Rosenzweig, the crippled Jew from Bavaria.

He turned toward that procession moving toward the northwest, people like himself who were moving away from the battle, who would never see the elephant, who were not worthy.

He drew closer. There was no break in the procession, no way for him to enter and join even those whom the world had designed to be his companions. Only one person, in all the time he waited, gave him recognition.

An old man with a white beard came by. His head was bare, and almost bald. Over his left shoulder hung a feather boa; an enormous silver serving fork stuck from his left coat pocket, the side toward Adam; in both hands, with exceeding care, out from his body, he carried a Wedgwood soup tureen, large enough to satisfy a dozen. Over the tureen his eyes were fixed straight ahead, and his lips moved constantly in a soundless discourse. His feet, shod in patent-leather boots obviously not designed for him and painfully too large, were set on the soft earth in a sequence awful in its slow methodicalness. It was this man who, snatched mystically from the rigidity of his walking dream, suddenly stared at Adam Rosenzweig.

He stared at him directly, a stare of ferocious and damning intensity, as though he could peer into the very soul; then spat.

Adam, with detachment, saw the sunlight flash silver on the ejected spittle. He saw the new brightness on the lower lip above the beard, the innocent and anomalously infantile pink where the dampness of spittle yet clung. He saw the glitter in the eyes fixed upon him. He saw, and classified each separate item as separate. No item seemed to have any relation to any other, nor even any meaning in itself. It was as though he were observing words in a language strange to him—no, rather, the characters in an alphabet strange to him. He recognized nothing beyond strange marks on the bright blankness of the world.

Then, all at once, his mind was saying: *How did he know I am a Jew?*

The eyes staring at him had glazed into fatigue, age, uninterest. They had withdrawn and swung away, up the thronged road. It was all over in an instant. Those old broken patent-leather boots had never missed a single, duck-flopping stride. They were carrying that old face and body, the feather boa, the silver serving fork, the noble soup tureen, into unfathomable distance.

No, Adam decided, the old man couldn't have known he was a Jew.

No, he thought, *this is not Bavaria.*

No, the old man could not have known that he was a Jew. Or if he had known he would not even have cared. The old man had done only what, living in the world, he had had to do. The others, those whose stare of uninterest had bleached him into nothingness —they, too, had done what they, each locked in himself and moving toward his mysterious destination, had had to do.

And as he thought these thoughts, another thought began to grow behind him. Whatever the old man and the others had done, he thought, whatever their reasons, or compulsions, for doing it, there was, somehow, a justice in the act. The act corresponded to something in himself.

His inner vision fell, fleetingly, on the face of Jedeen Hawksworth as he had last seen it. The face had been staring up from the shallow hole, back in the woods, and the shovelful of earth had been poised above it.

But I didn't do it, I didn't, Adam cried out in his mind.

No, he had not dumped the dirt on those staring eyes. Standing there, with the shovel poised, he had remembered, just in time, the face of the dead Confederate soldier, the body at Gettysburg lying in the trench with the jacket over the face, placed there by some nameless hand. So he, Adam Rosenzweig, had taken his own handkerchief and laid it over the face of Jedeen Hawksworth. It had been a clean handkerchief. It had been washed only the day before.

There was no reason for them to accuse him, no reason to spit at him, no reason to turn upon him that stare that bleached him to nothing.

Then, slowly, he thought: *They accuse me of being like them.*

But I'm not, I'm not, he protested.

Then: *But they hate me because I am.*

Then: *I hate them because I am.*

At that, the rage and shame roiled up in him.

"God damn!" he burst out. He lifted his whip and swung it. The horses plunged forward, edging in.

There was a ditch along the road, but here not deep

enough to matter. Even as the ditch grew deeper, Adam hung on, trying to crowd onto the road. The wagon was canting over a little now, but the right wheel was on the edge of the road. Adam looked up ahead and saw that the ditch was deeper. Already the off-horse was having trouble on the slant.

There was no break in the procession.

He struck again with the whip, and drew the right reins. The beasts swung sharply into the column, forcing aside two women with bundles on their heads. But the next wagon had pulled even, the nigh-horse of the wagon was crowding Adam's team, the front wheel of the wagon had locked with the right wheel of Adam's wagon.

The driver of the wagon looked over at Adam and uttered a wailing blasphemy, like a cry of pain. Then he disappeared from sight, over the far side of the wagon, and for an instant Adam had the crazy notion that the man was going to walk away up the road, abandoning his wagon as too difficult to deal with, escaping from some last outrage of life.

But no, the man had reappeared. He had turned and come clear around the rear of Adam's wagon. He waved his whip, the butt end up like a bludgeon. He was cursing Adam. He was making some demand that Adam get down and do something—something, Adam could not make out what, about the team. The man's face was contorted in such pain and ferocity that Adam could do nothing but stare into it as though trying to plumb some new dark dimension of life.

The man had struck him across the left leg with the butt of the whip. The man had seized his left ankle, was trying to jerk him off the seat. Behind them, down the road, men were yelling. Without premeditation, Adam jerked his foot back, and kicked him full in the face. It was the left foot, and therefore the unusually heavy boot Old Jacob had made for him, back in Bavaria.

Rapt, almost light-headed with sudden excitement, Adam looked down into the man's face. Blood was gushing from his nose; Adam looked down at his left boot. He wondered, curiously, if blood was on it. Then he looked up in time to see the man with the bleeding face draw a knife from his shirt—a long knife—and start at him.

He recognized the object. But there was scarcely time enough for that before the blade had been struck down. A big beefy man, somehow familiar in appearance, had struck down the weapon with the butt of his own whip. Now others had seized the man with the knife. "You durn fool," the beefy man was saying to the man with the bloody face, "help git them wagins untangled and stop killing folks."

A stranger had gone to take the bridle of the near-horse of the man's team. Adam realized, all at once, what demand the man had been screaming at him. He got down from the wagon and went to take the bridle of his off-horse.

"That's it," the stranger holding the bridle of the stranger's horse said, "ease it up. Pull towards you a mite. But easy—God damn it, I said easy!"

It was working. Inch by inch, the wheel drew out. Adam's wagon stood there canting down in the ditch. Adam waited, passive, for an order. Everything—everything in the world—seemed to be out of his hands.

"Pull in front thar," the beefy man said, and Adam led his team out of the ditch up to the road.

But the owner of the other wagon was screaming that it wasn't fair, it was his place, he was ahead.

"You better shut up and git in thar and drive," the beefy man bellowed at him. "You better be glad them sodjers ain't taking you off to hang you fer murder!"

The beefy man turned contemptuously away and stepped to Adam's wagon. He came around to the right and without any by-your-leave swung up. "Move on," he said amiably. "You want to set here all day?"

Adam looked up the road. The procession had drawn on away. There was an empty space of a hundred—no, two hundred, three hundred yards. He lifted the reins.

"Lucky I showed up," the beefy man said, and took out a red bandana and mopped his red face.

"Yes," Adam said, "I am grateful."

"Whar's Jed?" the man asked.

Adam looked at him. He felt the cold spreading from his guts. The man knew. He knew he knew.

And all at once he knew who the man was. He couldn't remember his name, but he knew that he had been around with Jed Hawksworth.

"Pick yore ears, son," the man said, without heat. "I ast you whar's Jed."

"He's—he's—" But Adam stopped.

"Up ahead?" the man demanded.

Adam nodded.

"Jes like him," the man said. "Ain't got no patience. That's Jed Hawksworth fer you. Bet he was so restless he started a-fore light."

"Yes," Adam said.

"The nig with him?"

"Yes," Adam said.

Adam looked up the road, steadily. The gap was closing a little. The sun was very bright.

"I got me a feller helps me," the man said. "He's back thar driven now. Four wagons back."

"Yes," Adam said.

"Good fellow, ain't no nig," the man said. "But he's leaving me. His pappy's sick and he's got to go home to the farm."

The man was looking sideways at Adam. Adam did not take his own gaze from the road.

After a time the man said: "Jed—does he treat you good?"

"Yes," Adam said.

"Yeah," the man said. "Ole Jed." He paused, thinking about Ole Jed. Then said: "Yeah, Ole Jed. He's a good ole fellow."

Then he fell silent.

Then, in a tone of sudden aggravation, he burst out: "Durn it, he ought to treat you good. A young fellow like you. Steady and honest and ed-jicated. I don't keer if you are fur'n. But them Rebs."

He paused and studied Adam, sidewise. "You know Jed was a Reb?" he demanded.

"I knew he was from Carolina," Adam said. "They drove him out for being against slavery."

"Maybe," the man said. "Yeah, maybe. But you know, I bet he don't give a toot who wins this-here war. So long as he's making his." Again he gave the sidewise look.

"What's he paying you?" he asked softly.

"Ten dollars," Adam said.

"And found?"

"My food," Adam said. "If that's what you mean."

"Jesus Christ," the beefy man breathed in despair. He sank back in his thoughts. "He owe you any money?" he demanded.

"Three months," Adam said.

"Ole Jed fer you," the man said, and shook his head. "Looks like he can't let loose of money. Not even when it belongs to somebody else." He paused. "Well," he resumed, putting on an air of sardonic gaiety, "you're lucky. It mought have been six months."

The man fell into meditation.

"God durn it," he burst out, "you so honest Jed Hawksworth goes off and leaves you to bring a wagin full of stuff, and he don't even pay you yore money. Tell you what, you oughta take thirty dollars' worth of stuff out of his wagin. Thirty dollars wholesale, too, and not them robber prices he charges them pore sodjers. Yeah, you take it and put it in my wagin and you drive up to him tonight and tell him you done collected yore time."

Adam said he didn't think it would be necessary to do that. He would collect from Jed Hawksworth more directly.

"Well, I'll be waiting up the road when you do," the man said. "You come with me. Yeah, tell the ole booger you're coming with me, I don't care. A smart fellow like you and ed-jicated—he kin git rich. This country is gonna be full of money. It is gonna be as full of money as hog meat is of grease. Hell, walk in the right place and money will stick to you like cockleburs. Hell, money is gonna be as common as cholry-morbus in dog days, and a sight more pleasant. I tell you what—"

And he told him what.

He told him what he would do for him. He would pay eighteen dollars and a percentage. Yes-sir-ree, he would go that far fer a young fellow like this who was honest, steady and ed-jicated, even if he did have a kind of fur'n brogue and wore a funny boot on one foot, it wasn't his fault, no-sir-ree. He warn't no real cripple, no way.

He would make him a partner in no time. He would make him rich. Didn't he want to be rich?

243

Yes, Adam said, he wanted to be rich.

"Wal," the man said, "I'll be waiting fer ye tonight. You'll find me. I'll be camping beside the road."

And he dropped off the wagon.

When, an hour later, Adam pulled off the road, he had no plan. He had seen the lane leading off into the woods, that was all. He simply pulled off, climbed down from the wagon, and pretended to be inspecting a wheel. He did not know what he would say if the beefy man got off his wagon to come and help.

Out of the tail of his eye, he saw the beefy man's wagon draw even, and saw the beefy man staring at him. In that instant, he knew that the man was, for that instant, caught between conflicting impulses. So, without thought, he straightened up from the wheel, waved, and shouted: "It's all right! I'll be there! Tonight! I'll find you!"

The man waved back, grinned, and passed on in the slow grinding pace of the procession. Adam bent back over the wheel, sank himself into a profound contemplation of it, rubbing his hand gently back and forth on the ironbound felloe.

Behind him he heard the sound of passage, the grind of axles, the innumerable small creakings, the innumerable strains and torsions of leather and chain, the susurrus of innumerable hooves on earth or gravel and of turning wheels, all absorbed into one pervasive sound. Now and then, in the distance, some human cry rose thinly above that unremitting undersound. The undersound filled the world, and his head, as he stared

244

at the wheel. He thought of wheels turning, of people passing forever, in an endless procession, and the sound was always there, filling the air.

He thought that now the beefy man would be too far up the road to see him. So he straightened up. He turned and looked at the road. He looked at the people passing, at the individuals with their eyes fixed ahead, at the procession winding into the anonymity of distance; and his heart contracted in a pain of lostness. He had, he thought, come all his years and the thousands of miles to stand, with the woods at his back, and watch that procession wind away from him.

Then the pain of lostness was gone.

He found himself looking at that thronged road with distant disdain.

I did not come here to go with them, he thought.

I came here to find something, he thought. *In Virginia,* he thought.

And now he was free to go. It did not matter what had made him free, what murky complications or blind accidents of the past. Suddenly, all the past was nothing, and joy flooded his heart.

He was free, at last, to go.

12

Deep in the woods, the lane had become little more than a trace. Turf absorbed the sound of hoof and wheel. New grass was up to the fetlock. Here and there some bushes, or a switch of maple or gum boldly rooted in the very lane, brushed the length of a horse's belly, then bowed beneath the axle. Boughs hung with fresh green, and leaves fully formed but not yet thickening to summer fleshiness, brushed the sides of the wagon. They might brush his shoulder, even his cheek.

A little stream crossed the trace. The water was crystal clear. The stones by the water were furred with moss, dark green in the deep pile but with a pale glimmer of new green over all. The sun glittered on the water. He realized that he was dying of thirst. He had not had a drop of water all day.

He got down and flung himself flat with his face against the cold silkiness of the water. He sucked the water in, feeling the cold go veining out from his stomach. Under the crystal water he saw tiny flecks of something like mica caught by the sun and glittering against the velvet blackness of the stream bed. He rolled over on his back and looked up at the brilliant sky.

He thought how beautiful was the world.

Three hours later he got down again from the wagon to investigate a deadfall across the trace—if it could be called a trace any more. He saw the cabin. For the first instant, as he parted the leafy brush that screened the spot, he thought it was abandoned, it was in such grim disrepair, the door sagging, and the mud-and-stick chimney crumbling under weather. But then he saw the woman.

She had been crouching, and now his gaze caught her as she rose. He came into the open space, an area rank with new growth already knee-high, the green broken here and there by the black stalks of ironweed from the year before. The woman had moved into the trodden space near the cabin door, which gave inward on a blackness like a cave.

"Good day," he said.

"How-do," she said, and made a jerking motion of the head. Her hands, he noted, were twisting the slack, earth-colored cloth of her garment, just below the waist.

He came closer. From the face he could not tell what her age was, the face so drawn and of the same ambiguous color as the dress. The hair, however, showed little or no gray. It was dark brown, not without luster, and though disheveled showed that, in a last flicker of self-respect or vanity, some care had been taken to plait and pile it. She was looking at him out of dark eyes unremarkable except for the sharp, wary suspiciousness, like eyes spying from a thicket.

"I'm lost," Adam said.

She made no answer. Her hands were twisting the cloth. Looking down, he realized from the slight motion of the long skirt that she must be rubbing one foot over the other. Then he saw the bare toes emerge from beneath the sagging hem, and withdraw.

"It's getting late," he said. "I wonder if I could stay here?"

A dog barked, suddenly, back in the woods, and she threw a glance in that direction.

"I want to pay," he said.

The dog barked again, closer.

"Him," she said, jerking her head toward the sound in the woods. "Got to ast him."

When the woman spoke he noticed that one of her upper teeth was missing. When she spoke she tried to hold her upper lip so that the black gap would not be observed.

They stood there, waiting. They avoided each other's eyes. He looked down and could see the slight motion of the skirt. Once more he saw the bare toes emerge, withdraw. The world was so quiet he thought he could detect the tiny rasping sound of the rough, calloused, scarred sole of one foot being drawn across the top of the other.

The man came out of the woods. He carried a rifle, lightly like a twig. He was a tall, thin, stooped man— a torn black felt hat low on his hairy face, a flannel shirt that once had been red but was now a yellow-striped angry brown, linsey-woolsey britches held up by a length of rope tied cruelly around the waist, bottoms of the britches stuck into fine, rather new military boots. The big bony, brown dog, some kind of hound, stood close to the man's left foot and stared up at Adam from bloodshot, unforgiving eyes.

"He wants to stay," the woman said, and jerked her head toward Adam.

The man was looking at Adam. Then he looked beyond Adam. He was looking at the wagon. "How many?" he demanded.

"I am alone," Adam said.

The man studied him with a dark dubiety. Then he nudged the hound with the toe of his left boot. "Huh?" he demanded of the brown hound, "huh, Red?"

The hound seemed deeply engrossed, then relaxed and leaned against the man's leg.

"Yeah," the man said, leaning to scratch the hound's head. "So you're by yoreself."

Adam nodded.

"Whar you comen from?" the man then demanded.

"The army," Adam said.

"You—" the man said, and studied him. "You," he resumed, "you doan look like no sodjer to me."

"I'm a sutler," Adam said. "I was selling things to the soldiers. That's my wagon." He pointed.

The man ceased to pay any attention to Adam. He was looking off in the direction of the track, in the woods beyond. He looked down at the hound, and the hound stared back. He looked up at the sky. Then back at Adam, and demanded: "Whar you headed?"

"I want to cross the river," Adam said. "I want you to show me how to cross the river. I'll pay. I'll happily pay you for your trouble."

"Carryen stuff to the Rebs, huh?"

Then before Adam could answer, the man leaned at him: "How you know I got any time fer them Rebs?"

"I don't know," Adam said. "But I am not carrying anything to the Rebels. All I want is to get across, so when Grant crosses I can catch up with the army quickly and sell things."

The man was studying him.

"Yes," Adam said earnestly, "look at me. I am not an American. You can know from the way I speak. I am a foreigner. I came from Bavaria. That is in Germany. I am a Jew. I do not care which side is which. I want to sell things."

The man's face, under its hairiness, was twisting into some sort of a grin. "Me," the man said, "I ain't no Jew. But I shore-God doan keer who kills who."

"May I stay tonight?" Adam asked, leaning, sensing an advantage.

"What kin you pay?"

"I'll pay a dollar," Adam said.

The man hesitated.

"I'll bring food in," Adam said. "Yes," he said, "enough for us all."

The man was looking at him, saying, yes, he could stay. Then Adam saw something like a grin growing under the hairiness, some inwardness of humor, and the lips twitched back to show the strong, stained teeth, and say: "Yeah, and make that-air grub good, son. Les all have us one real nice supper together, son."

Adam caught sight of the woman's face. Her eyes were dark and wide as she stared at him. She looked as though she had just discovered him. He could not decipher the expression of her face.

That night, after supper, Adam rolled up in his blankets, against the wall. The man—whose name, it had developed, was Monmorancy Pugh—had already got into the bed in the far corner beyond the fireplace, a bed formed of sapling lengths led from the corner walls out to a post set in the floor, and covered with shorter and more flexible lengths. The man was snoring already. He had drunk three tin cups of whisky before and during the meal.

Adam wondered why he could not go to sleep. He opened his eyes and idly watched the woman, who was doing some last chore at the hearth, pouring something into an earthen pot. She leaned, and all at once, against the glow of the coals, he saw her face in profile.

He had seen, before, the strained face, the dead, earthy color of flesh, the broken tooth. But what did those things matter? What did anything matter in the great emptiness of the world when now he saw the calmness and purity of the silhouette against the rosy light?

Then the woman turned away. It was like the loss of a memory.

He shut his eyes. Irrelevantly, but with a clarity to stop his breath, he saw the Mutton—poor Mollie the Mutton—as, under an evening sky of spring, among the staring faces, the lash fell. He thought of the torn, twisted stockings on the pipe-stem legs, of the feet in broken brogans twisted pigeon-toed against the earth.

He wondered what had happened to her now.

What could have happened to her now? Had anyone carried her away? Had anyone eased the pain? Had anyone bathed that flesh abused by the lash and by all the years? Had anyone adjusted a pillow to her head to make sleep more readily come?

He wondered what would have happened if he himself had done those things. He imagined himself lying in some cabin like this, deep in the woods, away from the world, spying on the beauty of Mollie—Mollie the Mutton—as she leaned in darkness, profiled against the glow of coals.

A strange excitement took him. He felt himself trembling on the verge of a revelation. It was a revelation not, he suddenly decided, about Mollie the Mutton. Except insofar as Mollie was a part of the world. For it was a revelation about the world. The whole world. It was not about flight from the world, but about the nature of the world. He was about to put the truth into words.

Then, all at once, he was asleep.

When he awoke it was full day, and the cabin was empty. Yet lying in his blanket, he looked around the place, the spent hearth heaped with ashes and charred wood, the table of puncheon in the middle of the puncheon floor, the floor long unswept, dried mud ground into the wood, a few dead leaves in a corner as though dropped by an eddy of air. The only light was from the half-open door. It was bright morning outside, he could tell, but this place was more like a cave, a den, than a constructed habitation. Even the objects constructed by human hands scarcely bore the mark of hands upon them; the fabricating hand had, in some dire contempt for the human need that had demanded the object, left only the merest mark of its humanity.

He got up, found some water in a wooden pail, drank from a gourd dipper lying on a stool, then splashed his face and hands. He dried himself on his shirt tail. He saw a piece of corn bread lying on the table, on the bare wood, and a few beans in a rude wooden bowl. He ate what was there. His appetite was ferocious. He felt rested, full of confidence and strength.

He went out into the bright morning. No one was in sight. He saw his team tethered to a tree some yards away, where he had left them the night before. He went to the wagon, rummaged for a sack of beans, a half-dozen tins of beef, and a tin of molasses candy. With this burden he came back and was almost to the cabin door when the woman came around the corner. She stood there under the oak tree, as she had stood yesterday when he first saw her. Now, standing there, she held a few dog violets in her hand.

Adam stopped.

"Good morning," he said.

She wet her lips, gathered herself, and said: "Mornen."

He saw her eyes on the objects in his arms.

"I'm sorry," he said. "I was just—" He stopped, embarrassed under her gaze.

"I mean," he said, "I hope you won't mind. I mean I—"

With her unwavering, blank gaze directly on his face, he couldn't go on. Something that seemed like guilt forbade his words. It was as though he himself were, in the great complication of the world, guilty for the dimness, filth, and deprivation beyond the door, and anything he could do now, or say, would be shameful and disingenuous; even his gifts would, in fact, compound rather than extenuate the guilt.

She again looked down at what he carried.

Then he managed to say: "I don't need this. I mean —I have some more."

Her eyes, staring from their distance, never wavered.

"If you don't mind—" he burst out, in desperation.

"All right," she said, in her flat voice, and looked down at the violets in her hand as though bemused by their irrelevance.

He went in the door. He looked around for a place to leave the burden. He avoided the open space of the empty table. He went to the dim corner where the dead leaves lay on the puncheons, there he let down the objects, quickly as though in fear of detection. Then he went back to the door, and out.

The woman was crouching under the oak tree, over to his right. She was crouching there in the same spot as she must have been the day before when she rose to meet him. He moved toward her, and stood a couple of paces to one side. He could not make out what she was doing. She lifted her gaze toward him, over her left shoulder.

"I thought you was gonna sell that-air stuff," she said. "To the sodjers."

"Yes," he said.

She was staring at him.

"I mean," he said, "I have more to sell them."

She continued to stare at him, rebuking him it seemed, for the foolish inadequacy and dishonesty of his words.

"I mean," he burst out, "I mean I wanted you to have it here. Anyway, it isn't beans I sell them."

She turned back to her occupation. Crouching there on the bare ground, amid the fallen acorns of the season before, she was arranging the violets in a cup of water. It was, he saw with surprise, a china cup, a piece of white china. It looked very delicate. She was arranging the violets with great care. The cup was on a little mound, oval, some two feet long, not high.

"They are pretty violets," he said.

" 'Bout the last," she said, not looking up. "Had to go way back in the woods fer 'em."

He waited, then said: "It's a pretty cup."

"Right purty," she said, after a moment, in her flat voice, still not looking up.

She adjusted the last violet, and inspected the cup. "The other one," she said, "it was more purty."

"Other what?" he asked.

"The other cup," she said. "It had flowers painted on hit. Roses, they was. I found it. Lak I found this here"—she touched the cup with a forefinger—"in a house whar we was hiden."

"Hiding?"

"Yeah," she said, "hiden. It was ruint. The house, I mean. Burnt out and nigh to fall. But the cup," she said, "it was a-setten thar. Not hurt, and them flowers painted on to hit."

She waited a moment, the forefinger touching the rim of the cup.

"But he come out the woods," she said then. "It was after we had done found this place to lay hid in. It was the first day I set the cup out here. It was the first day I found me some vi'lets. I had me some vi'lets in hit, setten here, and he come out of the woods. Yonder," she said and pointed to an opening beyond a lightning-split beech, dead at the top.

Adam looked yonder at the opening. There was no stir there, nothing in the late morning stillness. It must have been getting on to noon, he thought. It was the time of silence in the woods.

"I was standen by the door," she said. "I had done fixed me the vi'lets, the fust ones, and was standen back thar, looken. He ne'er seen me when he come out of the woods. He come here and he seen the vi'lets in the cup. Then he done it."

She stopped. He saw the forefinger move on the rim of the white cup, ever so slightly, back and forth.

"Did what?" Adam said.

"He jes drawed back his foot," she said.

He waited.

"It was his right foot," she said.

She waited again.

"Then he kicked," she said.

Suddenly she swung her gaze up at him. He recoiled from that gaze, it was, in its defensiveness, so ferocious and unrelenting.

"Durn it," she cried, in that rage directed at him, at Adam Rosenzweig. "Durn it, don't look at me that-a-way," she cried out. "He couldn't help it! Durn it, it jes come on him, and he couldn't help it!"

She waited; then said: "But I reckin I ne'er knowed it then. I mean how he could not of helped it."

She looked down at the cup.

"He come towards me," she said, "and I reckin I would of killed him, or somethen. If I had me a gun, or somethen. He went past me lak I warn't thar, and in the house. I run to the woods. I laid me down on the ground. It was the place whar I found them fust vi'-lets, that selfsame day. I laid down and I wanted to die. I laid thar till dark. I come back to the house.

"The fire was out. I hear'd him breathen and grunten in the dark. He had not even et. He had drunk out the jug till he fell down and lay. He was on the floor and I let him lay. It came in my mind how I could a-stuck a knife in him and him not even knowen. Fer breaken that cup. But I ne'er done it."

She touched, rearranged a violet.

"I ne'er done it," she said. "I laid down in the dark on the bed. I shut my eyes. But I got up. After a time

258

I got up and put something under his head. I put some kiver on him."

"Why?" he asked.

She studied him, with a flash of that defensiveness and rage of a few minutes earlier. Then said: "Lak I tole you. It come on me how he couldn't help doen it. Kicken the cup." She paused.

"Ain't ever-thing in the world a man kin help," she added.

She brooded for a moment. Then said: "I might of knowed it. How he couldn't help it. When he died—"

She stopped. She looked down at the cup, then at the mound on which it was set.

"Who?" Adam said.

She looked up at him, as with an air of rebuke for stupidity, or forgetfulness. "The boy," she said. "He was two year old, and he died."

She was looking down at the earth. Her forefinger again moved on the rim of the cup. He could hear her breathing. He could, as a matter of fact, hear his own breathing, too. Beyond the shade of the oak tree the noon light blazed down.

"Him," she said.

"Who?" he said.

"My husband—him," she said, "he couldn't pray fer the boy—fer Joe—his name was Jotham—to git well. His thote swelled up and he couldn't breathe. Joe's thote, I mean. And my husband, he couldn't pray. You know what he said?"

"No."

—

259

"He said, 'The world, it ain't no place fer prayen.'"

She waited. Then said: "And Joe, he died. Then him—my husband—he ne'er cried. I said warn't he gonna cry. You know what he said?"

"No," Adam said.

"He said, 'The world, it ain't no place fer cryen.'"

Abruptly, she stood up. She stared distantly down at the cup of dog violets, then out into the blaze of light. "Maybe it ain't," she said.

She wheeled angrily at him. "A thing ain't ne'er what you think it is!" she cried.

She waited, peering into his face. "Did you know that?" she demanded.

"But Jotham, he died," she said. "And we buried him here. Here was whar he best fancied. 'Twas here he fancied to roll in the dirt and play with them a-corns."

She paused, collecting herself.

"But him, my husband," she cried, "—he was always a prayen man. He was always a Bible-man. A-fore. A-fore they fit the war," she said. "That was how it happened."

"What happened?" Adam said.

"He was a Bible-man and wanted to do lak Jesus says. He did not want to kill ner harm. Then they come."

"Who?" Adam said. "Who came?"

"The 'scripters," she said. "To get him fer the army and make him kill folks. The Rebel 'scripters, he knowed they would come and seek, but he ne'er knowed what to do. He did not aim to kill nobody. But he did not aim to be took, neither. He laid in the night and prayed to Jesus, what to do. I said to him how Jesus was took. He said, 'Oh, Lawd, I am not Jesus, and how kin I let a man lay a finger on me? Oh, Lawd, how kin I unhook my sinful pride and bow down my heart to be took?' "

She was twisting the slack cloth of her garment, with both hands, at the level of her waist.

"We was hiden out," she said. "It ain't no way to raise a young 'un, hiden out, but we done the best we could. But they found us, them 'scripters." She paused. "He taken the head off one of them, them 'scripters," she said. "That 'scripter, he was gonna lay a hand on him, and thar was that-air scatter-gun. Him—my husband—he picked it up."

Adam watched the fingers work the cloth, which was earth-colored.

"It was runnen and hiden then," she said, "worse'n a-fore. We lived lak a varmint and the dogs on him. One night I laid sleepen and I woke up. It was him busten out laughen that woke me. I ast him why. When he could stop hisself laughen, you know what he said?"

"No," Adam said.

"He said the Lawd God shore taken a pleasure to joke and prank. He said the Lawd God said thou shalt not kill and then put a fellow in a tight whar he had to kill to keep from killen. He said the Lawd God let a fellow grab holt of a hickory limb hung out over Hell-fahr and then taken a chicken feather and tickled the bottom of his bare feet till he bust out laughen and let go the hickory limb to scratch.

"Yeah," she said, "that's what he said. When he could stop hisself laughen."

She waited, pondering. "Then you know what he said?" she demanded.

"No."

"He said, well, he had let go to scratch one time, and he was shore goen to keep on scratchen till he hit Hell-fahr and bounced. Whene'er he got a itch, he said, he aimed to scratch. He bust out laughen agin. Next I knowed he was sleepen lak a baby."

She leaned over and picked up an old acorn from the earth. She inspected it, with great care. Still inspecting it, she said: "That night—it was a time after Joe had done died. Since then ever-thing is different. Since he bust out laughen in the night. I don't know nuthen 'bout him no more. He goes and he comes, and I don't know."

She inspected the acorn with excessive care. "Them boots he's a-wearen," she said. "They's new. But I don't know."

She flung the acorn to the earth.

"I don't want to know," she said.

He stared at her. She met his eyes, then turned sharply away.

"I'm sorry," he said.

"Fer what?" she demanded listlessly, not looking at him.

He reached out and touched her arm, and she faced him.

"For that," he said, and pointed to the mound of earth.

"That," she said, with no expression, and turned her gaze down where the mound and cup of dog violets were, and where the old acorns were scattered.

Early in the afternoon she came to call him from where he sat on a fallen log by the spring. She had some food ready, she said. He sat at the table and she served the food which was, he knew, from the supply he had brought. She said nothing until he had finished. Then she said that he better lie down and get more rest. He would be traveling all night, she said.

He lay down and shut his eyes. In his mind's eye he saw the new boots the man wore. *Well*, he thought, *at least my boots won't be much good to him.*

He did go to sleep.

When he awoke, the room was dim. Then in the dimness he became aware of her presence. She was crouching on the floor near where he lay.

"Has he come?" he asked.

"No," she said. Then, studying him in the gloom, said: "You could of left here this mornen. You could of been back outa the woods by now."

"I could have," he said.

"You could go now," she said. "You could still git a good start."

After a moment, he shook his head. "No," he said.

She peered at him in her slow, studious way. "I know somethen," she said, finally. "You ain't crossen that river to sell nuthen."

"No," he said.

"You said you come acrost the ocean," she said. "You come a long way."

"Yes," he said.

"You could of stayed home acrost the water," she said, "and not come."

Then: "What did you come fer?"

He had been propped on an elbow facing her as she crouched there, her eyes gleaming in the dimness. Now, slowly, he let himself down and rolled to his back. He looked up at the rafters, at the unpeeled saplings on which the shakes were laid. He could barely make out the pattern up there, it was so dark. The dark seemed to hang down from the rafters, like cobwebs in an old attic. He stared at the depending shadows and thought of his life.

He thought of his mother dying in a shadowy room in Berlin, how her eyes gleamed with fever and unforgiveness. No, she had not forgiven him, her son, because she knew he had not forgiven her her own unforgiveness of the father, who had walked away from her to take his musket at the barricade.

He thought of his father dying in the shadowy room in Bavaria, saying, yes, he had trusted in man.

He thought how short his own life had been. He

thought of the swift emptiness of his time. It was, he thought, like wind. He thought, suddenly, with a strange unspecified despair, of all he had not had.

He had never had his arms around a woman. He had never had a friend to talk with about the way life was. He had never had money in his pocket to buy the respect of the world. He had never, he thought sadly, been sure that he had found Truth. With a sweet yearning that seemed ready to break his heart, he thought how a man has to have something in order to be ready to die.

He rolled on his right side and again propped himself on an elbow, and found her crouching there, the eyes gleaming in the darkness.

"A man has to have something," he said to her, slowly. "To live."

"Then what did you come fer?" she asked again, with no pity.

He thought a moment then managed to say: "To fight."

He kicked the blanket off his legs. "But that," he said, lifting his left leg, waggling the foot, "it isn't exactly—exactly *schnurgerade*."

"What?" she demanded.

"It isn't exactly—exactly straight as a string," he said, staring at the foot. Then he let it sink.

"They wouldn't let me fight," he said.

"Fight fer what?" she said.

"Freedom," he said, and heard his own breathing now, in and out. It was as though the word had cost him some effort from which he had not yet recovered.

"Freedom," she repeated at last, trying the word on her tongue, musing on it.

Suddenly, she rose.

"Killen," she said bitterly, "that's what they is fighten fer. They all done got the habit. They is killen fer killen. Anything else they done long forgot."

She stared down at him from her height and disdainful distance. "Freedom," she said. Then demanded: "That why you was aimen to cross the river?"

He pondered the question. He wondered how late it was getting. He wondered when the man would come.

"Yes," he said, looking up at her. Then painfully, he said: "At least, I thought so. I hope so. A man has to have a reason."

He considered that thought, feeling naked and small in the thought. "Perhaps I don't know why," he said. "Don't know why I am crossing the river."

He pondered it deeply. He felt slow and stupid. His head felt large and full of cloudy, painful distance.

"I just don't know," he said, again.

But all at once he stood up. He knew one thing.

"But I know one thing," he said. "I know I have to cross over to find out what I have to find out. I know that if I do not cross over, I shall never know what I must know to live."

She seemed not to hear him. She took a couple of steps to the door and looked up at the sky. "Still bright day," she said, and turned questioningly back toward him.

When he made no movement, she shrugged, then said: "One side a durn river, it's jes lak t'other."

She went out.

After a moment he followed. She had disappeared. He looked up at the sky. Yes, beyond the gathering shadow of leaf, it was still bright day. He wondered when the man would come.

He took the animals to water, to the spring, brought them back, and tethered them. He inspected the harness to see that all was in order. He was rearranging odds and ends of the load in the wagon when he became aware of the presence, and sharply turned.

It was the woman. Her bare feet had made no sound. She held something wrapped in her skirt that he could not make out.

"Listen," she said, speaking rapidly, almost in a whisper. "He will come to a big sycamore. They is a moon tonight and that-air sycamore, it will stand up white and big. Let him be a-driven and if'n he turn to the right side of that sycamore, you do it then."

"Do what?"

"Durn fool," she said. She unwrapped what had been hidden in her skirt. She thrust it at him. It was a pistol.

He stared at it.

"Stick it in his side," she said, in her contempt, "and tell him to git to the left side of that tree. Tell him you ain't to the ford in a hour you will do hit. Throw his rifle back in the wagin whar he can't git at it easy. Git his knife out the top of his boot. The right boot. Tell him to drive on acrost the ford and git on the trace."

She thrust the pistol at him.

But he stood there, staring at it. "I don't want to shoot him," he said.

"I don't want you a-shooten him neither," she said. "He is all I got."

But she still held the object at him. He did not reach for it.

"It ain't loaded," she said querulously. "But he ain't a-knowen that. It will feel loaded, stuck in a man's side."

He reached out, slowly, and took it. He inspected it curiously.

"Put it in yore pocket," she commanded. "You don't want nobody to see it and know."

He obeyed.

She looked up at the sky. "Gitten on," she said. "Ought to be here soon."

She turned to face him. "You said you was gonna pay him. Fer taken you over."

He nodded.

"Now don't you fergit to pay him," she said.

He promised that he would not forget.

13

A whippoorwill was calling. Above the black tracery of boughs the stars were out now. In the underdark you could hear the leaves brushing the sides of the team, the canvas hood of the wagon. Ahead, sudden in the shadow of the woods, the sycamore loomed spookily white. Adam, sitting by the man, could sense the tightening of the reins. He waited a moment to be sure. Then he did it.

He was, in fact, greatly surprised when he found that he had done it.

But the man did not seem surprised. When the muzzle pressed into his side, he did not even turn his face toward Adam. He let the reins fall slack; the team stopped. "I must of made a mis-take," Monmorancy Pugh said.

"Yes," Adam said.

The man picked up the reins and clucked to the team. He sawed the reins, clucking, and the wagon began to back up.

"All right," Adam said.

The man drew to the left of the sycamore. Adam, with his left hand, managed to pick up the carbine propped between him and the man, and shoved it back under the hood of the wagon. He reached down and withdrew the knife from the man's right boot, and dropped it behind him. The man was immobile in the shadow. The team moved on, down slope now, breasting the dark growth.

After a time, the man, not turning, demanded: "How did you know?"

"Know what?"

"Know it was left side of that-air sycamore?"

Adam waited a moment. Then he said: "You don't go uphill to find water."

The man pondered that. "Naw," he said, "you don't."

For a moment he sank into himself. Then said: "I did'n reckin you was that smart."

The man waited again, pondering. Then said: "But that don't make you put no pistol on a man."

"Listen," Adam said. He discovered a tendency in his voice to crack, and stopped.

The night was beautiful. He thought: *If the night were not so beautiful—*

But the thought did not complete itself. He was afraid he might weep. He had not made the world the way it was.

"Listen," he said, mastering his voice. "I don't know why you took the right fork. I don't want to know. All I want is for you to get me over the river in a reasonable time. Do you understand?"

The man drove on, not answering. The whippoorwill was calling.

After a time the man spoke. "You gonna shoot me?" he asked.

Or was it a question? Adam could not be sure.

"No," he said, slowly. "I simply want you to guide me over the river. I told you that."

They moved on in silence except for the dry brushing sound of leaf and twig against the animals, the axle, the canvas.

"Hit wouldn't be no great spite to me," the man said.

"What?"

"I mean if'n you did," the man said.

"Did what?"

"I mean I wouldn't much keer if you did," the man said. "I mean if you did it quick. Not in the gut ner nuthen lak that."

"You mean shoot you?"

"Yes," the man said.

The wagon drew on sibilantly through the dark growth.

"A man gits tahrd," the man said.

The wagon lurched in the dark. It was a length of deadfall, or a stone.

"Weren't you—" Adam began and stopped. But he resumed: "Weren't you going to do it to me?"

He paused, collecting some force in himself. "Kill me?" he demanded.

In the darkness the man seemed to be considering the question.

"Mought of," he said, finally.

"You know," Adam said, "I would have given you anything you wanted. Half my load. More. If that was what you wanted."

He hesitated, embarrassed. "I did leave a few things," he said. Then, after a moment, added: "In the corner of the cabin."

At first the man did not seem to hear. But after a time, when anything he might say seemed irrelevant, he said: "I seen hit in the corner. Wisht you hadn't."

"Why?" Adam asked.

The man did not answer.

"Why?" Adam repeated, softly.

"God durn you!" the man burst out. "God durn you—you know!"

It was darker. The boughs were now interlaced overhead, netting the stars. More often now a wheel lifted on some obstruction, and dropped. The man's body swayed in the dark. It was difficult to keep the pistol pressed to his side.

The man gave a dry, short laugh.

"What is it?" Adam asked.

"You leaven that stuff," the man said, and laughed again.

"What?"

"It was lak you was cheaten me. It was lak you was cheaten me outa the whole durn load."

The man fell silent for a moment. Then: "If'n you hadn't left that stuff in the cabin, wouldn't nuthen been on my mind. I could of been easy in my mind."

The wheels were moving more smoothly now. Over the creak of axle and leather, there came, from the left, the muted musicality of water.

Suddenly, the team had pushed through a screen of brush. There was a little open space, calm in starlight, giving on the stream. The man let the reins drop and gazed up toward the stars. "Gitten on," he said.

"How late?"

"Past midnight," the man said.

"Let's get on," Adam said.

The man stared out at the stream. Across the river there was blackness of brush merging with the blackness of water. In midstream the water slid glossily, and stars gleamed in that darkly burnished surface.

Across the stream peepers were calling.

"I don't see the ford," Adam said.

"Yander," the man said, nodding. "You kin hear it."

Adam looked downstream. There, forty yards or so off, was a riffle. You could hear the water on stone. That was the source of the sound they had heard, descending the track, before they passed on west of the ford. They would now have to double back, downstream.

"The ford, hit's yander," the man said. "But nuthen to brag on. Not like them fords down lower. Or that-air ford at Germanna. Nigh drowned out here. But," he added, that's why you ain't lakly to git shot crossen over. The Rebs ain't watchen it so close. Road ain't been used fer years."

Adam stared across at the blackness of growth on the far bank. It was absolutely black. After a moment, he said: "Now. Let's go now."

The man picked up the reins. The wagon drew into the starlight, doubling back toward the river to an old track that had come in from the west toward the ford. The wheels ground on gravel now. The team was entering the ford. It deepened quickly.

"Lak I tole you," the man said, "nigh drowned out."

The team was floundering, almost.

" 'Druther git shot than drownt," the man said. "Fer me, I mean. Allus said so."

The current, broadside, was sliding the wagon sidewise on the gravel, at an angle to the team.

"What you 'druther?" the man demanded.

Adam held the pistol against the man's side and stared at the dark shore.

The man laughed his short, hacking laugh. "You ain't sayen, huh?" he said.

"No," Adam said. "No—I hadn't thought about it."

The man waited a moment. "Mebbe," he said then, "mebbe you're right. Mebbe dyen is lak when a man gits in his short rows, don't matter much who 'tis he got a grip on." He paused, and gave his hack of a laugh. "Or drownen or shooten," he said, "which one got a durn grip on you."

The team had found good footing. The wagon lurched forward.

"Hell," the man was saying, "time comes nuthen don't make much diff'runce."

They had drawn out on the bank, into the pitch dark of the trees. The wagon stood motionless. In the dark you could hear the heaving breath of the animals. When that sound had subsided, Adam asked: "Do you know the country over here?"

"Yeah," the man said.

"What is that way?" Adam asked, pointing east.

"Country," the man said. "Nuthen to brag on."

"Then?"

"The Pisen Fields," the man said.

"What?"

"What I said," the man said. "That's what folks calls hit."

"Poison Fields?" Adam asked.

"Yeah," the man said. "Lak I said. Ain't worth

nuthen. Worse'n nuthen. Sass'frass. Briar. Scrub. It is sahr ground. Then them woods."

"The Wilderness?" Adam asked. "What they call the Wilderness?"

"Yeah," the man said. "And they don't call hit that fer nuthen. It is that-a-way. It is shore-God a place a man can wander and not know."

"All right," Adam said. "Let's go."

"They's a road down that-a-way." The man nodded to the south. "Ole Turnpike. But you git on that them Rebs will find you. They will cut yore thote."

"Yours, too," Adam said, "if you don't find the right way." He felt, suddenly, gay.

"When you gonna let me go?" the man asked.

"Before dawn," Adam said, feeling very strong and competent. He felt stronger than ever before in his life.

Before dawn he let the man go.

When they stood beside the wagon, which was drawn off the track behind a dense screen of growth, Adam held out to Monmorancy Pugh a greenback for five dollars. "I told you I'd pay you," he said.

The man held the greenback in his hand, waiting.

"I don't know what to do about your weapon," Adam said at last.

"It's one of them new Spencer carbeens," the man said. "Repeaten."

"I might pay you for it," Adam said. "Not that I want it."

276

"Skeered of me, huh?" the man said. "If'n I had my carbeen."

"What did you pay for it?" Adam asked.

"Nuthen," the man said.

"You mean—" Adam began, and stopped.

The whiskered face was grinning in the shadow of the hat. Adam could see the teeth.

"Listen, mister," the man said then, "if'n you don't give me that-air Spencer I'm gonna have to find me another sodjer boy somewhar with one of them things, and he ain't gonna thank you."

He waited, then grinned again. "He won't be in no shape to thank you," the man added.

"You mean—" Adam began again.

"Yeah, I mean," the man said. "I mean they puts out pickets sometimes ain't ne'er been in the woods a-fore." He was watching Adam's face. Then he added, softly: "And sometimes, them pickets, they jes stays there. They jes can't find them the way out. In fack, they ain't in no shape to try."

The man was grinning, under the shadow of the hat.

"Listen, mister," the man was saying softly, "you jes break them bullets outa my carbeen and gimme it. They is fed up from the stock. Holds seven but ain't but two in now. I ain't got no more bullets on me. You see"—and he grinned more wolfishly, pleased with himself—"you see, I ne'er figgered I'd need but one no-way."

Adam stared at him, feeling foolish and lost. "You mean—" he began.

"Yeah, you durn fool," the man said. Then added: "Or mebbe two. If you laid and kept on jerken."

It wasn't fear that Adam felt. It was a strange light-headedness, as though he were about to faint. He thought that if he only closed his eyes he would fall down. Then nothing would matter any more.

"Listen, mister," the man was saying, "you look sick. But you'd a-been real sick back yander crossen the Rapidan if'n I had taken me a notion. You know what?"

Adam shook his head.

"When that-air wagon jounced once in the river you clicked that pistol you had stuck on me. You warn't keepen yore mind on yore business. Yeah, you might of kilt me."

"I'm sorry," Adam began, "it's just that I—"

"Hell, mister, you never knowed what happened. You never even knowed you clicked it. I figgered then I could of grabbed you and thowed you in the water." The man paused.

"Hell," he repeated, "bet that durn pistol ain't even loaded."

He reached out and took it from Adam's hand. Adam did not resist, did not even move. He felt a peculiar relief.

The man examined the revolver. "Yeah," he said contemptuously, and stuck it into his waistband. "Now git me my Spencer down," he commanded.

Adam climbed back into the wagon.

"Git me my knife, too," the man said.

Adam found the carbine and knife and climbed back down.

"Give 'em here," the man said, and Adam held out the carbine for him to take.

The man took it.

"Why—why didn't you?" Adam asked. "Back yonder, in the river?"

"Hell," the man said, "a man jes gits tahrd." He fingered the carbine, hefting it a little. "Could do it right now," he said. "If'n I had a mind to." He paused. "'Course, it would make noise," he added judiciously.

He leaned toward Adam with an insinuating camaraderie, and reached out a hand. "Gimme the knife," he said, almost whispering.

Adam did.

The man held the knife in his right hand, the carbine grounded by his left boot. He balanced the knife lightly in his hand. "Wouldn't make no noise," he said. "This-here wouldn't."

But he leaned, and stuck it in his boot top.

"One thing I'm gonna do though," he said, when he had straightened up. "Gonna slap the pee outa that woman."

He turned, as though to walk away, as though something were finished.

"But she—" Adam said. He had taken a step after the man, reaching out.

The man stopped, and looked back at him.

"I know she done it," the man said. "Knowed it as soon as I tetched that-air Colt pistol. Knowed 'twas the one I brung in. Knowed she give it to you."

"But she—"

"Did'n load it, huh?" the man finished for him. He paused. "Gonna slap pee outa her anyway," he resumed.

"Please," Adam said. "She didn't load it. She didn't want you hurt. She made me promise to pay you. It was just because—"

"—because she was messen in my business," he said dourly.

"Please," Adam said, stretching out a hand in entreaty. "It was only because—because we got to talking. Out under the oak tree. Out where she'd put the violets. Out by the—"

"God durn you!" the man burst out, "you want me to blow yore son-a-bitchen head off?"

The carbine was at his head.

But it sank.

"Hell," the man said, "a man gits tahrd."

He again turned away.

"You won't do it?" Adam asked.

"You kin live or die, fer all of me," the man said sourly. "Rebs gonna cut yore thote anyway."

"Her—your wife—" Adam began, and stopped. Then: "I mean you won't do anything to her?"

The man seemed not to have heard. "Her," he repeated then, finally, but not to Adam. "Her," he repeated, then lifted his face. "Yeah," he said, "time wuz I done plenty things to her. In a man-way."

He sank back into himself a moment, then again lifted his head. "Seven year," he said, "nigh on seven year."

He paused again.

"Purty," he said. "She was purty, them days. Yeah," he said. "Yeah," he said, "and she taken a relish."

Suddenly the man straightened up. He spat on the ground in the dark, and put his foot over what must have been the spot.

"That," he said, "that was then. It ain't now."

He turned away.

"Please—" Adam began.

The man looked back at him. "Listen, mister," he said, "time I git back, lak as not I ain't even remember'n to slap the pee outa her. A man fergits. A man gits tahrd."

He had, without a sound, slipped into darkness.

14

Toward noon Adam rose from his blanket in the thicket, and came into the clearing to see about the animals. They were grazing, as peacefully as the flies would permit. He ate some hardtack and the last of the meat from an open tin, and drank from the sluggish little branch. He lay down again, on his back, and stared up into the leaves. In general, the cover was thick, a shadowy green on the underside toward him. But here and there, in some little spot, only a single leaf divided him from the brightness of sky. He would stare at such a leaf. It was pale, filmy, translucent—

the merest diaphragm of lyric green cutting him off from that powerful flood of light beyond.

Now and then, he heard one of the horses stamp, or sigh.

Dusk fell. He bestirred himself to make ready for the coming of darkness and the journey. He watered the horses and put them to the wagon. He ate and drank. He filled his two canteens. The last red now stained the west. He returned to the wagon. He picked up the reins. Joy stirred in his heart.

He thought that if he tried to say why that joy was there it would go away.

He said to himself: *I don't want to think.*

The wagon was moving now. He surrendered himself to the slight motion. A tree frog kept up its utterance, and would not stop.

He thought: *I do not know what there is to think about. It is there, but I do not know what it is.*

It was full dark now. Somewhere a whippoorwill was calling. All night long, as he moved across the shadowy land, in the darkness of trees or in the dim openings washed with starlight, sometimes with the scent of unseen blossom in his nostrils, sometimes the sour smell of rotting earth, that thought, in his very resolution not to think, moved with him. Until in the later hours it changed its form. He moved now in the certainty that though he did not know, he would come to know.

It was the next night when his wandering track led

---

him across what he took to be the Old Turnpike which Monmorancy Pugh had mentioned. From a track in the deep trees, tangled with mist, he debouched, with startling suddenness, into the starlit space. The pike extended pale in the starlight, east and west. Lying on the paleness of the pike there was, he saw, a little cluster of dark objects. He got down from the wagon and leaned above them. They were horse droppings.

He prodded one with his foot. It was, he discovered, fresh. In panic he jerked up to look both ways. But the Rebel cavalry had passed into the night, wherever it was going, east or west. It must have been the Rebel cavalry, he thought.

Then, all at once, his fear was lost in loneliness. He stared down at the horse droppings and felt as though he might weep.

It was morning.

The place was a little glade, set around by sizable timber, oak and gum, and a thick tangle of brush. The glade was, clearly, man-made; the scattered stumps, even in their late decay, still showed the mark of the ax. Among the stumps, fern grew knee-high. To one side ran a thin trickle, scarcely a stream. With summer it would be gone, but it would serve for now. Beyond the trickle, downstream, the animals were tethered. Adam lay on his back, on the blanket, in the shade of the wagon, eyes closed. But he was not asleep. He could not go to sleep.

At noon, or past, he heard it.

It was a thin, flat sound, very far off, a sound that came, in the heat-throbbing, muted susurration of the woodland, with a peculiar emptiness. He had the feeling that if he could only put his mind on the problem he would know what it was. But he was too tired.

Then he knew.

He found himself standing by the wagon, straining. He was straining for the next repetition. There was another. Then repetition after repetition rolled together to make a dry, nagging crackle, like green briar burning. The noise was to the west, the way he had come. The crackle lifted and spread northward, as though a breeze were fanning flame through a green thicket.

Then the crackling broke out to the south. It fell slack; then resumed.

He sat in the shadow of the wagon. He sat there and felt strangely disembodied and pure. He felt as he had once felt when, as a boy, he had been recovering from a long fever. He had awakened that morning, years ago, feeling himself adrift in air, light as a feather, pure. For a moment now, in the shade of the wagon, while sun beat down on the glade, it was a breathless happiness to remember that long-lost waking.

His mother—she had come and laid a hand to his brow and looked down at him, her dark, beautiful eyes swimming with such tenderness that guilt and unworthiness had whelmed over him. Yes, even now as he saw, in broad daylight, in this distant, wild forest, that gaze upon him, he experienced again, as strongly as on that lost morning, the same guilt and unworthiness in the face of such love.

That was the last time, he thought; and the thought stopped.

He waited for it to resume.

It resumed: *That was the last time she ever loved me.*

He had never thought that thought before; but he knew it was true. She had, he could think now with distant sadness, come to hate him, her son, because he had not forgiven her for not forgiving his father.

"Your father," she had once said, "he thought more of something else than of me. Or of you."

And the boy, caught up in rage and rapture, had cried: "And so do I! And so do I!"

Sitting here now, in broad daylight, he heard, with a wrench of the heart, the very words the boy had cried, and saw, again, the woman's stricken face. In the vividness of that vision, here in the woods of this far country, he was about to rise, to cry out, no, no, it was not that he didn't love her, it was something different, something he had to explain to her, if she would only listen, if she would only—

But the noise had, all at once, burst near. It was like the sudden rising of wind.

Then the windy roar had fallen in volume, or retreated. He lay down again. He rolled over on the blanket, on his side. He noticed that ants had discov-

286

ered crumbs near the edge of the blanket. They were dragging fragments as big as boulders through the gigantic forest of grass and more gigantic fern. He stared at them in their work, and could feel, in that effort, the creak and strain of tendon and the rasp of horny integument. His involvement became intense. His breath, he discovered, was coming in short, jagged gasps.

Once, as he lay there watching, he thought he heard a human voice, a cry. It came as a single cry, wild and silvery and pure in distance, in irrelevance. But then he was not sure that he had heard it at all. Perhaps it was only what, all the while, he had been expecting to hear: the cry.

He continued to stare at the ants.

At dawn light he opened his eyes, and gazed up into the sky. The air was trembling and clotted. In that first instant of waking to the dawn flush yet in the sky, amid ferns wet with dew, he asked himself what was that increasing shudder of sound.

But yes, he knew where he was.

In the afternoon he was staring at the ants. It was then that he heard what he now thought was, beyond a doubt, a human cry. In a sudden lull of sound, when there was only the natural hum of woodland, the cry came. Then, as before, he was not sure that his ears had not deceived him. He strained to hear. If he could only hear the cry. But he heard only the sound

287

of insects. The cry had been, he decided, only a delusion. Loneliness overwhelmed him.

He leaped to his feet.

"I came here!" he cried aloud. "I came here to fight
for freedom!" he cried.

He stood there sweating in the brilliant flood of
afternoon. In that far, windy swirl of sound there
were strange, fat clottings, cottony and dull, like gas
exploding from the depth of mud. His nails were
clenched in the palms of his hands.

He opened his hands and looked down at them,
embarrassed. Looking down at the emptiness of his
hands, he thought how he had not been permitted.

At that moment one of the horses gave a wild snort,
and even as Adam turned his head, had jerked loose
from the tether and was plunging through fern across
the north end of the glade. Then the beast crashed
into the brush, and was gone.

Adam went to the other animal. He untied it, led it
through the fern to the wagon, tethered it to a wheel,
and stood there patting its neck. He noticed that each
time one of those strange clotting, cottony blobs of
sound rose from the general swell, the animal quiv-
ered under his hand.

No, he had not been permitted, his mind was saying, as he stroked the trembling neck of the animal.
No, they did not want me, he thought.

Then thought: *But I had to come. I had to come,
because—*

Under his hand the animal was still now. He came

---

and sat again on the blanket. He thought: *Because*—

He waited.

Then: *Because you have to know if there is a truth in the world.*

The sound of battle swirled farther and fainter. He sat there and wondered if it was to be permitted him to have that truth.

But, he thought, *others have been permitted.*

He hung his head and thought how, that very instant, far in the woods, men plunged through the greenery, and found their truth, and died. He thought, all at once, of Simms Purdew, somewhere in this forest, rising gigantically from a thicket and swinging the clubbed musket, his face shining like truth. Yes, even Simms Purdew.

But not only Simms Purdew.

He thought of Stephen Blaustein, who, just a year ago, had come, with his truth, into these woods, and had died. He thought of Hans Meyerhof, who had come into these woods. He thought of Maran Meyerhof, who had, at last, cried out her truth. He thought of the black cavalryman who had lain under the lights of the hospital tent, and the blood had run out of him, and he had died in his truth. And he thought of Mose —Talbutt, Crawfurd, oh, what did it matter?—who had lain in the hut in the dark, in the agony of shame, and had cried out: "God damn it—I wish it was me—me layen quiet and bleeden—oh, I wouldn't keer—oh, I wouldn't keer!"

Yes, Mose—even Mose—had, in that moment, found his truth.

And sitting there, thinking that, Adam was filled with a tenderness, even a love, for Mose Crawfurd. *Let him go in peace,* he thought. *Oh, God, lead him to peace.*

Adam heard the windy roar sweep north, then south. In the center of the whirling of the storm, he remembered having read, there is a cold, minute eye of stillness. He bowed his head and heard the swirl of sound, and thought that he, he himself, was the cold center of stillness in the storm which was the world.

Then the world broke into the thicket. It plunged into the glade.

15

The eight maniacal scarecrows burst into the glade.
They rushed toward Adam as he stood witlessly by
the wagon, frozen in astonishment, appalled in in-
credulity as though his fantasy had conjured up reality.

The first scarecrow, tatters and beard streaming
with the violence of his passage through the air, came
leaping over the ferns, in one hand a rifle to which was
attached the glitter of a bayonet. He came leaping
with a comic awkwardness that was all knees and elbows and angles and ferocious speed. He was uttering little yelps, like a puppy.

The others came plunging after the leaper. They

did not leap over the ferns. Their feet swung through with a small savage ripping sound. The nearest was hatless, and Adam saw how gold was the sun on the tossing pale hair. Then he saw how blue were the eyes. In all that motion the young face looked calm. In that instant in which the ferocity of motion was frozen for his inspection, Adam saw how calm and clear was the brow of that boy.

Then the instant in which all had been frozen for his inspection exploded around him. It crashed like an enormous glass demijohn hit by a brickbat. It crashed and flashed in all directions.

A bayonet was prodding Adam gently in the belly. Beyond the bayonet he saw the calm brow of the boy. The bayonet was attached to a rifle which the boy held.

Hands were trying to tear the canvas top off the wagon. Bayonets were ripping it. "Jesus, sumpen to eat," a voice kept breathing, "right here in the woods!"

All another voice could do was make a sound like a whimper.

Suddenly the rending of canvas ceased. The wagon heaved up on one side, teetered, was over. In the big crash and crack, objects splayed out in all directions. The horse now stood with head lowered to the shortened tether—it led to the down-side wheel—and jerked and jerked.

The men were scrambling on the ground, grabbing, ripping open tins, stuffing their mouths, making gulps and little whimpers. All except the one who kept on saying: "Jesus, Jesus." He said it as well as he could under the circumstances of a crammed mouth.

The boy with the gold hair, blue eyes, and clear brow kept prodding Adam in the stomach, ever so gently, and pleading to the men in a beautiful voice, in a cultivated tone: "Get me something! Get me something, do you hear? Some son-of-a-bitch get me something to eat. Some son-of-a-bitch!"

Some son-of-a-bitch did. It was the tall angular leaper over ferns who rose to his knees now, his cheeks bulging so tight the hairs of his whiskers stood out like quills, and handed an open tin of beef to the boy. The boy dropped his weapon, forgetting his duty, and grabbed the tin. He scooped two fingers into it like a spoon, opened his mouth, crammed the substance in, and began to chew. As he chewed, he closed his eyes.

When he finally swallowed, his eyes popped spasmodically wide, his face went crimson, and for an instant the effort seemed too much. But he managed. He gasped. "Two days," he was saying, "two days and—"

But his own hand interrupted him. The hand crammed food into the words. The jaw began to move, the eyes closed, sweat gathered on the clear brow.

In that instant outside of time and place, as though he were there invisibly staring at that clear face that was sweating with its effort and gratification, Adam felt a sweet sadness fill his heart. He loved the boy because the boy had been very hungry and now had food.

But the crouching scarecrow cried out: "Look, Tadpole!" he cried to the boy of the clear brow, whose eyes were open now, and were fixed where the hairy scarecrow pointed.

"Boots!" the hairy one cried in rapture, and in that instant, Adam saw that the feet of the hairy one were bare. That was all he saw before the hairy one, never rising from his crouch, had seized him about the knees, lifted him up, and with shattering force, flung him to the ground.

The man was tearing at the laces of the right boot. Adam, half stunned, tried to jerk away.

"God durn, Tadpole!" the hairy one was yelling to the boy with yellow hair, "God durn it, stob the son-of-a-bitch or grab holt!"

The Tadpole elected neither course. Instead, he elected to sit on Adam. He turned and dropped his behind with such sudden impact that the breath was knocked clean out of Adam's chest. "Please," the Tadpole was saying in his beautiful voice, "please lie still. Please don't make difficulties."

Adam lay still, and the boy, sitting on him as on a log, scooped out meat from the tin and crammed it into his mouth, closed his eyes, and chewed.

The right boot was off. The hairy one was jerking the other boot off. He suddenly rose. "The son-of-a-bitch!" he was shouting in outrage.

He stood there, quivering with cosmic grievance,

holding the boot up against the bright blue sky. "Look!" he cried to the Tadpole, "look at that durn thing!"

The Tadpole obediently looked up at the boot.

But now the hairy one was pointing down at Adam's foot, the left foot.

"The son-of-a-bitch," he cried, in unassuageable anguish, "the son-of-a-bitch—he is mulefooted!"

The anguish was too much for him. At some risk to his own bare toes, the hairy one gave a great kick to Adam's side. But the toes, apparently, had suffered little damage, for the man said, "Oh, the lousy son-of-a-bitch," and kicked again.

Adam uttered a grunt, or moan.

Dispassionately, the Tadpole turned on Adam's chest to look down at the deformed foot, then up at the boot still held against the blue sky.

"It doesn't really help to kick him," the Tadpole said calmly.

"The son-of-a-bitch," the hairy one said and drew back for the kick, still holding the boot high.

"Listen," the Tadpole said in a reasonable tone, "why don't you try on the good one?"

The hairy one began to try on the good boot. The Tadpole swung back to a normal position on Adam's chest, took food, and began to chew.

"Fits!" the hairy one announced.

The Tadpole swallowed. Then he managed to say: "Perhaps you can fix the other."

The hairy one was tying the laces of the left boot

---

to his belt. "Ain't no time to fix it now," he said. "But durn it, one is better'n nary!"

The Tadpole was cramming meat into his mouth. He closed his eyes to chew. Then, with their sudden blueness, they popped open again. But this time it was not the result of the strain of forcing down into the clamoring emptiness of stomach a great gob of half-chewed food.

The eyes popped open because from the greenery to the north of the glade had come a smart crack; because a hornet of peculiar velocity and vindictiveness had come *zinging* past; and because the horse, apparently stung by that insect, had reared, had uttered a peculiar blubbering snort, had plunged, had snapped the tether, and had fallen on its side.

Adam saw the blue eyes pop open in the boy's face. He rolled his head and saw the wisp of smoke in the greenery to the north of the glade. He rolled his head the other way and saw one hind leg of the horse jerk and jerk. Again he rolled his head the other way and saw men burst from the woods. These men were in blue. Sunlight was on their steel.

The Tadpole had risen from Adam's chest. He had made a plunging scramble toward his weapon, which lay on the ground, some two paces off. He had not laid hand on it before he flopped to one side, rolled over once, and sat up, clutching his right shoulder. His face expressed great irritation, even anger. Blood was beginning to come between the fingers of his left hand, which was pressed against the right shoulder.

The men in blue, some six or seven of them, had swung around the far end of the wagon, all except one. He and the hairy scarecrow, now with one boot on and the other swinging and jouncing at his belt, were exchanging thrust and parry with bayonets. Five times Adam saw this, and five times heard the smart clash, or clink, then the small grind of metal at the instant of disengagement. The two men went at their work with great staunchness and preoccupation, as though their lives depended on it. Their breathing was labored.

The Tadpole, Adam became aware, was gone. From beyond the wagon there were certain sounds, for the most part oaths and clashings. Then a cry.

A scarecrow—but one with no beard—came around the end of the wagon. He leaped over the fallen horse and with bayonet on rifle approached from one side the man in blue who was working so sturdily with the hairy scarecrow with one bare foot. Seeing the second scarecrow approach from the side, Adam, in his peculiar lethargy and detachment—for that was what the pain of the kicks had become— thought: *He shouldn't do that. It is not fair.*

It was a sharp access of moral repugnance that made him roll over, half rise, and reach out. At least, whatever it was took the form of such repugnance. His hand was on the weapon that the Tadpole had never recovered.

He leveled it, and for the first time in his life, pulled the trigger of a charged weapon.

Long practice could have made no improvement. The beardless scarecrow lowered his bayonet, seemed for a long moment to reconsider, as though with the pang of an awakening conscience, his original intention; shook his head in a motion of self-reprobation; dropped his weapon in a sudden decision to mend his ways; took two steps backward; and stupidly stumbled back over the dead horse.

He did not get up. You could not see him, but you could see one foot propped on the belly of the dead animal over which he had fallen. The toes pointed skyward.

The man in blue made a desperate lunge at the hairy scarecrow, a lunge clearly intended to be definitive. But the scarecrow parried, made a riposte, wavered to one side like a weed swaying in a stream, and leaped sideways, light as a cat.

Men were running across the glade, beyond the wagon, toward the woods.

The hairy one had leaped again, over the dead horse and fallen scarecrow, in a great burst of awkward, angular energy that was, somehow, as beautiful as a dance; and with those crazy, cranky leaps over the ferns, one boot on, one boot off, beard whipping in the wind, rags flapping, bayonet glittering in jagged arabesques, tethered boot snatching and jerking at the waist, was gone. At that instant of disappearance into the greenery the head had turned, the mouth had opened, and a quavering of heart-broken sound had come forth.

—————

Two men in blue, the last in the glade, plunged after him.

After all the pother, the quiet was sudden, and delicious. Adam lay face down and drew in the quiet. For one thing, he had discovered from his recent activity that any movement could make his abused side hurt mortally. Now, however, the pain was subsiding to a throb.

Soon he would have to move, he knew that, but he did not want to move yet. He lay with his face in the crook of his left arm, his right arm outflung, the hand yet touching the metal of the weapon he had fired. He wondered what time it was. He thought it must be getting late.

But he did not move. His hand yet touched the metal of the weapon.

He thought: *I have killed a man.*

He held that thought in his mind, and marveled. He lay there and marveled that a strength should be growing in him, that with the death of that nameless man he himself should feel so much more a man.

Yes, he thought, *I have killed a man.*

But, he finally thought, *that is why I crossed the ocean and came all the miles. To do that.*

Yes, he had come. Everything in the world had tried to stop him, temptations, disillusion, fear, the blankness of the world and time, all the betrayals of his dream. But he had come. By God, he had come here.

———

He did not look up. His fingers felt the metal under his touch.

Nothing had been able to stop him, he thought. He felt a surge of pride in that, a manliness.

He thought: *We always do what we intend.*

He lay marveling, filled with awe, and terror, at that discovery.

He became aware, all at once, of the movement of air over his feet. He wriggled his toes. Yes, the hairy one had taken the socks, too.

Abruptly he sat up and peered at his feet. He swung his gaze around the glade, the trampled ferns, the wrecked wagon, the scattered debris, the dead horse, the woods leaning closer, darkening.

A strange light was now in the sky, northward. The roaring sound was farther off, and fainter.

He looked down again at his bare feet. He thought how white, friendless, and unfended they looked in the middle of the glade, with the woods darkening. All at once he felt sorry for them—not for himself, but for them as though they were stupid, ugly, unlovable children, lost, not knowing.

He let his head sink in thought.

We always do what we intend, he thought.

But now the strength, pride, and manliness that had accompanied that thought were flickering out, like the rag wick of a slush lamp, slowly sinking and guttering down to darkness as the grease gives out.

He thought how he was lost, was barefoot, and the night would come. But somehow it was all justice.

He looked at the whiteness of his twisted foot, and thought of the terrible justice of the world. The world must be just, he decided, for he felt overwhelmed with guilt. If the world were not just, would he have felt guilty?

But no, I'm not, he protested, *I'm not guilty.*

He lifted his eyes and gazed at the foot of the dead man propped over the dead mule.

What I have done, he thought, *I did for freedom. I would have died for freedom.*

That thought, the thought that he would have died if necessary, made him feel better. It was true, he knew. He would have had the courage to die for freedom.

But all at once, faintly as in distance, in the hollow darkness of his mind, he heard the wild jocularity of the cries, "Für die Freiheit, für die Freiheit!" followed by the wilder laughter.

But I did nothing I did not have to do, he thought. *I had to come.*

Yes, he had had to come.

But he thought how, if he had stayed with Aaron Blaustein, Aaron Blaustein would not have died.

I had to come, he thought in rebuttal and defense. Even Aaron Blaustein had admitted that.

But coming, he knew now in sudden painfulness, he had come in hardness of heart. Oh, if—

His mind slid away from that *if*.

He thought how Jedeen Hawksworth would not have died if—

***

His mind refused it.

He thought how Mose Talbutt—Mose Crawfurd—would not have been driven forth, with crammed money belt, greasy alphabet cards, and bloody hands, if—

He could not think that *if*. But he had to. He knew that, in the end, he would have to think every *if*—every *if* which was life.

If he, Adam Rosenzweig, had not told the black man to shut up, to stop talking. If he had not called him the name he had called him, the name of insult which, it seemed now in absolute clarity, he had always been doomed to call Mose Talbutt, Mose Crawfurd.

Thinking that, feeling again as he had felt that night when, after having called the black man that name, he had stood panting in the dark, he realized that Mose might have killed him, not Jed Hawksworth. Why hadn't Mose done that? He lay and wondered. Then he thought he knew. Mose had not been able to kill him because he had once saved him.

Yes, he thought, *you cannot strike down what you have lifted up*.

So Jed, he decided, had had to die in his place. And then, with that thought, he wondered if every man is, in the end, a sacrifice for every other man. He did not know. He could not read the depth of the thought, but stared down into it as into a deep well where a little light glimmers on the dark water.

Then he could bear no longer to stare down at that depth.

But they all betrayed me, he cried inwardly— Aaron Blaustein, under the glittering chandelier, exalted in grief, pronouncing the curse; Jedeen Hawksworth, staring into the campfire and denying the only thing that had ever given his life meaning; Mose with that shameful *W* puckering the black flesh.

Yes, they had betrayed him. The world had betrayed him.

And my father, he thought, *he betrayed me.*

He looked down at the twisted whiteness of his poor foot. He stared at it.

My father, he thought, *that is what he gave me.*

He felt that he was on the verge of a great truth. He felt that everything he had ever known was false.

Ah, he thought, *that is the greatest betrayal.*

He leaped up. He stared at the dead horse, at the foot stuck over the belly of the dead horse, the toe pointing upward.

"By God!" he cried aloud, and felt energy flooding him like wine.

Ah, he thought, *this is it!*

He felt the exaltation of one who discovers the great secret. He felt that if this was the way the world was, it was a joy to know it. He rushed to the dead horse, to the foot propped there. There was a boot on the foot. It was a good boot. That was the way the world was, and he would put on the boot.

303

He tore at the laces of the boot. He was dizzy with a sudden access of power. He had never felt anything like this. Deep in his being he was aware, fleetingly, of an image, a rich room glittering with crystal and silver, yellow hair falling unbound, candlelight winking redly through wine, a white breast lifted to his hand. He was dizzy with an angry lust as he tore at the boot. In that rage all the betrayals of life were consumed like straw.

He was stripping the boot from the foot. There was no sock. But the boot, it was a good one. Holding the boot up to look at it, he noticed that the strange light northward was more marked now. He looked at the west. Yes, the sun was setting, but that light, it was to the north, that heaving rosiness streaked with green and gray.

He dropped the boot and stared at the white foot propped, in such frailty, over the animal's belly.

I killed him, he thought, *because his foot was not like mine.*

With that thought he felt suddenly pure, and young. All the past was suddenly nothing. He leaned and looked down, for the first time, into the dead man's face. It was a most commonplace face. It was entirely unremarkable. It expressed nothing. It seemed to have no experience to express. It was the face of a man who, clearly, might as well never have lived. The eyes were staring up at the sky with complete lack of comprehension of anything.

Adam fell to work on the other boot. He unlaced

it, jerked it off. Yes, it was a very good boot. He held it up for closer inspection. It was a splendid boot. That, he realized, meant only one thing. It was a Federal boot. And the man who lay dead there, the Rebel —he, too had taken that boot from a dead foot.

Now, Adam thought, *now I am taking it.*

He felt like giggling. Something was very funny.

Now it is my turn, he thought.

He went to the wagon, near the debris, and began, · methodically, to put on a boot, the right boot.

He was about to tie the boot when he saw it.

It was the little satchel his uncle had given him. It had been flung from the wagon, torn open, or burst open. It lay there on its side, beyond the dead horse, the dead man, in the clutter from the wagon. It seemed to be empty.

Adam cast his glance about. He saw something under the shadow of a fern. At first he did not recognize it. Then he knew that it was a phylactery. He peered about. Yes, and there was the *talith.* He wondered where the prayer book might be.

He had, of course, thanked the maid back in Aaron Blaustein's rich house, the maid who had sat up at night to dry the prayer book, the *seddur,* and press its pages with a mild iron. But he had not looked inside to see how well, after the soaking in the dark cellar, she had restored the pages. He wished he had. He wished he had opened the book before her eyes and praised her. Why hadn't he done it? It would have been so easy.

———

305

Stupidly he looked down at the boot, not yet tied, on his right foot. He stared at it along time. He could not decipher that boot. The boot was infinitely precious to him, and he had it—it was his now, by God! —but even as he stared at it on his foot and knew that it was his, he knew, with a sense of desolation, that something was going to happen. Before what was to happen actually happened, he had this dim foreboding of it.

Then it did happen: he took off the boot.

He picked up the other boot, too. He rose and moved, with barefoot stealth, across the ferns. He crossed to the other side of the dead horse. He set the boots on the ground, very tidily, near the body of the man. Near enough, he realized, to be within easy reach.

In a numb, quiet way he thought how foolish this was.

He again looked at the face of the dead man. The face, as before, expressed nothing.

But he lived, he thought, *he had a life, there must be something in his face which I cannot see.*

He stood there, peering, and wondered what his own face would be like in death. Would it wear a mask of anger, of pain, of outrage, of despair, of peace? Or would it wear no mask at all—nothing over the numbed blankness? What, he wondered, could he hope to have on his own dead face from the life that would lead to his death?

Am I different from other men? he demanded.

He found, now, that he was breathing very softly, as though not to awaken the man.

He felt ashamed of his foolishness. But with the same stealth, the same control of breath, he withdrew. He crouched on the ground, near where he had been making ready to put on the boots. He peered at the objects among the ferns. His gaze found the book now.

But carefully—as though by a weighty effort of will—he refrained from reaching out a hand to touch any of the objects.

He looked up at the sky. West, the color was fading, but in the north, that heaving rosiness, now definitely streaked with gray, was more positive. He stared at the phenomenon with an air of painful speculation. But he was not now speculating about the nature of the phenomenon. Now he was trying to deny, as long as possible, the certainty of what it was.

For he knew what it was. In a moment, he would allow his mind to say what it was.

He allowed the certainty to take words.

Yes, the forest was on fire.

He listened most attentively. If he listened attentively enough he might now, at last, hear it: a cry. If he could hear it, he might, somehow, in that instant, be freed from something. He might be able to leap up, to run, barefoot, into the forest, to drag some wounded man from the nibbling, or gusty, encroachment of flame.

He listened as hard as he could; but he could hear nothing.

If only he could hear it: one cry.

He shut his eyes, and strained to catch the cry. To shut the eyes—that was a mistake. For immediately the darkness of his head rang with a thousand cries. The cries had the strange, clear, beautiful, vaulted and vaulting hollowness of a cry uttered in the deep woods. Cry after cry rang in his head, with that soaring purity. Hands reached out in the darkness of his head. The red reflection of the flame glowed on faces from which the eyes distended maniacally, and in which the mouth made the perfectly round *O* of the scream, the scream he could not, in fact, hear.

Then he was on his knees in the ferns, eyes shut. He was saying the words: "What dost Thou? O Thou who speakest and doest, of Thy grace deal kindly with us, and for the sake of him who was bound like a lamb. O hearken and do—"

He had last heard those words on that winter afternoon, long back, across the ocean, in Bavaria, over the body that was being deposited in the earth, the body of Leopold Rosenzweig, and he was saying them now, and as he said them that place and this place, and that time and this time, flowed together. He was saying the words: "Just art Thou, O Lord, in ordering death and restoring to life—"

He was saying: "Far be it from Thee to blot out our remembrance—"

And at last, he was saying: "Have mercy upon

the remnant of the flock of Thy hand, and say unto the Destroying Angel, Stay thy hand."

He crouched in the ferns, saying nothing now, head bowed, breath coming hard and slow. After a while he might, he thought, be able to raise his head and see what he would see—the naked foot of the dead man propped over the belly of the dead horse, the heave of far flame on a darkening sky above thickets where, miles away, the steam of sap in vernal wood would be exploding festively like firecrackers, and wounded men, those who were able, would drag, pull, claw, hunch, hump, roll themselves, inch by inch, over the ground in a lethargic parody of flight until the moment of surrender when the summarizing scream of protest would be uttered, but heard by no ear.

Adam Rosenzweig crouched there. He did not strain now to hear a cry. But he had begun to feel, with a slow, painful, dawning sense of awe, like dawn through clouds, that after a little, soon now, he might be able to rise. He might be able to rise and do what he would have to do, as he had done what, in the compulsion of his dream, he had had to do. Yes, he had done only what he had had to do, he decided, good or bad. He decided that much—slowly, carefully, painfully, his mind making the motion of an old man who bends to lift a weight beyond his strength because there is no one else there to lift it. Yes, he was only human, he thought. Yes, and if necessary, he would do it all again, he decided. He stared at the rifle lying there, absurd and lost like a toy. Yes, he thought, staring at the rifle, he would do it all again.

But then cried, in his inwardness: *But, oh, with a different heart!*

He did not know what he would have to do now, or with what heart. He knew, however, that he would have to try to know what a man must know to be a man. He knew that he would have to try to know that the truth is unbetrayable, and that only the betrayer is ever betrayed, and then only by his own betraying.

He thought: *I must get up. Soon.*

He knew that he would have to rise, and go pick up the boots, and put them on, and walk out of the Wilderness. He would walk—hobble, if he could find some way to bind and brace his left foot—out of the forest wearing the boots that had, in the fullness of time and human effort, been passed from one dead man to another. He did not, he thought with sadness, even know their names.

He would never know their names.

Then, quietly, he realized that that thought was not without its sweetness. He could try, he thought, to be worthy of their namelessness, and of what they, as men and in their error, had endured.